SOMETHING EVIL THIS
WAY COMES . . .

Jarry looked at the stars, staring at them with dull hatred. He was a veteran of fifty-plus missions; this one should have been routine. Except they hadn't told him about the Other.

He giggled, a mad sound, faint amid the escape pod's busy clicking and beeping. The Other in his mind pressed again, and Jarry knew he couldn't fight it much longer. Soon it would have total control.

Tumbling into a shipping lane, the escape pod was able to broadcast its emergency call unhampered by static.

Jarry, unaware, stared sightless into space, his mind totally immersed in its silent war.

By Johanna M. Bolton
Published by Ballantine Books:

THE ALIEN WITHIN

MISSION: TORI

MISSION: TORI

JOHANNA M. BOLTON

A Del Rey Book

BALLANTINE BOOKS • NEW YORK

A Del Rey Book
Published by Ballantine Books

Copyright © 1990 by Johanna M. Bolton

Library of Congress Catalog Card Number: 90-92909

ISBN 0-345-36340-X

Manufactured in the United States of America

First Edition: June 1990

Cover Art by Richard Hescox

This book is in memory of Leonard Thomas Bolton, Jr., my father, who once told me not to tell him what I was going to do, but to show him what I'd done. And so I ended up doing a lot of interesting things I might otherwise have only dreamed about. I've won a lot of awards, but the best one I'll ever receive was the day he said, "I'm proud of you." I hope I can continue to make him proud of me.

CHAPTER 1

Jarry realized that the end was near—not only of his journey, but of his life as well.

His life?

No, *mind* was a better word. His body might live on, but the essential something that made this person, this particular collection of chemicals unique would be gone.

It was the end of his mind.

Yes, that sounded right.

The end of his mind.

Flashing lights pulsed with the beating of his heart. Or had his heart altered its rhythm to be in time with the lights? He didn't know, and it didn't matter now. Irrefutable fact: his heart and the flashing were synchronous. The sound pounded in his ears, each pulse throbbing in his temples, the veins in his head stretched beyond limit, blinding him with bright pain.

Even though they hurt him, the lights had a purpose— they meant something. A warning? His hands knew what to do, tried to move, reaching out.

Hands of bone, flesh torn from fingers, blood dried black.

The hands tried to reach the controls, to make the lights go away, even though the remnants of his mind knew it was useless. For him the lights were eternal. Even with his eyes closed, they shone red through the membrane—on, off, wink, blink, bright, bright, bright. Like some radiation eating away at his will.

Radiation.

Yes, that was it. Radiation overload. The pod had malfunctioned. Just like his body. Mal function. Bad works. A bad scene all around, he thought.

Outside the escape pod he could see more lights, frantically signaling. Some of them were stars. Some of them were reflections off the asteroids. Rocks, really. All sizes of rocks.

Someone was throwing rocks at him?

No, he told himself. Not throwing rocks. He was in the Stone Field. His pod was trying to escape through one of the most wicked asteroid fields in the known galaxy. Stupid mistake. Not going through the Field, but trying to deal with that planet in the first place. He never should have accepted the job. Stupid. But he didn't know what he was getting into then. No one knew. Troubleshooting, problem solving, that was his job, and he was very good at it. Correction: he had been very good at it. This time he'd slipped up, and now it was going to kill him.

Now the end was in sight. The end of him. Of Jarry.

And finally, there was the end of the Stone Field. But he didn't know that—or did he?

Acrid smoke burned his eyes, coloring the air faintly blue. Some iridescent liquid dripped from a ruptured hose, pooling beneath a torn console where his foot rested. He could see it all clearly, but he felt helpless to do anything about it.

Yet the pod kept on, radio beacons screaming for help, even though there was no one to hear, for no ships would willingly enter the Field to face the rocks, or risk blinding their sensors in the chaos of outlaw radiation. Asteroids from the size of pebbles to small planetoids filled this section of space, giving the Field its name, constantly in motion as they churned through dust, clouds of gas, and each other. The pod bore scars, dents, and scrapes from more than one collision in its desperate flight, but the round shape had enabled it to escape with no more than superficial damage.

Which was more than could be said for Jarry.

Somewhere ahead lay his destination—if the autonav was still functional; somewhere across parsecs of void, among billions of others, one small star glowed, a star called Sol by the inhabitants of its third planet, Earth. Earth meant home, safety, and hopefully the end of the constant war he had been waging with the invasion of his mind. Earth . . . home . . . very, very far away. And in the shape he was in he doubted he'd make it.

"Are we going to make it?" a voice in his mind asked, speaking very clearly.

It wasn't his voice, he knew that, and so he ignored the question.

But that was another mistake. Whenever he ignored it, it tried to take over.

"Get back, you bastard!" he screamed, sound muffled in the pod. Something hissed in rage behind the ruined console.

Jarry strained against the webbing that held him immobile, hands fastened too far away for fingers to touch the release plate—he'd made sure of that when he entered the pod. If the thing won . . . no, when the thing won, he didn't want it to be able to use his body. It could do anything then and he would be powerless to stop it. It might even sabotage the ship, and the ship was all he had left . . . his only chance . . . his only, his last hope.

Stars in the small, round viewport drew his attention, for a moment banishing chaotic thoughts. The stars, numberless in blazing color, jewels against velvet black, like a treasure hoard. Between them swirled dust as brightly lit as the stars. And the black . . . the great void of black. The space was deceptive . . . it only looked empty; Jarry knew it was not.

Terror forced its way into his consciousness as the presence of the Other made itself known.

"No," the sound a moan forced from between cracked and bloody lips. His eyes glazed as he concentrated on . . . on anything, anything to help him defeat the Other.

"It's easy to think of space as empty, a void of black and white," a voice said in his mind, the sound so matter-of-fact and totally sane that it shocked him. "It is easy, that is, for someone who has never been in space."

Jarry accepted the calm words as just another facet of his madness. Yes, he thought, yes, that's what they told us at the Academy. But they were liars. He was certain of it now. It was a conspiracy, a gigantic plot, and everyone at the Academy was in on it. But they had to lie, otherwise we wouldn't go . . . we wouldn't trust our fragile flesh to this great void protected by nothing more than a tin can full of air.

Air. Oxygen. Atmosphere.

Remember to breathe. Jarry drew a huge breath, feeling the recycled air burn against the raw lining of the back of his throat. That hurt too, but the pain was only a small part of the agony his total flesh had become. He held his breath a second and then let it out.

Mankind doesn't belong in space, he told himself. There's nothing out here for us . . . nothing, except death.

"Space is not empty," the remembered voice lectured. "It is as full as can be with both the visible and the invisible."

Invisible. Jarry focused on the word. Things invisible. Things like death. Death is invisible. Despite his distress, his mouth made the motions of laughter, but his body could no longer produce the sound. Tears ran down his face, his breathing harsh as he fought to regain control. The Other pressed, and he realized that the words, dredged from forgotten recesses of his mind, were the result of the alien's delving.

"No" came from him again. But one word couldn't stop the probing.

"Space is not black and white. It is every possible color, and some not possible . . . clouds and cosmic dust, dark as soot or bright as rainbows. Stars . . . fires burning in the eternal night, radiation like cosmic smoke curling through an endless void, in unseen tides . . ."

Tides.

Jarry remembered the seas of Earth . . . blue-green,

cool . . . waves frosted with sunlit foam . . . waves, gentle, graceful as they came and went . . . ebb and flow . . . Except the waves here were invisible, attacking, bombarding the ship . . . radio waves, gravity waves, ion waves, electromagnetic, ultraviolet radiation. Waves that were spherical, cylindrical, simple, complex. Yes, waves in tides, trying to get to me, trying to get in, trying to get into me!

The calm voice went on, cutting through his rising hysteria. "And through it all the impartial stars dance the slow, elegant dances of an expanding galaxy. They are the sirens of space. They are . . ."

He focused his will, denied the voice, and it died away.

Jarry looked at the stars, staring at them with dull hatred.

He remembered how it had started. It had been a job just like all the others, and like the others, there had been the potential for danger. He'd known this before he agreed to go. No one forced him, right? He was a veteran of fifty-plus missions; this one should have been routine. Except they hadn't told him about the Other. Or had they known? He didn't know . . . or say no . . . or know what he now knew.

As his mind played with the sounds, he giggled, a mad sound, faint amid the pod's busy clicking and beeping.

The Other pressed again, and Jarry knew he couldn't fight it much longer. The periods of unconsciousness, when It ruled, were coming more and more frequently. Soon It would have total control.

"God, help me!" he cried in silent supplication.

His eyes were gritty, red-rimmed, and underlined with dark shadows. A filthy jumpsuit hung on his emaciated frame.

Tumbling into a shipping lane, the escape pod left the Field, and for the first time its emergency call went forth unhampered by static.

But Jarry, unaware, stared sightless into space, his mind totally immersed in its silent war.

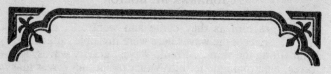

CHAPTER 2

Mier Silver sat on the public bus, her forearm resting on the edge of the window as she watched the city streets. People do not change. From planet to planet they spread into the galaxy, but no matter where they went, they remained essentially the same. Man. Humanity. Humankind. Individual bodies might age, wither, and die, but there were always others to replace them, all the same in their need to find some meaning in their short existence— or to hide from the necessity. They all had potential, but most of them never learned what to do with it, and most of them were hiding.

Karr used to complain about the common herd: Why should they be so mindless? He once told her that there were three kinds of people. Just three. Those who created things, those who repaired things, and those who used things. And the last group were the parasites, and the majority. He had despised them, even though they were his audience, the ones who made him famous. He couldn't understand a life without creativity. When he wasn't on assignment, he was always making things, their apartment cluttered with paints, plastic, a bit of electronics. The galleries took everything he did, and until the end, he had been the critics' darling. Following this lead, the people loved him, and bought his work as fast as he could make it.

Mier let the thoughts of Karr drift through her mind. As long as she remembered him, as long as his work remained, a part of him was still alive. But, oh, how she missed him, his warm arms around her, his laughter, his brilliant, sarcastic mind. She had never been able to share so much of herself with anyone else.

She leaned against the window and watched the people with lazy eyes beneath long eyelashes, seeing much more than one would suspect, especially if one neglected to look beyond the tawdry finery that barely covered her lush figure. She relaxed against the stained plastic, body swaying slightly with the bus's movement.

Twin suns slid down toward the horizon, the dense orange atmosphere filtering their light. The upper reaches of Belosa City shimmered in a golden glow, towers floating above deep blue darkness, the odd, twisted shapes of industrial structures alternating with the more traditional styles of business and residential areas. The picture resembled a surrealistic painting, beautiful until one got close enough to see details and realized it was really a madman's dream. It was a hodgepodge of styles, old and new, carelessly mixed, and all of them beginning to crumble around the edges. Mier didn't like it—she didn't like any of the megacities. She felt closed in, suffocated, depressed by the decay she saw all around her. The suns cast a grid of shadows from elevated pedestrian walkways crossing high above the streets; closed walkways serving people as elevated in the planet's social strata as they were physically raised above the working classes that plodded through the perpetual dusk below—people such as the ones in the bus, their smell an overripe compound of bad breath, sweat, and stale perfume. Only her eyes moved as she glanced at the children in the seat ahead of her. They were a mixed group of teenagers, and she wondered what they had to look forward to, growing up in the bowels of this awful city. A momentary flash of her own childhood came, long sterile tubes of Theta station,

spiritually not much better than this, despite the physical
difference. Avoiding the memory, she looked out the
window again.

The lower streets were uncovered, and Mier wasn't
happy with what she had to breathe, despite the morning
report, which rated the air quality acceptable. Nose fil-
ters helped a little, but her eyes burned, and the irritation
did nothing to improve her temper. Nonetheless, she fixed
a smile on her lips—a tight, cynical smile—as she
climbed from the bus and made her way along the con-
gested walkway.

Music blared from the open doorways, competing with
loud voices inside and out. This part of the city was
rowdy, the unstructured energy—physical, aural, and visual—constantly changing. Bright signs flashed, clashing
color over everything, and holograms beamed samples of
pleasures onto the sidewalk. The holograms crackled and
dissolved around Mier as she passed through them.

She moved slowly, chewing a wad of cinstim, and
swinging her hips seductively. The synthetic gremlin silk
she wore clung to her body like a shiny pink skin, revealing the generous contour of padded breasts and hips.
A grav net covered the suit, and all around her 'lectrogems—those that still worked—flashed on and off. More
'lectros winked from her earlobes and the big bracelets
circling her slender wrists.

A couple of potential customers approached her, but
she put them off with a word and a grin, and passed on.

"Hey, Pinky," a prostitute called after she had gone a
block. "Yer in big trouble."

Dressed in a tarnished costume of metallic green, the
streetwalker leaned against a storefront, watching everything with predatory eyes and breathing in the smoke
from a narcostick. The lit end bobbed in front of her
mouth as she spoke.

The smell was cloyingly sweet, and Mier held her
breath as she paused. "Whadayah mean?"

"You gotta protector? Better get'm fast." The woman
raised one long-nailed finger to scratch under her gilded
hairdo. When the nail had done its work, she nodded to
the street. "This Bernard's territory, an' he owns all the
street ladies, an' I know he never seen you before."

"An' I ain't heard of no Bernard." Mier looked into the traffic and noticed a flashy red groundcar making its way toward them, grav lifters under the chassis illegally loud against the surface of the motorway.

"You mean you come here an' jus' steal business, nothin' said?" The woman bared her teeth in a grin, narrowed eyes surveying the competition. Not as young as me, she mentally noted. Then her mind shifted to Mier's costume, deciding she liked her own better. But maybe Bernard would give her the 'lectro net. Yeah, real nice.

"I'm new. Jus' started. Ain't done no business."

"So maybe convince him. Maybe sign up, huh? But he be mad you didn't find him first."

"That be his problem," Mier said, more to herself than to the whore. "I don't want trouble. Maybe good idea I go away." Mier didn't have time to convince an enraged pimp she had no intention of poaching in his territory. Just ahead was the mouth of an alley, and, if she wasn't mistaken, it would take her where she wanted to go. "Thanks for the warning," she said, moving away.

"Hey! Where you off to?" the woman called. "You can't hide from Bernard! He find you everywhere!"

But Mier had increased her pace as best she could in the tight skirt, and didn't reply.

Mier entered the alley, a dark tunnel running behind a row of warehouses on the right, bars and crash joints on the left. With no people, the environment contrasted sharply with the street. Mier's high heels clicked on cracked pavement, sound echoing between gray native stone and plasticrete, streaked and crusted with dirt. The noise of the street had faded, muffled by high walls that trapped smoggy air, strangely still and sour, the smell a combination of decay, apathy, and rocket exhaust. Garbage spilled from a broken dispos-all, and rats and other scavengers hunted, rustling and squealing. She caught a glimpse of the greenish-brown body of a mutated rodent that was easily the size of a house cat. The creature rose on its haunches and stared at her, eyes glittering like pieces of broken glass, yellow teeth bared in a frustrated snarl as he realized she would not be easy prey. Very careful to keep moving, she stayed in the middle of the alley. Men she could handle, but rats made her skin crawl.

She glanced back and saw the red hood of Bernard's car turn into the opening, silhouetted against the kaleidoscope of street light, but as she watched it paused and then pulled back. It would seem he didn't want to risk the flashy vehicle in such an unsavory avenue—or perhaps he didn't consider her so great a threat as the whore implied. She grinned to herself and moved on.

The passage opened into a yard filled with long rows of enormous freight trailers. Old-fashioned surveillance cameras clung to the walls on either side, high above head level. One of them had a shattered lens, and the other dangled uselessly from its bracket, trailing torn wires. Mier shook her head disparagingly as she checked further. The electric fencenet across the alley was torn in several places. She slipped through and crouched under the end vehicle. From here she spotted a guard shack near the entrance to the street. Luck was still with her, for there was no one visible through the glassine walls.

She left her hiding place and went boldly across the yard. Scratches and dents marred the sides of the trailers, revealing their age and lack of care, while identification numbers and company seal faded toward invisibility. Mier could just decipher the name on one of them as she turned down the row: Galactic Union Terra. No one was in sight, yet she remained in character, her face vacant, as if chewing gum and walking took all of her attention. She went slowly in the direction of the street, passing the big warehouse doors. They were tightly closed, all of the workers gone for the day.

Mier paused. She took the cinstim gum from her mouth and disposed of it by sticking it under one of the trailers. Tucked into the gum was a tiny device that had been disguised as one of the 'lectrogems on her costume. She wiped sticky fingers on her skirt before resuming the undulating walk.

Before she reentered the street, she glanced quickly to the left and right without spotting the noisy red car. Feeling secure, she stepped into the crowd, now heading toward the spaceport. Reaching an intersection, she crossed the sunken motorway, moving with the other pedestrians.

''Hey, Sweet Pink,'' a husky voice whispered in her ear. ''Somebody wanna talka you.''

Before she could reply, her arms were linked by two men in worker's overalls, and she was almost carried from the walkway into the darkness between two buildings. Fear came unbidden and with it anger that anyone would dare to manhandle her. Banking the rage, Mier waited for the right time to react.

She could see the low-slung red car in a strip of light farther down the alley. Bernard's timing couldn't have been worse, for her.

Two more men waited, one of them tall and well muscled, staring at Mier with unfriendly eyes. The other man smiled, jewels set in his teeth flashing even in the shadows.

''So,'' Teeth said. ''Talk is you plan to work my street an' not pay my dues. How come you thinking this thing?''

''I didn't know anyone had a monopoly,'' Mier replied, wondering if she could talk her way out. Rage waited, suppressed, boiling. Soon.

''Mo-nopoly,'' Teeth repeated, grinning and nodding. ''Lady use big words. Fancy talk. How come you working the street an' you got education?''

''Jus' tryin' to make my way. Need credit to live, you know? So maybe I cut you in?''

Teeth laughed. ''Name's Bernard. You wanna work for me?''

A bark of laughter came from one of the bodyguards.

''Fax, you an Slam take the car and pick up resta today's chits,'' Bernard said to the men who had brought Mier in from the street. ''Come back in maybe fifteen minutes.'' He grinned at Mier. ''Me an Gummy here got to do some inter-viewing.''

Faces grinning with knowledge and anticipation, they relinquished their hold and started toward the car. Bernard would take proper care of this one. Too bad they couldn't be in on it. But then, Bernard had a nasty way with people who didn't obey him—as the whore in pink would soon find out.

Mier held her anger with a tight rein. All of this was a waste of time.

"Now, my pretty, educated, little lady," Bernard said very slowly, a leer on his face.

Mier felt a flash of revulsion, and the hairs on her arms rose, electric. She couldn't believe they didn't feel her anger, but then, they weren't tuned to anything but their lust: for power, control, money—for her. Still she held herself in check, ready for what would come next.

"Maybe I gonna have me a little taste of what you gotta sell. You a little old for the business, but maybe . . . some jacks like ex-perience." He extended a very dirty finger and flipped the 'lectro net, making the gems flash crazily. "You see, I can use big words, too."

She took an involuntary step back but came up short against the bodyguard. He gripped both of her wrists, twisting her arms together so he could hold them with one big hand. Bernard came closer, and she could feel his breath in her face, foul, drug-filled. Gummy held her firmly, his free hand tangled in her long hair.

Rage broke free and Mier reacted. She stiffened her arms and, with a sudden twist, pulled both hands free. The wig came off as she moved, leaving Gummy with his mouth open and a handful of false hair. She jerked her leg up, knee smashing into Bernard's groin. As he bent forward, pain-forced breath erupting from between his lips, she slashed the edge of her hand into the back of his neck. He dropped. In almost the same movement she pivoted, her foot extended in a kick that connected with Gummy's stomach. His mouth opened even wider as air was forced out of his lungs. Body limp, he slid down the wall to sit in the filth there, gagging and gasping.

Mier picked up her wig, replaced it, and straightened her clothing as best she could. A tear in the skirt went almost to her waist, but it didn't matter now.

Rage had been satisfied, but still its heat filled her. She took a deep breath, suppressing the remains of adrenaline that raced through her system. While her heart slowed to normal, she counted the wasted minutes. There was still enough time. She took one last look at the pimp and his bodyguard; they wouldn't be troubling anyone for awhile. She smiled, eyes glittering like the rat's, as she turned away.

When Mier reached the street, she blended into the crowd and resumed her careful walk. Before long she reached the steps of the shuttle station and paused, searching for a concealed stud on the inner surface of one of her bracelets. When her fingers found the button, she pressed.

Blocks away, from the direction she had just come, there sounded a dull blast, and a sudden, bright light filled the streets. A distant alarm went off, accompanied by shouts and screams. All around her people stopped, turning, trying to see, to understand what had happened.

Mier walked briskly down the steps and into the station. Her timing couldn't have been better, for a shuttle was just loading. She pressed her palm on an ident plate and, when the computer verified her reservation, joined the last of the passengers to board. As soon as she was in her seat, the doors were sealed and the shuttle lifted, its destination a huge liner in orbit above the planet.

CHAPTER 3

Above the planet, in one of the orbiting liner's cabins, harsh amber light from a computer screen limned a seated figure in the dark shadow of the room. Hester lit a cigarette, the end flashing bright for a moment as she inhaled. Yellow smoke trickled slowly from between thick lips as she studied the information scrolling up the computer screen.

Belosa's only importance was commercial. She had no idea what the planet had been like when the first settlers came there, but whatever it had been—sylvan beauty or vast wasteland—the world was drastically changed, succumbing to man's insatiable drive for power and wealth. Almost the entire surface of the planet and even deep underground warrens were devoted to making more and better products. A prime example of what could happen to a world where profit and expediency were allowed to prevail over ecological concern, Belosa could boast of dead, polluted seas and an atmosphere resembling an organic stew rather than something fit to breathe. If unrestricted growth continued, it would soon be necessary to install an atmospheric generator. It wasn't completely in jest that the editor of one of the largest interplanetary news services—a well-known curmudgeon—pointed out that the greatest fortune on Belosa still waited for the person who could invent a way to mine chemicals from the atmosphere. Some adventurous souls had tried, but atmospheric pollution increased faster than they could clear it.

Despite these problems, however, the planet was wealthy in raw materials and high-tech products. Fifty-seven major cities dotted the continents, each one boasting at least one good-sized spaceport. With off-world consumers clamoring to buy, the transport companies were equally as important and numerous as the manufactories. And with all those ports and freight companies, Hester realized their agent had been fortunate to find the one specific business that had decided to become rich in a less legitimate way.

Legitimate? Hell, no—immoral. And what did the Belosan government do about it? Nothing! They needed more proof, they said, proof that the substance was dangerous—as if the near destruction and then takeover of an entire planet wasn't convincing! This excuse meant the same thing as "no comment" in the vocabulary of the uninvolved. And thus the Federation had been forced to interfere.

Hester's eyes remained on the screen as her fingers ground the last inch of the cigarette into a dish and then lit another. It was time. The last and most difficult part of the job should be just about over. There shouldn't be anything to worry about. Mier Silver was a good agent, a survivor. But they were all survivors, she reminded herself, until the one time they didn't make it back. And Silver had been out of contact for the past forty-eight hours. If she ever had to work with her again, Hester decided, she would end up with gray hair or an ulcer, or both, despite modern medicine. The woman was too independent . . . or dead. Either way, it meant complications.

Hester lit another cigarette, watching as the information on the screen ended with a list of cross-references. She snapped off the machine, already more than familiar with the material. Reviewing had been a way to pass the time while she waited—the hardest part of her job. There would be one more shuttle before the liner left orbit, and hopefully Silver would be on board. In any case, Hester was going down to the planet, to clean up after Silver, or to finish the job herself, whichever was necessary.

A soft chime sounded, startling her from immobility and silence.

"Come in!" she bellowed.

Mier Silver sauntered into the cabin, looking like a whore who'd been in a cat fight, and lost. But at least she had returned in one piece.

"Is there a power shortage?" the agent wanted to know.

"I knew you preferred it dark," Hester replied. "And you're late. I expected you yesterday."

"And you sat in the darkness all this time? I'm flattered."

"Don't be! Why didn't you report on schedule? And what kept you?"

"There were unavoidable delays."

"But you managed to stop the shipment?"

"Check the newscast. There was a mysterious explosion in the freight yard of Galactic Union Terra. And there should have been quite a fire."

"Good," the control grunted. She sat back in her chair and waved her hand, indicating the portable computer on the table. "Show me what you found."

Mier took a seat and pushed buttons. There was a slight visual vibration in the air, and a three-dimensional cube appeared, defining a space about two feet square. Then she removed the bracelet from her wrist, tugging it straight before she plugged one end into the side of the keyboard. A cascade of sparks filled the space, shifting and coalescing into a slowly revolving, holographic model. Colors changed as various mutations were indicated.

"These are some of the popular, high-yield grains developed to meet conditions on the various colony worlds," Mier explained. "I found the file in a computer at the research center. Cabbing and Jameson were responsible, as we suspected. Now watch this." She pointed to the hologram as a group of angry red cells grew and began to invade the model. Within seconds the original sample had been replaced with something completely different.

"So that's the virus," Hester commented. "Nasty thing."

"It's artificial, but once established, self-perpetuating. The biologists on Dexter called it the Red Scourge, and it was responsible for destroying almost the entire harvest there, and on Brace's World. I can't imagine why anyone would want to create such a thing."

"Economic advantage. Just be glad we caught it in time. You recorded enough to indict Cabbing and Jameson?"

"All of their records as well as conversations and phone calls."

"Good." Hester got to her feet and unplugged the bracelet. "I'll go down, take care of the arrests and clean up. Your part's finished."

"And I can go home?"

"I booked you a sleeper, as you requested."

"Sounds wonderful."

Living mostly on adrenaline and stimulants until the job was over, Mier could finally give way to exhaustion. While Hester took a shuttle to the planet's surface, she went to the sleep-tank deck. Entering into a small prep room, she dimmed the lights before flipping the contact lenses from her eyes. With a sigh of relief, she stripped, dumping clothing, bodypads, and wig into the disposal chute. The flash shower removed the makeup and cheap scent. When she was finished, short sandy hair stood out from her head like a halo, each strand charged and crackling with static electricity, until the damper discharged the field.

Mier went to look into the mirror, to be sure she was herself again. Some white strands lightened her hair . . . more, she thought, than the last time she'd checked. But then, this job would turn anyone's hair white. There was a suggestion of sag around the eyes, too, she decided. It would soon be time for a rejuv treatment, if she ever stayed in one place long enough.

High cheekbones slanted her brown eyes—mystery-eyes, someone had once called them, admiring the large pupils. Mier knew that women in ancient Europe dropped poison into their eyes to dilate the pupil, believing it made them more alluring. The poison was eventually named after this practice—belladonna, beautiful lady. But Mier often wished her eyes were normal and could see without discomfort in strong light. Still, there were certain advantages, and not only cosmetic. She blinked her dark lashes, and made a sound halfway between a yawn and a sigh as she left the room. Rows of tanks awaited the passengers who preferred to travel asleep. An attendant came to escort Mier, and to make sure she was comfortable. Electrodes were fastened to her forehead and chest, a monitor turned on, and the reading checked. While Mier watched, the tank's controls were set to revive her in forty-eight days. As the top closed, a narcotic was pumped in and her lids dropped. The suspension field came on, cradling her body as she slept. She wouldn't wake until the liner was in orbit above another planet, named Earth.

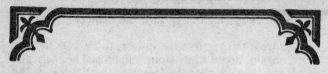

CHAPTER 4

"What do you mean, there's a survivor?" the man's voice demanded over the comlink.

The screens at both ends remained blank despite the heavily shielded line.

"Precisely what I said. He was recovered three weeks ago."

"Then it's too late. The treaty's already been signed."

"That's not the case," the other speaker was at haste to explain. "He was in an escape pod, barely alive. There's no way a treaty could have been negotiated."

"But you don't know that for certain."

"I don't. But I will soon. We're sending in another agent."

"You'd take that risk? How will it be justified?"

"The situation will be different. We won't send her as part of a mission this time. She'll go in alone."

There was reluctance in the man's voice. "I don't know . . . Who is this agent? No, I think it's time we send one of our own people."

"I don't think that's wise. We'll attract too much attention."

"I'll take it up with the committee; let them decide. Who's the agent you're proposing to send?"

"Mier Silver. She's good, and she's experienced. And I don't think she'll give us any problems when it's over."

CHAPTER 5

Mier Silver was tall and slender, built for nervous speed rather than strength, but years of training had taught her to compensate. Strength, she had learned, did not depend on muscle alone; there were other sources of power, and they could be much more devastating.

For the past twenty-three years she had been contracted to the Federal Administration, seventeen of those years as a field operative. She entered the Academy at sixteen, and spent six years in the rigorous mental and physical training that produced Special Intelligence Agents. Not every one of the students made it to this branch of the service; constant testing and monitoring weeded them out until maybe one in twenty exhibited the right combination of intelligence, nerve, and reflexes. And these agents were the very best—they had to be; they were expected to do whatever was necessary to complete their assignment, or die trying. So far Mier had survived, but not without mental and physical scars, reminders of the more advanced lessons she had had to learn, lessons in improvisation that could never be taught in a classroom.

Back home on the orbital station named Terra III, she worked out in the gym, trying to flush the accumulation of stress from her latest assignment out of her system. She went through a series of slow, graceful movements

that were part martial arts, part dance, timed to her
heartbeat and breathing. Every muscle in the body was
involved in the workout, for it required intense concentration and a focus of energies. Afterward she usually
felt drained, but also clearheaded and peaceful.

Over and over again she repeated one sequence, her
mind relaxed and calm, as if in a trance. Opposing forces
were used to amplify strength; certain gestures were designed to confuse the opponent's eye, to hide where a
blow would come from. The sum total was power ex-
pressed in grace, energy in breathing, while the mind
remained apart though a part. A meditation, this dance
without music. A deadly dance, a warrior's dance. Bare
feet sure and light on the polished floor—a cat stance, a
blow, a block, and back to ready, at rest . . . then the
dance was over.

"Bravo!" The sound of clapping tore into her awareness just as she was about to begin again. She turned to
see Inspector Brian Palo standing in the doorway.

"This a social call or business?" she demanded.

"Heard you were back. Thought I'd come and congratulate you. Mind if I turn up the lights a little?"

"Yes." Mier felt the weight coming back to her body
and mind as she wiped at the sweat running into her eyes.
She donned a pair of tinted glasses as the lights—against
her protest—came up to half-normal. The glasses were
something of an anachronism, but she usually wore them
between assignments since they were easier to put on and
take off than contacts.

Despite his flippant manner, she knew the deputy director of the agency wouldn't have come to find her without a good reason. She was beginning to think of him as
a bearer of bad tidings—every time she saw him it heralded another nasty job. But he always smiled. He'll be
grinning like that when he dies, she thought as she crossed
the floor toward the dark man. He was undeniably handsome, and many of the women on the station welcomed
his attention. Mier, however, found him irritating, although professionally she had to admire his efficiency. It
was his apparent inability, or perhaps unwillingness, to
take anything seriously that grated on her nerves. She'd

once seen him kill a man with his bare hands, all the while wearing the same grin on his face.

"The Professor sent me for you. You're shipping out on a shuttle tomorrow."

"What's so important?"

"We'll brief you in the Professor's office."

"Do I have time for a shower first? A water shower?"

"Of course, Babe. Take all the time you want. You know the Professor doesn't mind waiting."

"Like hell he doesn't," she snapped. "And don't call me Babe."

"Loosen up, Silver."

Mier brushed past him and started toward the locker room.

"You did a good job on your last assignment," he said, falling into step beside her. "Have any problems?"

She paused, leaning against the wall, well out of the way of the other people in the corridor. "It was tedious. I spent a lot of time holed up in Highport with nothing to do but fight off bandybugs and wait."

"Your report said the lead we gave you worked out."

"I was able to get to the computer in the Science Center, and went from there. But even then, I spent two nerve-racking nights hiding in a pitch black warehouse while I tried to find out when the virus would be shipped."

"You know I'd feel sorry for you if I didn't know you can see in the dark as well as I can in daylight."

Mier capitulated, grinning. "Well, after all that, the ending was almost an anticlimax. Planting the explosive was easy."

"We're grateful you were able to do it. I'd hate to think what would've happened if that stuff got to Felix or one of the other agricultural worlds."

"But it didn't. Look, Brian, I'm not too happy about going out again so soon. I was looking forward to a couple of weeks off. I have it coming."

"I know, but this job's important."

"According to you, it's always important! Isn't there another agent you could send? Why me?"

"The Professor thinks you're perfect for the job."

Brian paused. "Besides, you're the only agent available."

"You're joking!"

"No. Diaz is in the hospital, Su'ha's still in rehab, and everyone else is out on assignment."

"What a great career I picked," Mier grumbled quietly. "It's nothing but one exciting mission after another. If I didn't know better I'd think you were deliberately trying to get me killed. Maybe I should opt for retraining."

"Don't complain. At least you eat regularly, which is more than a lot of people can say. And with no time to spend your credits, you're getting rich."

"If you keep me going at this rate, I won't live long enough to spend anything."

"You've still got a few good years ahead of you, if you're careful."

"Not the way I'm aging. I've been out five months straight. I'm tired and I want some peace and quiet before I forget what it's like. Besides, according to the regs, you're required to give me time off between assignments."

"That's true—on paper. You're dealing with the real world here."

"Spare me your real world!" She went around him toward the dressing room, but he followed.

"I could scrub your back," he offered softly, a suggestive twinkle in his dark eyes as he held the door open for her.

Mier scowled. "Not a chance. If I can't have time off, the least I deserve is five minutes of peace in the shower."

"Never say I didn't try. I'll meet you at the Professor's office at twelve hundred."

"All right."

"See you there . . . Babe." Brian's laughter was muffled as the door swung shut between them, cutting off her retort.

The smile left his face as he made his way to the administration level. He could tease Mier, and enjoyed pushing hard enough to get her riled, but both of them knew he wasn't serious. His flirtations were a game to him, something to be enjoyed for a night or two, but nothing more. This, he insisted, was understood by his partners before they got involved. In reality, his ideal was rarely realized—although he refused to admit it—for his partners, being female, often took on him and the game as a challenge, resulting in a number of sticky emotional scenes when they invariably lost.

Mier, on the other hand, preferred other kinds of challenges and tended to form longer-lasting ties, which was both a strength and a weakness. It made her emotionally vulnerable, as her relationship with Karr had proved. And this, Brian had argued once, proved his point: Life in their business was uncertain, so why not get the most out of it while there was still time, without entanglements that could prove disastrous in the end? Karr had been killed on assignment, and Mier had almost died as a result—not a happy ending for anyone. No, he realized, despite the occasional confusion, his way was best.

A frown creased his brow as he walked, his mind returning to the assignment. This time, Mier was right; she had been out too long without leave. But the mission was important. And it was also true that the Professor had insisted she be the one to go. Strange about that: the Professor usually took better care of his people, preparing and scheduling assignments so that his operatives worked under optimum conditions. This meant the best information, equipment, backup, and support available, as well as rating the agent's own physical and mental readiness. Mier wasn't ready to go out on a new mission. The problem of Tori had waited this long and could probably afford to wait even longer, right? But the Professor insisted: the time had to be now, and the agent, Mier Silver. Brian couldn't think of a reason for such haste, unless . . . He stopped dead in the hallway, the man hurrying along behind him narrowly avoiding a collision. Oblivious, his mind fastened on a new thought, and when he moved again, he was walking fast.

There was no reason for haste, he reasoned, unless someone else had learned the secret of Tori! Yes! That had to be it! But why hadn't the Professor said so? Even

though Brian was second-in-command of SIA, he knew
there were things his boss kept from him. It was all part
of another game, this one called galactic secret agent.

And with these thoughts, all his consideration for Mier
dissolved. Again she was little more than a tool, something to be used as long as possible and then discarded.

After a moment more of deliberation, Brian went to a
link box. There was no way to insure privacy on a public
line, but at the same time, it would be difficult to monitor
without advance warning. And lately he had the feeling
that his office was even more public than this box.

He deliberately left the screen blank as he punched in
an access code.

"It's me," he announced when a male voice answered. "Your old sailing buddy."

"Which has to be a clue, since I know you have an
advanced case of agoraphobia."

"Yeah, well . . ." Brian had the grace to be discom-
posed for a second. "Did you get my note?"

"It's all set. In fact I was about to leave. You still think
we can bring this thing off?"

"I have faith in you. It will be like old times. We sure
pulled enough crazy stunts in our younger and wilder
days. And this one's for the best possible cause."

"Wish you could convince my father of that."

"You're not going to back out, are you?"

"Of course not. I'll give it a try."

Brian gave a satisfied sigh. "All right then. See you
later."

Mier tilted her head back and closed her eyes as water
beat against her lids and plastered her hair to her head.
It felt good, and she leaned back against the wall, relaxing until the ration buzzer sounded. When the water au-
tomatically switched off, the dryer turned on, blowing
warm air against her skin.

Emerging from the shower, she palmed open her locker
and took out the clothes she had bought earlier that day.
She looked at them for a moment before starting to dress.
The outfit was too formal for work because she had
planned to wear it for quite a different occasion. With a

sigh she pulled on the skintight bronze bodysuit and shrugged into a black tunic, the sculptured shoulders holding the panels slightly away from her body so that they dropped in a straight, elegant line to her knees. So much for R and R, she thought as she stuck her feet into soft, leg-hugging boots. There was no time or need for makeup, though she quickly brushed her hair.

When this was done, she strapped a holster onto her right forearm, pulling the tunic's loose sleeve over it. The pistol it held was a custom ML-Delta that shot light or explosive pellets, and it was her favorite weapon. One of its best features was the neurolink, created just for her; at a thought the pistol would be in her hand, aimed, and fired before a conventional handgun could be drawn. She wore it everywhere, despite the problem every time it set off a weapon scanner.

She went quickly to one of the main tunnels and stepped onto the passenger walkway, moving to the faster middle lane. Promptness wasn't her strong point, and her boss didn't like to be kept waiting, especially not by his agents.

Mier checked her chronometer—eleven fifty-five. She started walking on the moving strip, dodging the other pedestrians. Fortunately at this hour there weren't many people to slow her down. Unfortunately there was a new security guard in the Tower's lobby. He took a long time at the computer, checking her identification and weapon permit while she fumed, and the timepiece on the wall pulsed on past twelve.

CHAPTER 6

Three people were waiting in the Professor's office when Mier finally arrived. The Professor didn't comment on her tardiness beyond a faint tightening of his lips and a curt nod to her quiet, one-word apology. Brian raised his eyebrow in an exaggerated gesture meant to say "I warned you."

The third man, a man in a tailored, metacord jumpsuit, stood silently in front of the viewport and paid her no attention beyond a brief glance when she came in. He stood at ease, gazing outside as if deep in contemplation of the view of Earth almost filling the window.

The current head of the Special Intelligence Agency was called the Professor, for as well as his government position he held several academic degrees. Probably the best director the Service had ever known, he was determined to keep his spotless reputation, and thus tended to be as demanding of his agents as he was of himself. This didn't mean he wasn't fair; there just wasn't much latitude for failure in the department. He was of medium height, and his finely drawn features and smooth skin hid his true age. Mier didn't know exactly how old he was, but compulsory retirement was at seventy-five, and it seemed he was nearing that. He was neatly dressed, as always, in a semiformal gray suit, the pattern modified from an antique style currently in vogue in the downside cities. The most arresting feature about him was his eyes. They glowed a clear, bright blue from beneath dark brows. Many people found his direct gaze hard to meet—especially if they had something on their conscience.

"Mier, this is Hac," he said by way of introduction. "He'll be your partner for your next assignment."

Mier's stomach gave a sickening lurch, as if she had been suddenly dropped a great distance. "What do you mean," she heard herself ask. "I never work with a partner. I can't. You know that." How can they do this to me? her mind screamed. Shocked, she was nauseated and dizzy, and fought to maintain her equilibrium

"I am aware of your background, but these are unusual circumstances."

"Then you'd better get someone else to take the job. Whatever it is, I can't do it."

She stood stiffly, facing her superior, inwardly appalled by her defiance. Still she had no choice; she couldn't work with a partner, no matter what the circumstances.

There was complete silence as she waited for the Professor's anger. It didn't come. She caught a glimpse of Brian from the corner of her eye. He was grinning at her.

The Professor seemed unperturbed. "I didn't think you would mind working with Hac."

"Why not? What makes him different?" she demanded, voice tight.

"Silver," Brian warned quietly.

"Hac is an acronym. The letters stand for Human Analog Computer," the Professor said calmly.

"Analog computer? I thought they were obsolete?"

"Wrong connection, Babe," Brian explained with deliberate, almost condescending care. "It's not 'analog computer,' they *are* obsolete. Hac is a robotic computer that happens to be a *human* analog, meaning 'like unto.' "

Mier ignored him and bought herself some thinking time by crossing the room to where the figure stood. "I've never heard of such a thing. Robots, yes. But I didn't know they were making anything so realistic."

"The model is new. Hac is a prototype."

"How will the manufacturer feel if he's damaged on the mission? I may get into a situation where I don't have time to protect a valuable piece of equipment."

"Let us worry about that." Brian came to join her beside the android. "Look at him, Silver. You'd never know he wasn't alive. And in a way he is; the frame's duraplast, but they've actually developed a way to grow a surface covering of skin and hair. That part's completely organic."

She looked. The machine's chest rose and fell as he "breathed." His skin was dark, textured with lines and pores. She could even see where hairs "grew" from his head.

Mier touched his cheek and felt warm flesh. She recoiled. He was almost too real! The blue eyes were looking at her now, one brow raised. "Who built him? He's amazingly lifelike."

"He belongs to Geo-Mining," the Professor said. "They're financing the research at Nieman's. They're also the ones who insisted the android be included on this mission. His job is to record and report back to them. I didn't like it either at first, but then, I had very little to say about it."

Mier stared at the android, who was staring back at her, and had a sudden feeling, a suspicion. "Are you certain he's not real?" She felt foolish as soon as the words were out of her mouth, but her suspicion had been quite intense. Even now she thought she could feel heat radiating from his body.

Brian cocked his head, his eyes wide. "Of course he isn't!"

"Hac, show her please," the Professor asked politely.

At his words the android pulled up his left sleeve. Mier couldn't see what he did, but the skin on the inside of his wrist loosened so he could pull a flap away, revealing a complex frame of gleaming metal intertwined with wires and some of the smallest hydraulics she had ever seen.

"That doesn't look like flesh and blood to me," Brian quipped.

Hac pressed the skin closed and stood looking down at her again. Did the slight crinkle at the corners of his eyes imply amusement? She couldn't be sure.

"All right, I believe you. He's an android, and he's coming on the mission. But what am I supposed to do with him? I know nothing about working with androids."

"Treat him exactly as you would a human partner," the Professor told her. He leaned back in his chair behind the big desk in the corner. "You'll have to make the best of this, Mier. Seven of the Ruling Houses are funding the mission. It's vital to Earth's economic stability, and that's why the Geo-Mining boys are risking a piece of equipment as valuable as Hac."

"Right." She left the android and moved closer to her superior's desk. Without waiting for an invitation, she seated herself in one of the comfortable chairs. Brian moved with her and took the other seat.

"Exactly what is the mission?"

"We're sending you to a planet called Tori."

"Tori? I've never heard of it."

"Sigma Draconis Four. The only M-class world in that system," Brian supplied.

"Which still doesn't tell me anything. What's on this planet that's so important?"

"The government sent an S and D—Survey and Diplomatic—mission there four months ago. It was the second team. One of them managed to return."

"One of them what?"

"One person," the Professor told her. He broke eye contact as a shadow flitted over his face. It was gone almost immediately. "The project seems to have been plagued with bad luck from the start." He sounded annoyed, as if it were his department's fault. "Tori was discovered a little over two years ago. Since it already had a thriving class-four culture, it was closed to colonization. But once we had the translators working, we did receive permission from the natives to establish a diplomatic base. In fact the Torians seemed eager for us to do so. Very eager.''

''Then we got the first assay reports on the mineral samples from the planet,'' Brian interjected. ''Tori has incredibly rich deposits of tridenite. Probably the richest in the known galaxy. And a lot of other minerals as well.''

''That's why Geo-Mining is interested?'' Mier suggested.

''You can see why we were eager to get results from the mission. If the Torians could be made to understand the advantages of an alliance with the Federation of Ruling Houses, we hoped to establish a mining treaty with them.''

''What happened?'' Mier curled one of her legs under her, absently smoothing the soft material over her thigh.

''Nothing,'' Brian interjected. ''Absolutely nothing!''

''That's a bit of an exaggeration,'' the Professor chided. ''The mission set up a base station and began negotiations. Almost right away headquarters received a series of reports detailing the initial steps of contact. Then, as Brian so succinctly puts it, there was nothing for seven long months.''

The Professor lined up a stack of microtapes on his desk, and Mier decided she had never seen him so worried about a case. The thought gave her pause; there was more to this assignment than what appeared on the surface.

''That's when SIA was called in,'' her superior continued. ''When it was time to send a supply ship we included one of our people in the crew. A month later we received a very polite message from Tori. It seems that the supply ship crash-landed. There were no survivors. The Torians sent vistapes of the wreckage, and profuse apologies that they were unable to return the bodies— they don't have spaceflight capabilities.''

''How did they send the message?''

''Recorder drone from the diplo team's supplies,'' Brian answered.

''What about our mission? Didn't they have a shuttle?''

"Short-range only. They were depending on supply ships to rotate personnel."

"So we sent a second supply ship," the Professor continued. "With another one of our people in the crew. Then there was more silence until a week ago when we recovered a survivor. It was our man. We have no way of knowing how long he was in the escape pod. In fact, we don't understand very much about what happened to him. When we found him, he was nearly dead from starvation, yet, for some reason, he hadn't touched any of the emergency food supplies in the pod."

"You can imagine the shape he was in," Brian added quickly when the Professor paused.

As he spoke, Mier turned her head to face him. He stared into her eyes for an intense second, trying to send her a nonverbal message—something he didn't want to say out loud. There was definitely more going on here than the obvious.

Mier turned her attention back to the Professor. "You have his report? What's his explanation for all of that?"

"There is no report."

"But you said he was alive . . . Is he hurt? Unconscious?"

"She'd better see him, sir," Brian suggested.

The professor sighed and seemed to meditate on this for a moment. "Yes. I agree." He got heavily to his feet and led the way to the door.

Brian fell into step beside her as they left the office. "This is all the information we have. Not much for you to work with, I'm afraid." He dropped his voice. "Nice outfit. Is there still time for me to take you someplace where it would be more appropriate?"

"Sorry, I have . . . that is, I had other plans. Now it looks like I'll spend my evening studying—alone!"

He laughed at her angry reply and changed the subject. "I've put tapes of the supply-ship crash, as well as all of the reports from the first mission, in the computer under your password. You can review them before you leave."

Mier gave a curt nod, and looked at the android who was tagging along, wondering if he was to have access to the information as well. He's just a machine, she re-

minded herself. Just as expendable as the rest of the
agents at SIA. Her mouth pulled down slightly as she
dismissed her bitter thoughts. This was her job, and
right now there was nothing more important than the
mission.

CHAPTER 7

The Professor led them down the hall and into an express
elevator. After he tapped the destination and a code into
the keypad, they still had to wait for confirmation from
the main computer. Mier knew there were secret parts
to the satellite, but this time the elevator traveled much
farther than she remembered ever going before.

No one spoke. The Professor looked abstracted, not
only worried about something, but also strangely sad.
This mission was obviously troubling him a great deal.
Brian was smiling, as always, and he stood with his
shoulders resting nonchalantly against the wall of the car.
His posture was deceiving, however; from the faint wrin-
kles on his forehead she could tell that his thoughts
weren't untroubled. Only the android, Hac, looked un-
concerned. As if he felt Mier's eyes on him, he turned
his head.

She had to look up at him and found this disconcerting. Although she stood just under two meters tall, the
android topped her by most of a head. "Have you been
programmed for speech, or are you a mute?"

"I am capable of mimicking all human functions,"
Hac responded in a calm voice.

"I can't imagine why." She resented him and wanted
to take her frustrations out on someone, on anything—
right now even a machine would serve.

"I bet you could come up with something, Silver, if

you try real hard,'' Brian said, his grin growing even wider.

She ignored him. "You don't seem very interested in our mission,'' she told the android. "You didn't ask questions or add anything at the briefing."

"That is correct'' was the quiet answer. Hac gazed back at her, his face expressionless.

Mier couldn't decide if he was being deliberately provoking or not. Once again she imagined an amused gleam in his eyes. "Why not?'' she demanded.

"I had nothing to add to the information. My role is primarily that of observer." His voice was as expressionless as his face.

"Just think of him as a glorified computer, Babe,'' Brian suggested. "At least he won't bother you with needless chitchat."

"Unlike some people I could name . . .'' The car doors hissed open, interrupting the rest of her testy response.

They emerged into a short corridor of white tiles, glaringly bright after the dim cab of the elevator, and Mier's glasses darkened even more to compensate. A strange, faint smell colored the air, something sharp. She sniffed and recognized the antiseptic odor she usually associated with a hospital.

She followed the Professor through a door at the end of the hall into a well-equipped sickbay. A busy life-function monitor and a bank of video screens backed the desk, while against the far wall a glass-fronted case held medications. The monitor screens attracted Mier's attention; she recognized the hall they had just left on one of them. Others showed different views of a figure sitting slumped on the edge of a bed in a bare room. A nurse, dressed in the pale blue of the healer's guild, came to his feet as they entered.

"How is the patient?'' the Professor asked.

"The same, sir. There's been no change at all."

"Has he eaten yet?''

"No, we're still feeding him."

"This is the surviving member of the mission?'' Mier squinted at the monitor, trying to get a better look at the man. He seemed familiar.

"Yes," the Professor answered. He looked at the nurse. "Let us in, Saam."

After the nurse unlocked the door, the Professor waved Mier into the inner room. Then he allowed Hac and Brian to pass, while he remained standing in the doorway.

Mier went straight to the bed and froze. "Jarry!"

Jarry hadn't been young, but his thick brown hair had turned completely white since she last saw him. The lifeless eyes didn't respond to their entrance or to Mier's exclamation. He sat on the side of the bed without moving, emaciated—a tent of skin stretched over bones—and barely recognizable as the man she knew. There was no tension in his muscles, and his posture suggested that he would topple over at the slightest push.

"That was Jarry," Brian said.

"But what happened to him?" An alarm went off in the back of her mind.

Jarry had been one of her instructors at the Academy, and she'd known him well. An energetic individual, one of SIA's top field operatives, he was clever and resourceful. She couldn't believe this was the same man.

Mier knew that the Professor sincerely cared for his agents' welfare, even though he never hesitated to send them into hazardous situations. Now he kept as far away from Jarry as he could and still be in the same room, his stiff posture evidence of his discomfort. "We have no way of knowing how long he was in the escape pod. But however long, it still doesn't account for all the things that are wrong with him."

Brian hastily broke in. "He was almost dead of starvation and exhaustion, and covered with bruises. His arm had been broken and allowed to heal without being set."

Even after all of her experience, she couldn't help but feel a sense of horror at the wreck of the man before her. "He wouldn't have let that happen. And he knew enough field medicine to take care of himself if there was no one else around."

"I would agree with you," Brian said, "if I hadn't seen it with my own eyes. But this is Jarry, and his condition is real."

"Someone did this to him. The Torians? Someone from the mission?"

"That's another one of the strange things. We did a passive memory scan, trying to reconstruct what happened, but the reading was so jumbled, there was no making sense of it. And there's no evidence that he was physically restrained. Otherwise I would be tempted to agree with you."

"Do you know how long he was in the pod?"

"He had severe dermal ulcerations from sitting in one position for a very long time. Days, maybe even weeks. In places his jumpsuit was literally growing on his body."

"Jarry," Mier said softly, bending to look into the man's face. He stared back at her with no sign of recognition. "Jarry, can you hear me? It's Mier Silver."

The vacant eyes gazed straight ahead, and the man gave no indication he had heard.

"Mier, we're pretty sure he's not in there," Brian said softly. "That's not Jarry anymore."

"He's still alive. He's breathing . . ."

"Not according to his encephalograph."

She straightened up and turned to face Brian.

"You should see them for yourself." The Professor backed out the door and away from the sight of the man on the bed. He picked a stack of flimsies off of the desk and flipped through them until he found what he wanted. Mier looked over his shoulder.

"Here are the recordings that were made when we first recovered Jarry." He gave the sheet to Mier and removed another page. "This is the scan made just this morning."

The wavy lines were a mystery to her, but the difference in the two pages would have been obvious to anyone. "I don't understand. The ones from this morning are almost flat, but the first set show an incredible amount of activity. What does it mean?"

"We aren't sure. The readings when he was first brought in are abnormal . . . spiky, fast. According to Dr. Burton, the activity is doubled." His finger traced the line on the other sheet. "Beta waves are completely suppressed. They affect sensory reception and initiation of motor impulses. He is effectively catatonic: they assume it's some form of *flexibilitas cerea*, but how it happened or why they cannot say." He relinquished the papers to Mier. "As long as someone takes care of him, they believe he'll remain in this state. But his consciousness . . . his self . . ." The Professor shook his head, his lips held tightly closed. "We don't know what happened, and until we find out, there's nothing we can do for him."

"You said Burton was the physician in charge?"

"Yes."

"Who's he working with?"

"I'm not sure. I believe Gladys or maybe Dowling. They're both class-one empaths."

"But they still couldn't reach him?"

"No."

In the long silence that followed, Mier went to look through the door again. Jarry hadn't moved. Without a mind, he was no longer the man she knew. She shuddered. The varieties of death were as infinite as the worlds that spawned them. Even though accustomed to dealing with death in many forms, she didn't think she'd ever get over feeling sick about it.

Mier turned back to the room. "When do I leave?" she asked, her voice grim.

The Professor looked at the chronometer on his wrist. "You and Hac will leave for Tori in thirty-two hours. That will give you just enough time to requisition anything you'll need, and to study the background material. We've arranged a cover; Brian will provide the details. And now if you will excuse me, I have another appointment." He started toward the door, but paused and looked back. "All I want from you is an explanation. As usual, you'll act as you see fit under the circumstances you may encounter. If possible you will also arrange for the evacuation of any surviving members of the mission. We will have to find another way to negotiate a treaty with Tori."

"But you don't believe anyone on Tori is still alive?" she asked. She read the answer in his eyes before he spoke.

"In light of the evidence . . . what there is of it, no, I don't. Before we can make further plans, however, we need to know what has happened to the people we sent, and why. Report back as soon as you can.'' The Professor nodded farewell and left them.

CHAPTER 8

Mier had two pieces of irrefutable proof, one in her hands, the other sitting in the other room—Mission: Tori had aspects that went beyond the ordinary assignment. Or did it? she asked herself. There were perfectly ordinary reasons for what had happened to Jarry. A mishandled mindprobe could leave the victim brain-dead. But what about the earlier encephalograph? What about the frenetic activity of the brain then?

"What did Dr. Burton say about these first graphs?" Mier asked Brian.

"He didn't know what caused them. There are certain drugs—phencyclidines, he called them—that can cause similar brain waves, but there was nothing unusual in the blood workup. And he was very careful to check for drugs."

"What about mindprobe? Could it have gone bad?"

He shook his head. "Don't think so. Burton said the machine wouldn't have registered anything if that was the case. Besides, one of the empaths was monitoring the whole time. Burton's notes are in the file: you can see them if you want."

"No." Mier replaced the printed sheets and turned back. "Now what?"

"Let's go up to my office, where we can be more comfortable, and I'll brief you on your cover." He leered at her. "You'll love this one, Babe."

"Must you always mock? Jarry's in there as good as dead. You're an insensitive bastard; do you know that?" She drew a deep breath, regretting her outburst of anger.

He raised his eyebrow. "We're back to that, are we?

An agent functions better without a lot of useless emotional clutter, Silver. I keep telling you that. This is a dangerous profession. And Jarry knew it."

Mier gave a snort of disgust, but followed him into the hallway.

"Take a lesson from your new partner. He observes and says nothing. He doesn't feel and is therefore efficient."

"He's been about as useful as a shadow. I hope he participates more when we're in the field."

By this time they had arrived at the elevator. Mier and Hac stepped to the rear, leaving Brian to work the controls. The doors hissed shut and they began to move.

"I have just one question," she began.

"Only one?" he teased.

"Be serious, will you?"

"All right. What's the question?"

"We've already sent two agents to Tori. Why are you sending me? What do you think I can do if the others have failed?"

"We sent them as part of an official envoy. You're going in alone, through the back door, so to speak."

"Back door? I don't see how we can get around on a planet of aliens without being noticed. Unless they're humanoid?"

"After a fashion. There are holos in your files. But no, we don't expect you to be invisible. Just find some way to deal with the problem, and avoid whatever got Jarry and the others."

"Obese possibility!"

"You underrate yourself, Silver. At least you know there's a problem. The other agents went in cold, more or less. And you have a definite edge with some of your less common abilities. You're unique. That's why the Professor decided you were perfect for this assignment." Suddenly Brian reached out, pushing a button and stopping the car in the shaft. "I have a few things to add to what the Professor told you."

Mier caught her balance after the sudden halt and deliberately looked around her. "In the elevator? Charming surroundings for a briefing!"

"I know for certain that the elevator isn't monitored, but I'm not sure about the room back there or my office."

"You think there's a leak in security?"

"I don't know. It's the only explanation for some of the things that have been happening, but I have to admit, it's a pretty slim possibility. For one thing, it's next to impossible to penetrate a government complex like this one."

"But you are looking into it?"

"Of course. So far we haven't found anything. Agency offices have always been monitored; you know that—it's part of security. But either there's been an unauthorized use of the information, or there's an extra bug we haven't been able to find." For once Brian sounded serious.

"Then how do you know it exists?"

He gave a snort of laughter. "You know the agency. We have our ways."

Mier did indeed know.

"Anyway, the details of your cover," Brian continued. "There's a freighter leaving for Stonewall at three hundred hours tomorrow night. You're registered as a businessperson going to arrange a sales agreement for an outfit out of Denver called Three-C. All this has been in the works for a couple of weeks—reservations and so forth. We've sent 'grams ahead arranging meetings with some of the local businessmen."

"Names?"

"Mier Silver and Hac Andrews. We couldn't backstop complete new IDs, but these have been well documented. The data clerk got pretty creative with your file this time, Silver. You've even got a detailed list of hobbies including light sailing and, if I remember correctly, bonzai."

"Everyone's doing bonzai these days," she complained lightly. "So Tori's within easy range of Stonewall?"

"It's the freighter's destination, and the only transport we could find going in the right direction. You may be followed, so use the time on board to find out who it is. Also, Stonewall is only a two-day hop from Tori." Brian hesitated as if he was going to say something else, but then continued quickly. "We have permanent agents on Stonewall, and we've arranged for one of them to work with you. By the time you arrive, she'll have found a ship for you. I'm afraid you'll have to pilot yourself."

Mier was listening to his words with one part of her mind while another reviewed what she'd heard about Stonewall. The name was familiar for some reason, then she suddenly remembered. "You're sending us into the Stone Field, aren't you?"

Brian raised his eyebrows in surprise. "You know about that?"

"Yeah, I know about it. Stonewall is one of the planets on the edge of the Field. I've heard it has quite a reputation." Mier wasn't sure whether to be amused or angry. She settled for amazed. "That's why no one found Tori before now; it's in the Stone Field, isn't it?"

"No better place to hide a planet."

"But the Field is impossible to navigate."

"Almost impossible. And it isn't quite as bad as its reputation. We've had ships in and out of there for years."

"And how many have you lost?"

"Space travel is always risky."

"Which is all the more reason not to go into places you know are dangerous."

"You're not losing your nerve, are you, Babe?"

"What do you think?"

Brian grinned and then laughed out loud. "Don't worry about it. You'll have a navigational tape for the Field, and your nav computer will do all the work for you. Despite rumors to the contrary, we do consider our operatives' safety."

Mier raised a skeptical eyebrow.

"Why do I get the feeling you don't believe me?" Brian shook his head, and then changed the subject. "Be careful, Mier. You'll have to watch who you trust on this mission. Even agency people could be suspect, except me, of course."

"What about my contact on Stonewall?"

"We checked her thoroughly, and we're pretty sure she's all right."

"How bad is the security breach?"

"Probably worse than we know. It's what we used to call major serious."

"How do you think it will affect the mission?"

"We have reason to believe there are outside interests

who would do just about anything to get a treaty with Tori. The lease will be worth a fortune, and if control of the Torian minerals falls into the wrong hands, it would be very easy to exploit the resources. Once again, 'Whoever controls the economy, controls the galaxy.' They can push prices sky-high, and then take it from there.''

"But tridenite isn't that rare. There's a planet somewhere in the Triangulum—''

"Gemsbuck.'' It was Hac's first contribution to the conversation.

Mier looked at him, surprised. "That's right, Gemsbuck.''

"It isn't common knowledge, but the Gemsbuck mines are worn out,'' Brian added.

"There have been no new discoveries of tridenite in ten decades. The working mines on Gemsbuck, and in the asteroid belt, produce less ore every year, and much of it is of low quality and costly to refine. Four major shafts have been closed in the past twenty-four months,'' the android reported.

"Thank you, Hac,'' Brian said smugly. "See, Mier, I told you he was a computer. Ask him for some figures. I bet he could go on like this all afternoon.''

"No doubt,'' Mier said dryly. "But I can think of more interesting things to do than listen to mining statistics. Who besides Geo-Mining wants the tridenite?''

"About a dozen independent companies, small-fry mostly. There are a few jack miners interested, of course.''

"Jack miners are interested in anything that promises a profit.''

"And then there's one of the most powerful non-Federation merchantile groups today, the Consortium.''

"Right,'' she commented, appalled at the list. "Have you considered the possibility that the Consortium might be behind the problems we're having on Tori?''

"Yes.''

"No matter how powerful they are, mindwipe and sabotage are serious crimes. They should be investigated.''

"We haven't discounted that, and we do have people looking into it. But remember, the Consortium could buy the governments of a half-dozen worlds with their petty cash. Hell, they probably already have. But no matter how powerful they are, we can't let them get the Torian treaty.''

''Is there any evidence that they know about the minerals?''

''I wouldn't bet against it. And if they do, they'll follow you to the planet and kill you as a way to say thank you for being their guide.''

''How have you managed to keep the planet's location a secret?''

''It isn't easy, believe me. But the Stone Field has been a big factor. No one in their right mind would go exploring in there. And that's also why we're shipping you two out undercover, to try to keep anyone from following you. You should also know that no one in the home office is aware of your mission except the Professor and me.''

''And whoever put a bug in the Professor's office. How much do you want to bet that the Consortium already knows all about me and my destination?''

''No bets.''

Mier had a sudden thought and looked at Hac. ''He could be a walking transceiver.''

''Hac? Absolutely not! He's the safest one of us. He belongs to Geo-Mining, and they have more at stake in this than anyone. Remember, once you're out of here, don't trust anyone but him and our agent on Stonewall.''

''How do I contact her?''

''There's a hotel called the Four Star Inn. We've already reserved rooms for you. All you have to do is check in, and you'll be contacted.''

''Then there's just one more thing.''

''What?'' Brian asked.

''Hac. How do I explain him?''

''I don't know why you have to. No one will know he's anything other than your companion.''

''Do you really believe he can pass for human?''

''I don't see why not. He fooled you when you first saw him. He's capable of mimicking every aspect of human behavior. Just treat him the way you would any partner.''

Mier looked at the tall android. ''I don't know . . .''

"You'll feel better about Hac when you get used to him. And you'll probably forget he isn't real."

"If his contribution today was any example of his conversational skills, I don't see how you can say that. He isn't exactly what I would call verbose."

"Mier, Hac has a very complete memory system, partly to enable him to duplicate human emotional responses. You can talk to him exactly as you would to me. In fact to help establish your cover, treat him exactly as if he were me. Of course he doesn't have my charm and good looks, but . . ."

"Right." Mier looked at the android. "All right, Hac. What do you have to say for yourself?"

"Not very much at the moment," he replied.

"Oh?"

Hac smiled. "What Mr. Palo says is correct. Also what I told you earlier is true; I can counterfeit all of the human physical activities and most of the mental ones. I am, for instance, programmed for social conversation. It is this, I believe, which concerned you earlier?"

"Yes."

"Please let it worry you no further."

CHAPTER 9

Mier snapped off the monitor and rubbed her eyes. A glance at the chronometer showed that she had been up for almost twelve hours, the last four reading files on Tori and trying to make sense from them. She hadn't learned anything new; three missions, all lost, Jarry the only one who ever returned. It was essentially as the Professor and Brian had said. Still, she wished she could rid herself of the growing sense of unease. Both men—and Jarry, poor soul—had been holding something back, something vital. She wondered for the hundredth time what it was, and why they hadn't wanted to talk about it. Classified, top secret, need-to-know—catchwords of her business, but not knowing, if the information was vital, could get an agent killed. And there was often no way to judge the importance of information until the last minute, and by then it was usually too late. Was that what happened to Jarry?

Her thoughts went round and round like this until she decided she was just too sleepy to make sense anymore. Convinced they were hiding something from her, she was equally sure that, unless they changed their minds and told her, she wouldn't learn what it was. And she certainly wouldn't learn any secrets from these files. No, she was just too tired. Besides, she knew from experience that everything would look different in the morning.

With a jaw-cracking yawn she got to her feet and stumbled into the bathroom. Red, gritty eyes stared back at her from the mirror; despite the dim lights in her quarters, they were strained. Sleep. She needed sleep, she told herself, yawning again as she stripped and tumbled into bed.

Sleep came slowly, held at bay by the turmoil in her mind, but eventually blackness crashed down and the dreams began. Formless emotions came first, little more than vague apprehensions and misty fears that flitted in and out of her subconscious. Then a part of the mist began to take on substance, coalescing into a shadowy form. A figure walked slowly but steadily into the distance, where a light diffused through the fog. It became of prime importance for Mier to know who that figure was. She had a very strong feeling that it had some important information for her, something vital to her survival. She called out and started after it, running as fast as she could, but the fog wrapped around her legs, making it hard to move. Straining every muscle, she progressed inch by inch, but always the figure was just ahead. Despite her best efforts, gradually she fell behind. Lungs burning and heart pounding, she dropped to her knees, gasping for breath, fog swirling around her.

Then a shadow loomed over her, and she looked up to see the figure. She strained to see its face, for even her special sight couldn't penetrate this gloom.

Then a well-remembered voice spoke. "Mier? Is that you?" And the fog parted to show Jarry, his face wet with tears.

"Yes," she said softly, sorrow-filled. "Let me help you. What can I do?" She struggled to her feet.

"Nothing. It's too late for me." He looked over his shoulder. "I have to go. You must save yourself."

"Save myself? What are you talking about?"

"Keep away. Don't go."

"Keep away? From Tori? Is that what you're telling me? Not to go to Tori?"

He didn't answer.

"Jarry, you have to explain. I don't understand."

No words came, but tears began running down Jarry's face again.

"Please, won't you let me help?" she repeated, reaching an impulsive hand out to clasp his shoulder.

"No!" Jarry exploded as he pulled away from her.

The touch lasted only an instant, but the shock of it almost knocked Mier off of her feet. She staggered back.

What had she felt? She had always been able to sense the emotions of people she knew, not as well as a true empath might, but enough to guess what someone was feeling. Jarry, she realized, was a combination of terror, desperation, and pain, barely under a control that was fraying with exhaustion. But there had been more, and she desperately tried to analyze it. It was an invasion, a horrible invasion of body and mind, something too ugly to define or describe. Nausea burned at the back of her throat, and she trembled.

Jarry had turned and slowly, doggedly walked away.

"Wait! What was that!" she demanded, voice still shaking.

No answer.

"Tell me, please! I have to know!"

Jarry's form was being swallowed by the mist.

"*No!*" she shouted, trying to go after him, but the sound of her own voice woke her.

Lying in her bed, rigid and poised for flight, she realized it had been a dream. She forced herself to relax and still the pounding of her heart.

Why had her subconscious sent her such a message?

Danger was an inherent part of her work, and the beginning of a new mission always a cause for apprehension, but never such fear! She tried to shift her position and realized the sheet was wrapped tightly around her legs. She pulled them free, hitching herself up against the pillow. So there was a secret, if not more than one. She had been right, there was something she had to know before she could deal with the problem of Tori.

Shrugging into a robe, Mier went into the main room. The faintly glowing readout said four thirty-two, normally too early to be calling people, but anything having to do with a mission had priority over social niceties. She punched the sequence for the center and reached the night receptionist.

"Get me the Professor, please."

"I'm sorry, Agent Silver. The Professor is unavailable."

"Off-station?"

"I'm sorry, but that information is restricted."

She frowned. "Brian Palo. Put me through to him."

"One moment."

Not much longer than that, Brian's mumbling voice came over the speaker, followed by his sleepy face on the screen, eyes squinting in the sudden light. "Silver. I knew it would happen sooner or later. You can't sleep and need a back rub, right?"

"What I need are some straight answers, and I need them now."

"I'm all the answer you need, Babe. Want me to come up? Or will you come down?" He glanced off-screen and then back again. "On second thought, I'd better come up. Where do you want to meet?"

This last question told her that he would meet her, but somewhere outside of their quarters or the office. "The infirmary. I'll be there in twenty minutes."

"Infirmary? Mier, are you all right?" he demanded, his voice suddenly tense.

"I'm as well as can be expected. Twenty minutes." She cut off his anxious questions and smiled grimly to herself. He never gave up, did he? Even when someone else was in bed with him. She could imagine the word juggling that would be going on as soon as his current bedmate realized he was leaving.

Wide-awake now, Mier stifled a laugh as she jammed her feet into a pair of coveralls. She strapped on her pistol before pressing the seam closed and pulling down the sleeves. Feet in sandals, she went into the main hall, moving single-mindedly, intent on her destination.

So great was her preoccupation that she didn't notice the head that pulled quickly back as she emerged from her apartment. The watcher waited a second and then looked from his hiding place once again, just in time to see Mier's swiftly departing form round a corner.

CHAPTER 10

"Don't go," said the voice in the dream.

And she didn't really want to go. She was overdue for a break. No matter how much she liked her job—and surprisingly, she did get a great deal of satisfaction from the work she did—she also knew her limits. Going undercover in hostile territory was stressful. No, that was an understatement, she decided. Living day in and day out in situations where you didn't dare leave your back uncovered for even an instant wore down your nerve like nothing else could. It went beyond stress. After seventeen years, she didn't know if she could even exist in an environment where everyone wasn't a potential threat. What would it be like when she retired, supposing she lived long enough? She tried to remember any agent who had. There were those teaching at the Academy, between working an odd assignment, but that was all. No, she realized, agents didn't retire; they either died on the job, or continued to work in less and less demanding situations.

Mier rubbed the back of her neck as she turned into

the infirmary. The paranoia was ingrained, she decided. She felt as if someone was watching her even now. And if Brian was to be believed, not even the halls of the station were safe anymore.

"May I help you?" the woman at the front desk asked politely, after a quick glance satisfied her that Mier was not in need of immediate medical attention.

"I'd like to see Blain Nichols, please. Is he in?"

"I'll check." Rapid fingers played a keyboard. "He's off duty, but he left a message to be awakened if there's an emergency. Is this an emergency?"

"I'm afraid so." She willed the small tattoo on her left hand into visibility and held it up for the receptionist to see. The SIA logo appeared over Mier's ID number. "Official business. Special Intelligence. Priority."

"I'll alert him. You can wait in the consulting room over there. Fourth door on the left." She waved Mier to one of the hallways behind her.

"Thank you. I'm expecting someone else. Brian Palo. Would you send him in when he arrives?"

"Don't bother. I'm here," said a somewhat breathless voice as her supervisor came through the entrance. "Now what's this all about?"

"I'll tell you in a minute," Mier responded, aware of the receptionist's curious gaze. She led the way to the small room and sank down on one of the hard chairs against the wall.

Brian closed the door and sat beside her. "Well?"

"I want to see Jarry again."

"You got me up in the middle of the night to tell me that!"

"Brian, it's five, almost six o'clock. You'd be up in an hour or two anyway."

"Then why couldn't it have waited another hour?"

"There's too much to do. Now, do I get to see Jarry or not?"

"Why do you want to see him? And why," he looked around at the cubicle, "did you bring me here to ask me?"

"Because I want to have Blain Nichols there as well."

"Nichols? Isn't he your snooper? No, we can't do that. Jarry's Burton's patient."

"Get his permission."

"It won't matter. We've already had empaths in to see Jarry. Two of them, in fact. And nothing happened. The man's gone, Silver. Can't you accept that?"

"No, I can't. And I can't accept a couple of other things about this mission."

"What do you mean?"

"You're keeping something from me. You and the Professor."

Brian had the grace to look uncomfortable. "That's not true. We told you everything."

"I don't believe you."

"Mier! What can I do to convince you? Swear a blood oath?"

"Just tell me the truth."

"I am! Look, Silver. Maybe you were right; maybe you have been out too many times without a break. After this little job is over, I'll personally see to it that you get some time off. How about it?"

"Thank you. But all I need right now is information so I can do this 'little job,' as you call it."

"Mier, I swear to you. I've told you everything you need to know about Tori. Why can't you be satisfied?"

"I know you."

He frowned at her. Hurt? "Then there's nothing else for me to say."

Mier's conviction was shaken. What if she was just overstressed and imagining things? "What about yesterday in the Professor's office? You were staring at me, trying to signal something. I remember it clearly."

"In the Professor's office? Oh, yes, I remember. I knew the room was bugged. That's all. I was trying to keep you from asking too many questions."

Mier thought back. Was that really it? But Brian had a nimble brain and was more able than most to think on his feet.

"Okay, Silver. Listen. The Federation has sent three missions to Tori. No one has returned to tell us why everything is going wrong on the planet. We don't know what's happening. And we need to know. So we're sending you."

"And Hac."

"Yeah. And Hac. You've read the files, watched the tapes. You've seen Jarry. What more do you think I can tell you? What do you think I'm trying to hide?"

"I don't know," she said, backing down. She dropped her eyes. "The Professor's upset about this. More than I've ever seen him."

"The Professor's getting old. He's ready for retirement." She looked up sharply. "You didn't know that, did you?" he said.

"I suspected, but he's never allowed a mission to upset him like this, or at least I've never seen it."

"Well, it's about time. This thing with Jarry's hit him pretty hard. I've never seen him so upset about losing an agent."

"There's no hope for Jarry?"

"None at all. Which is why I don't think you should bother Nichols with this."

Mier shook her head. "I have to."

"Silver . . ."

"No, listen, Brian. There is something else going on here. Maybe you're not a part of it, but I know I'm right. And before I leave, I have to do everything I possibly can to prepare myself. And if that means deep-probing Jarry, then that's what we have to do. Do you understand?"

Brian stared at her in exasperation, his lips drawn into a thin line. Then he gave a sigh and relaxed. "All right, if it will make you feel better." He glanced at his watch. "I'll go call Burton and get his permission."

"Think he'll make trouble?"

"Hell no. He doesn't have any more hope for Jarry than we do. Is this Nichols?" he asked as a knock sounded on the door.

Mier opened it to admit a short, balding man in a blue smock, the small gold lapel pin proclaiming his esper rating.

He nodded to Brian. "Inspector Palo. Hello, Mier," he said in his soft voice. He looked at her closely. "Beyond some apprehension, you don't seem to be in any particular discomfort, so what is the reason for this visit?"

"I'll contact Burton while you fill Nichols in," Brian interjected, going out the door.

"I need your help, Nic," Mier told him. She omitted the details about the mission as she quickly told him about Jarry. "I'd like you to try to read him. Whatever's hidden in his mind could be vitally important."

"I assume Dr. Burton has had him read by other empaths. Why do you think I can succeed where they have failed?"

Mier inched out to the edge of her chair, her elbows on her knees. "Do you remember when you told me I could act as a resonator, someone who could naturally amplify an empath's reading?"

He looked dubious. "Yes."

"Well, I'd like to try."

"To amplify my reading of Jarry's mind?"

She nodded.

"Have you tried mental contact with anyone since Karr died?"

She broke eye contact, slid back in her chair, and shook her head. "No."

"Then this must be very important to you. Am I right?"

"There's something more going on than I'm being told. I don't know if Jarry has the answers, but I'm positive he has vital information. I have to know what it is."

"Mier, I'd like to read you, right now if you're agreeable."

"Now?"

"Yes, now."

She weighed his request and then sighed. "All right, if you must."

Nic laughed quietly. "Just relax. We've been through this many times." He moved his chair closer, and took her hands in a light clasp before he closed his eyes. Seconds ticked by before he dropped her hands and leaned back. "You're still carrying a lot of guilt around with you, young lady."

She gave a shaky laugh. "Goes with the job."

"Not this stuff. So you have been given a new partner."

She started. "Not really. Hac is an android."

"But it still troubles you."

"It did at first. I mean, I was surprised. But he's an android—a machine. It's not like being teamed with another person."

"Tell yourself enough times and you may begin to believe it. You have to learn to let go of the guilt for Karr's death. There was nothing you could have done to prevent it."

"In some rational part of my mind I believe you. But . . ."

"But?" He smiled. "All right, I won't trouble you with it just now. Perhaps you would tell me about your dream—the one that brought you here."

"You saw that?"

"The resonance is quite strong."

"It was Jarry. He told me not to go . . . to Tori, I presume."

"And because of this dream you want to try to contact Jarry's mind?"

"I think we might find something if we can go deep enough. You will help me, won't you?"

"Of course. And if you are willing to try to amplify my efforts, perhaps we can—"

Brian's return interrupted whatever he was going to say.

"Well, we won't need you after all, Nichols," the investigator told him.

"Dr. Burton wouldn't give permission?" Mier asked, coming to her feet.

"No. The whole issue's academic—Jarry's dead. He died about four this morning."

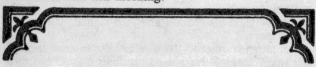

CHAPTER 11

The *Regina Douglas* floated within an electric blue force field, along one huge arm of Houston's orbiting terminal. Intricate latticework enclosed the cargo cubes, giving the little freighter the appearance of a gleaming net full of children's blocks. Work lights glowed within stout access tubes, illuminating a flurry of activity as robots and human porters passed back and forth, unloading freight, performing routine maintenance, and restocking the ship. Time was short; there were not only shipping schedules to meet, but a luxury liner was soon to arrive, to take its turn at the dock. In two more hours the *Douglas* had to be on her way.

"Your cabins are on deck four," the crewman told Mier and Hac as they moved from the tube into the freighter. "Even though we do take passengers, the captain asked me to be sure you realized that the *Douglas* is primarily a cargo ship. I'm afraid we don't have any luxuries."

"We understand," Mier said.

"Good. There's a deck plan in your cabin. The restricted areas are clearly marked. Other than that, you're free to move around, and to use the gym and common room. The grav tube's down this corridor and to the left." He smiled and turned to repeat this information to the next group of arrivals.

Mier couldn't think of a reason to linger in the entryway, but she took a close look at the other passengers before moving on. They all seemed sleepy, disoriented by the time difference between Earth and ship. Nothing suspicious about that.

"I'm exhausted," she said, turning back to Hac and yawning.

"Since you are tired, I will escort you to your cabin. While you are sleeping I can expedite matters by making a preliminary investigation of the ship."

"Hac?" Mier kept her voice soft, aware of other ears. "I would think you'd be tired, too." Maybe androids didn't need rest, but Hac would blow their cover if he acted like some kind of a superman. "We can explore together, in the morning. After we've both had some sleep."

Without waiting for his reply, she moved off down the corridor and stepped into the opening of the drop tube. Deftly snagging a loop with her toe, she exited at the fourth level. The android emerged behind her and obediently followed down the passageway and into a cabin.

It was small, the bunk as long as the entire back wall was wide. A door to the left led to a tiny bath, with a sonic instead of a water shower, Mier noted. But right now her most pressing need was sleep. She slung her shoulder bag onto the bed before she turned to her companion. "I'll take this cabin. You can sleep—or whatever you do—in there. But listen to me first," she added as Hac looked from the connecting door and back to her angry face. "I want you to stay there, with the door closed and locked, until I wake up."

"That would waste time."

"Think of it as a challenge, Hac. With all your impressive programming, I would imagine you could come up with something productive to do for six hours. Something that would keep you in your cabin."

"I can't imagine what would be more productive than learning my way around."

"I have faith in you. Think of something!"

"What?"

Her patience died. "I don't care! Meditate, listen to your transistors, turn yourself off—anything! But don't you dare go anywhere on this ship without clearing it with me first. Do you understand?"

"I understand you are giving me an order, but I don't understand your reasons."

Mier gave a huge sigh of exasperation. "All right, I'll try to explain, again. This ship is not only transport for us, but it's a chance to try to flush out whoever the Consortium has put on our tail."

"Are you so certain they could have someone on us so quickly?"

"Oh, yes. It's not only quite possible, but probable."

"Did you notice anyone suspicious on the shuttle?"

"No, but that doesn't mean anything." Mier yawned again. "So, while on board we'll seem to relax, enjoy ourselves, and blend in with the rest of the passengers. At the same time, we keep our eyes and ears open. You will do whatever is necessary to maintain appearances. That means you'll fake sleeping, eating, drinking . . ."

She paused as the thought dawned on her. "You said all human functions; that includes . . ." She hesitated.

"I both eat and drink. I can even simulate intoxication if it's necessary," Hac assured her quickly.

Mier frowned at him; was there a program for sarcasm, she wondered? She dropped down on the bunk, which gave under her weight and then re-formed to support her shape. "Look, I need sleep. Go away and turn yourself off for six hours."

"As you wish. But wouldn't it be useful if we could get a copy of the passenger list? Especially those people who boarded here?"

"The list should be available to anyone familiar with the magic of modern electronics, if we can get permission to use the ship's computer. We can check on it first thing in the morning. Until then, however, go." She pointed at the door.

Without another word, Hac obeyed.

Mier sighed and got to her feet one more time to check the door lock. Although she often went for much longer periods without sleep when she was working, she didn't like using stimutabs unless it was necessary. Too much of any drug and its usefulness diminished as the body built up a resistance. She quickly stripped out of her overall and flung it on top of the suitcase—which had actually made it to the right ship and cabin—and was immediately asleep.

Black night and the sound of drums—she had heard them before, though she couldn't recall where or when. Her mind felt strangely thick; thinking was more difficult than she could ever remember, except those times when she had been drugged. But then she had been in a hospital—sterile chambers, brightly lit, so different from this. Was she drugged now? The thought of that possibility faded as quickly as it had come, elusive as every other thought. Trying to think was too hard. The drum sound rode the smoky breeze that snaked through the town, spreading the ripe scent of ro blossoms. Shadows lay deep where she walked, though she had no idea how she had gotten there, or of her destination. Somewhere behind her, she knew that bonfires burned on the steps of the pyramid, lighting the way to the top. She could almost hear the chanting as black-robed Fedar snaked their way up the high stone steps.

Fedar? Yes! Now she knew, as one often did in dreams; this was the celebration of the black moon, and she had to be back on Lahkemba.

But this time she was walking away from the light, into the deep black beyond town.

"Mier," a well-remembered voice whispered.

"Karr?" she asked in amazed delight. "Karr, is that you?"

"Mier?"

But Karr was dead, her conscious mind intruded.

And now there was another voice. "Mier," it said as it had before, "don't go."

"Don't go where?" She turned, peering into the shadows, but there was no one and nothing except the pounding of drums and the smell of ro.

"Who's there? Come out. Please. I need to see you, to talk to you. Where are you?"

"Mier, don't . . ."

It was fainter, fading away, but she had the direction and started moving toward it.

". . . go . . ."

"No, don't go," she cried, breaking into a run.

Immediately it was as if she had gone through an invisible barrier, and she came to a startled halt. The sound of drums was abruptly cut off, and silence surrounded her. The town disappeared, and an empty plain stretched in every direction—empty except for the eerie glowing mist that swirled knee-high. Gingerly she moved again, eyes searching the distance. Suddenly her foot struck something soft and she stumbled, falling over a body. Instinctively revolted, she shoved herself away and scuttled backward on all fours, panting in fear, the fog eddying violently around her. Nothing happened, and as the shock began to wear off, she moved cautiously forward again. The body was still there. Mier peered into the thinning mist. She reached out and encountered warm flesh, felt a hand, an arm . . . and withdrew her fingers sticky with blood.

"Karr?" she whispered.

She crawled toward the head and realized it was Hac's face, the sightless eyes open, blood pumping from an ugly wound in his chest.

"God, no," she murmured, reaching for the wound, looking frantically for something to stanch this terrible bleeding. But the lids fluttered as his eyes rolled back until only the whites showed. He was dead.

Another partner dead.

"No! Hac, no!"

Her eyes snapped open, breath coming in short gasps as her system flooded with adrenaline. The cabin was dark. There was no sound here except the faint hiss of the ventilator, and the loud pounding of her heart.

The dreams were back again . . . the nightmares. She had thought she was rid of them forever after all those months of work with Nichols, but obviously her hopes had been in vain.

Damn.

Mier rolled onto her side and sat up, rubbing her face and raking her hair back with her fingers. She couldn't imagine why she was having the damn dreams again, unless it was the stress she'd been under lately. She had told Brian she needed a rest! Well, after this job, things were going to be different. She was going to take a vacation—a real vacation—maybe somewhere on Earth. Maybe she could get lost, go somewhere they'd never find her again.

She got up, drank some water, and returned to bed. Now she couldn't sleep. Her mind kept returning to the dream. Fine agent I am, she thought. The mission's only starting and already I'm falling apart! No, you're not, another voice in her mind argued. The problem was working with Hac, with a partner again. Her subconscious was reacting this way because he was along. Yeah, that was it. She lay staring into the darkness, attempting to reassure herself. Unless they could find a way to work together—which, despite Brian's assurance, she still doubted—he would be more a hindrance than a help. It might be best, she decided, to leave him behind on Stonewall. Perhaps the agent there would help. And if that didn't work, if she had to take him along on the mission after all, she had to remember that he was just an android. If something happened, his death—if it was possible to kill him—would be no more tragic than the loss of an expensive machine. Hac could be replaced.

Mier breathed deeply, consciously, using biofeedback techniques to eliminate the tension left from the dream. Slowly her mind stilled and she drifted back into sleep.

CHAPTER 12

The ship's purser introduced himself as David Scott, and cooperated readily when Mier requested access to the ship's computer. "It isn't an unusual request," he admitted. "We carry a lot of businesspeople, and they like to keep up with the markets." He led Mier and Hac to the cramped booth that held a keyboard linked to the BM22 that served the *Douglas*. "You can make a printout, if you'd like," he told them helpfully. "Just be sure you leave everything the way it was when you're finished."

"This shouldn't take very long," Mier told him.

"Don't worry about it. Take all the time you need. I've got to get going, though. I'm the only one assigned to the passengers, and they keep me pretty busy."

"I can imagine. Thanks for your help."

With a nod and smile, he left them.

"Are you sure you can do this?" Mier asked.

Hac sat down and activated the screen. "You're asking if a computer is capable of working with a computer. You want a passenger list. What else?"

"As much information as you can get as long as it includes address, destination, and business. I'd also like to know where and when the passengers bought their tickets. And if there were reservations, I'd like to know the dates they were made."

"Is that significant?"

"It would help to know who bought passage within the past two days. We can eliminate anyone who had a ticket reserved longer than that. And the more time, the less likely they're a suspect."

"Unless they used someone else's ticket."

"That's a possibility, too, but we have to start by looking for patterns. Do you think you can handle this alone?"

"Certainly. Where are you going?"

"To the kitchen. I'm hungry."

"And, after what you said last night, you're willing to trust me to do this job by myself?"

"If I can't trust you, I'd rather find out now."

"Logical." Hac busied himself at the keys.

Mier watched for a moment. What she said was true; she had to find out if she could trust him with a simple job before risking him—or herself—with something more dangerous. And it would be useful to have someone to do the more mundane tasks of sleuthing, tasks such as information retrieval.

The ship's mess was utilitarian, the seating arrangement including three large tables in the middle space, and two smaller ones providing a little more privacy. The only other concession to the passengers, a sophisticated food processor with an almost unlimited menu, occupied a large panel of the back wall. Mier made her selection and found a seat beside a taciturn man who wolfed his food, eyes fixed on his plate. Two equally silent women sat across the table, dressed in some sort of gray uniforms, their long hair pulled severely back from their faces. Such table partners suited her, however, the absence of chatter providing an excellent opportunity to study her fellow travelers—those who rose early enough to make it to the first meal. There weren't many; other than the two across from her, the only passengers were a rather deep-voiced woman shepherding a pair of small children who took in everyone and everything around them with awed faces. Mier amused herself as she ate by eavesdropping on the whispered comments of the girl and boy. Having little experience with children, she found them almost as fascinating as they did their novel surroundings.

"The little groundlings interest you?" a quiet voice asked as a short woman slipped into the empty place beside her. She juggled a small bowl, teapot, and cup onto the table.

Mier turned to see a small woman with cropped blond hair smiling at her. She wore a blue healer's tunic, the small, diamond-studded star on the shoulder proclaiming a class-one empath.

Mier smiled back. "Yes, they do."

"You do not have children of your own?"

"No."

"Prohibited by your work, I suspect."

Mier thought of the altered genes that she bore, which prohibited her from obtaining a permit.

"But I shouldn't pry. It's an occupational habit, hard to break, and too often disconcerting to would-be friends," the woman continued. "My name is Leah Roget."

"Mier Silver."

"The time necessary to raise children is a luxury few can afford anymore. And I don't think the community nursery system is nearly as rewarding. I give you good morning, Sister Aveda, Sister Fassa," she said to the two women in gray who had finished their meal and risen to leave.

They responded with polite nods before gliding away.

"Who are they?" Mier asked. "I don't recognize the uniforms."

"They're nuns of the Yehudan sect, a group that colonized a very difficult planet called Margus Four," Leah answered as she speared a piece of fruit from her bowl.

"I've heard of them."

"A hard people, but that's what it took to tame Margus. But what about you? What brings you off-world?"

"Business. I have to establish some contacts on Stonewall."

"And all very secret, I'm sure, so I won't inquire any further. I'm not bothering you, am I? Not many people feel comfortable talking to an empath."

Mier was startled for a moment until she understood why this might be. "Invasion of privacy?"

"Exactly." Her breakfast partner grinned. "Too many

people still confuse empathy with telepathy. They're afraid I'll 'read' their deep, dark secrets. Have you worked with an empath before?"

"I have."

The woman nodded. "I also have the feeling that you're not completely without talent yourself. Have you been rated?"

"No. I'm afraid my ability is limited. I was born on Tamerin, you see. And even with that, I'm only an amplifier."

"So you didn't receive the complete genetic package. That's too bad. But even an amplifier would be helpful to the Guild. Have you considered applying? We're always looking for new people."

"I'm already under contract."

"You can still apply. And if you're accepted, the Guild would buy your contract."

"Thank you. It's always a good feeling to know I'm wanted somewhere." Mier collected her dishes and started to rise.

Leah nodded, her attention seemingly on her bowl of fruit. "Please be careful with yourself. Great danger awaits you," she said in a low voice without looking up.

Mier paused, startled. Was Leah a precog? "Thank you again. And, yes, I will be careful."

As she moved to the counter to dispose of her breakfast things, two other passengers entered. When the woman and man greeted the youngsters and took places across the table from them, Mier realized these were the parents. That would make the deep-voiced woman a nurse. She was saddened to see that the little girl and boy viewed their mother and father with as much awe as they did the ship. They might be biological parents, but they apparently had little to do with raising their children. Maybe there were extenuating circumstances, she told herself. She had spent her own childhood in a government creche, and couldn't remember her biological parents.

Mier moved through the corridor, her mind on business. By now Hac should have finished, and they could begin to match names with faces. She hoped he had thought to get the cabin numbers as well, just in case she had to do some unauthorized investigating. She waved her hand over the lock plate of her cabin. The door opened onto blackness as the automated lights failed to come on. She had stepped inside before she realized this, and by then it was too late. Something hard connected with the side of her head, dropping her into a pit even darker than the cabin.

Mier couldn't have been stunned for more than a couple of minutes. She slowly became aware of activity around her, a door closing and feet coming quickly to where she lay. Someone gently brushed her hair aside and felt for the pulse on her neck. She reached quickly, fingers seeking pressure points on the unknown hand as she sat up—and just as quickly fell back dizzily.

"That's what happens when you're impulsive," Hac chided as he freed his hand, his other arm supporting her head and shoulders.

She rested against him for just an instant before her physical condition made itself known to her in no uncertain terms. "I have to get up," she gasped. "I'm about to be very sick."

With Hac's help she just made it to the bathroom before she threw up. She felt miserable, her head throbbing, tears running down her face.

"Thanks," she managed to gasp when the paroxysm was finally over. She put her head in the sink and splashed a handful of water on her face, movements slow and deliberate lest she start the humiliating process all over again. Hac guided her searching fingers to a towel and then helped her to a seat on the edge of the bunk.

"Stay here a moment," he instructed.

"What are you doing?" she asked, trying to get her breath and fighting the cabin's disquieting tendency to sway.

"I want to see if I can get the light fixed," he said from the darkness. "So that's how he did it."

Annoyed at her weakness, Mier felt her patience stressed to the breaking point. "Damn it, what's going on?"

The cabin's lights came on, and she blinked, the throbbing headache accelerating to major pain. But this was not the time to coddle herself. A quick look convinced her that nothing except the light had been disturbed. What did the intruder want?

"There was a piece of foil over the sensor." Hac held out the shiny piece of plastic. "It's the same—I mean, a rather common trick."

"Yeah, I've heard of it," Mier responded, gingerly feeling her head. "Did you see who hit me?"

"I didn't get a good look. Short. Could have been either male or female."

"That's all?"

"It happened very quickly. I heard you, or I assumed it was you, open your cabin door . . ."

"It was me. You didn't hear anything before that?"

"No. The intruder must have been very quiet."

"My cabin door was locked, so he either faked it or had a passkey," she said, thinking out loud. "Describe everything that happened."

"When I reached your cabin, someone was bending over you . . ."

"But you didn't see who it was?"

Hac shook his head. "No. As soon as the intruder heard me coming he ran. I started after him, but when I reached the corridor, he or she had dropped into the lift."

"And you didn't bother to follow?"

"I was concerned about you."

"Damn."

"Can't you make an identification? You were much closer than I."

"Too close," she said, wincing as her fingers found a very tender place on her skull. "No, I didn't see anyone. He must have been hiding, probably over there so he could be behind me when I came in. I was surprised when the lights didn't come on and that's when he struck. Or she."

Or you, she added mentally. Could it have been Hac who struck her down? Her head was throbbing, and she wanted to curl up and try to sleep off the migraine.

Hac looked around the stark little room. "It doesn't look as if he got into anything. If he searched your belongings, he was very neat about it. Or perhaps he didn't have time."

"Or," she said thoughtfully, "maybe he wasn't looking for anything. Maybe he came to leave something.
Dim the lights, please." When he obeyed, she slowly
turned her head, eyes searching the cabin for a mini-spy.
There was a cluster of tiny, gleaming dots above the bathroom door, tucked between the molding and an angle of
the wall. Mier pushed herself shakily to her feet.

"What do you see?" Hac came forward, ready to catch
her if she fell, but she waved him off.

"I feel a lot better, but I need to move around." She
made it to the bathroom and checked the walls and inside
the sonic cabinet. Nothing. "You were in your cabin all
morning?"

"Yes."

Mier gave a cautious nod, pleased when her head didn't
come off. "Come in here, please." It was a close fit, but
she managed to pull the door shut behind them.

"What is the purpose of this?"

"Whoever hit me planted an audiovisual monitoring
device—a mini-spy. It's shielded to be invisible to the
normal eye."

"Then how do you know—"

"Because I can see it!"

"I still don't understand."

Mier clamped down on her pain-fed impatience.
"Look at my eyes. Haven't you noticed anything unusual
about them? It should have been in the file you were
given."

"It wasn't." He studied her face. "You have unusually
large pupils. How is this significant?"

"My home planet had an unusually dim star, which
led to some interesting adaptations of the colonists—in
essence, I can see in the dark. That's the significance."
She sighed. "The device is shielded with a light-reflective
material. In the absence of light, however, it becomes visible. The shield works because people usually can't—"

"See in the dark," he finished for her. "And that's
why normal light is painful for you."

"Right."

"We must dispose of the mini-spy."

"That's also right."

Back in the cabin, Hac steadied her as she stretched

up, her fingers reaching for the spot above the door-frame. There was a faint popping sound and she brought her arm down, looking closely at something that shimmered in the palm of her hand.

"Expensive little toy," she commented.

"It seems a waste to dump it in the converter," Hac said as the tiny bug disappeared down the waste tube.

"There are more where this came from."

"You think the intruder will return to plant another one?"

"I don't think so. They know we're suspicious now. The frightening thought is that their plan might have worked if I hadn't come back when I did."

"They might put one in my cabin."

"They might. But don't worry about it. I'll check both of our cabins regularly from now on."

CHAPTER 13

"I believe it is considered polite behavior to indulge in light conversation while dining," Hac commented. "Or is your headache still bothering you?"

He sat across from her at the end of a large table in the mess. The last meal was almost over, and most of the passengers and crew had already finished eating and gone, leaving them a certain amount of privacy.

"The headache's tolerable. Let's go over the passenger list again," she suggested in a low voice.

"You could have a concussion. I don't know why you wouldn't let the ship's medic check you out. Or why you didn't report the incident to the captain."

"It isn't necessary to involve them."

Hac accepted this, but still couldn't accept her assurances about her health. She had been very quiet all through their meal. "Are you certain you feel well enough to have come here tonight?"

"Yes," she insisted. "All I have is a slight headache, and it will be gone in the morning. Now can we get back to what's important?"

"If you insist. Other than you and me there are twelve passengers. Since ten of them have long-standing travel reservations, we can probably eliminate them as suspects. They include Regis and Harryet Garske, husband and wife en route to their next assignment as Federation Reps; their two dependent children, Jamus and Catrin; the children's nurse, Marine Lavery; a businessman, Wes Began, traveling with his assistant manager, Ttar Began, and a paid female companion, Lady Wanda Hipp; a pair of nuns from Margus Four, Sisters Aveda and Fassa. Which still leaves two we know nothing about."

"You forgot Georgi Jovanovich, but he bought his ticket four months ago. The other is Leah Roget, a licensed healer. I met her this morning at breakfast. I'm certain she's legitimate. The fact that she's a sensitive and bound to her guild should eliminate her."

"Which takes care of everyone. But we know someone on the ship is aware of who we really are."

"We haven't considered the crew. Did you, by any chance, check personnel records while you were in the computer?"

Hac shook his head ruefully. "No. I was too busy running the passengers."

Mier sighed. "It's my fault. I should have thought of it. You'll have to go back. Think you can come up with a reason for being so interested in the passengers and crew?"

"One of the operators came by while I was working, and when she saw what I was doing, asked me if I was from FSA."

Mier stopped eating, and her eyes went wide. "What did you tell her?"

"I didn't actually admit I was, but she probably suspects I'm doing an audit. This will provide a good reason for us to gain access to any of the ship's records."

"She thinks you're from the Federal Space Administration? Oh, great." She dropped her head in her hands.

"What's the matter? Did I do something wrong?"

She slowly raised her head. "Did you stop to think this might give someone completely uninterested in our real mission, a reason to bug our cabins?" she asked in a tight voice.

"No," he said slowly. "You mean . . . ?"

"I mean, if word of this reached the captain—and I imagine it did—then he would have a very good reason for wanting to know what we know."

Comprehension dawned. "Oh."

"That's right: 'Oh.' At this rate we'll soon have the attention of everyone on board. Why don't you just use the ship's intercom and make an announcement."

"I'm sorry if I inadvertently placed our mission in jeopardy. It seemed like a good idea at the time."

"Yeah. Well, maybe it did. And maybe I shouldn't have left you in the computer room alone."

"I said I was sorry. I won't repeat the mistake."

Mier continued to glare for a moment, but then dropped her eyes to her plate. "Let's finish eating and get out of here."

He picked up his fork and thoughtfully chewed a mouthful. "Have you considered that there might not be a spy on board after all?"

"Yes, I have considered the possibility."

"Still, how else would he get to Stonewall?"

"There's always alternative transportation."

"Brian Palo said the *Douglas* was the only ship bound for Stonewall until sometime next month."

"There are private ships."

"Too expensive."

"Not for the Consortium."

"That is true."

"Hac, I hope you realize we're up against someone at least as good as an SIA agent. Whatever you do, don't underestimate them, or their resources."

"They also have the advantage of knowing who we are, while we do not know who they are."

"Yes."

"And so we must continue to expose ourselves, watch and wait for them to reveal themselves."

"And be careful." She was beginning to recognize the times when his logic seemed more human—and therefore flawed—than machine, and once again she was amazed at the programming necessary to produce such an android. And, as usual, Brian had been right; she was beginning to relate to Hac as if he—no, it—actually was human. "Curiouser and curiouser."

"I beg your pardon?"

"An old saying." She had finished her meal and poured tea into her cup. "After I've run the crew list, I think I'll go back and check the passengers again. I have a feeling I've missed something."

"You just said 'I.' "

"What?"

"I'm supposed to be your partner. I know I made a mistake when I let the communications officer think I was from the FSA, but I won't do it again."

"Good."

"When you say 'I' does it mean you intend to eliminate me from your plans? Officially, I am here to observe, but if there are times when I can be useful, it would be foolish not to take advantage of them."

"Yes."

"So I should be the one to check the crew's records. Will you let me do it?"

"I'll think about it." She drank more of the tea.

"You need me, Mier. The sooner we know who, or how many people, are set against us, the easier our job on Tori will be."

"Also true."

"If we can neutralize this person or persons while we're still on the ship . . ."

"I said I would think about it."

Despite her testy response, Hac wasn't finished. "There's something else we might try."

Mier refilled her cup. "And what's that?"

"A person at the far end of the room has been watching us."

She raised her head, but refrained from turning to see. "Do you know who it is?"

"No, but he appears to be interested in meeting us." Hac nodded in response to the man's wave. "Such a friendly individual might be an excellent source of information. He might enable us to broaden our knowledge of the other passengers."

Mier glanced at the small table in the far corner of the mess. The man, expensively but not necessarily tastefully dressed, beamed and waved again. Then her attention was caught by the beautiful young woman at his side. She saw that Hac had noticed her as well. "Are you interested in the man or his companion?"

"The man, of course" was the quick reply. "The woman, although admittedly attractive, is, I suspect, a paid companion."

"Attractive? You are capable of understatement!"

"Aesthetic appreciation, as well as curiosity, is necessary to make certain judgments. Appreciation of beauty, whatever its source, is an important part of my programming."

"I see," Mier drawled.

"Your tone would indicate otherwise. I don't understand why you don't believe me."

"Oh, I believe you; I know what you really are. So, come on. Let's go 'broaden our knowledge.' "

CHAPTER 14

The stranger came to his feet as they approached, and greeted them like long-lost friends. "I was hoping you'd notice I was looking your way. It's been dull as space on board this ship. I thought you and your pretty lady could help us think of something to pass the time."

"Thank you," Hac answered. "Your invitation is very kind."

"Of course, Lady Wanda keeps things from getting too dull. And then there's my brother—he'll be here in a minute. Talked him into joining me for a little cruise to Stonewall, you know? But here, sit down and make yourselves comfortable."

"I'm Hac . . . Hac Andrews, and this is Mier Silver, my partner."

Mier sat with her back against the wall, and the android settled beside her.

"This here's Lady Wanda, and I'm Wes Began," the man said. "And here's my favorite no-good brother," he added hastily, indicating a short, redheaded man who appeared at his side. "What's a matter, Ttar? Don't tell me no one wants to play?" He winked at Mier. "Trying to find a little action for later tonight. Thought we might interest someone in a game of smash."

"They play it all night and all day sometimes," Wanda added. "I think it's boring."

"You think everything's boring except yourself," Began said fondly.

"I liked that casino you took me to," she ventured.

"And I said I'll take you to one on Stonewall. You'll like that, too. How about a drink, everyone? I'm buying."

Mier felt her headache begin to pound again, thanks to their overly jovial host, but she recognized his affability as forced and was curious to know the reason behind it. He wasn't one of the suspects, for she'd recognized him as the businessman traveling with paid companion and assistant manager, who was apparently his brother as well. "I think I'd like a glass of wine—"

But Began cut her off. "Nonsense. A real drink is what you need. And I know they have booze on board. I wouldn't have come if they didn't."

Mier glanced at Hac, who was obviously waiting for her decision. "All right. Let's see if the synthesizer can come up with a reasonable brandy. Are you going to Stonewall on business?"

"Is there any other reason to travel? I've got interests all over this galaxy, it's starting to look like I'd save money if I just bought my own liner." His deep laugh punctuated the statement.

Mier smiled politely. "Where have you been?"

"Oh, here and there. From one colony to another. Sounds exciting, but it's starting to get a little dull. I mean, see one colony, seen them all, right? Say—" Began turned to Hac, "—what did you say your line of business was?"

"Ceramics. Our casings are on the new Explorer line they're building at the Gallandry yards," he supplied smoothly, seemingly unaware of Lady Wanda's admiring glances.

Mier, however, had noticed the other woman's growing interest in the android. If only you knew, she thought.

"Why are you going to Stonewall?" Ttar asked.

"We're negotiating a trading permit."

"You don't say," Wes broke in. "With the amount of traffic through an outpost like Stonewall, there should be a lot of interest in your product. You know, I've read about some of the new molecular bondings. With a casing like that a ship could probably plunge into a star without melting. Do you have any idea of the temperature of a star?" He asked this of Mier, who didn't seem to be paying attention.

"I'm sorry?" She looked at him and was rewarded with a broad wink.

"Well, it doesn't matter. Even if the ship survived, everyone inside would be cooked," he finished with a laugh.

"Where's your base?" his brother wanted to know.

"Old Denver, Earth," Mier told him. "Hac and I work for Cee-Co Ceramics."

Began beamed. "The old Three-C! I've heard of them. So they're expanding out to Stonewall."

"And you?" she prompted.

"D.C. Central, of course. Like you, I started out west, but then things got so big, I had to open an office on the east coast."

"To be closer to the Federal yards."

"Well, that, too. Except we got some pretty good yards in Houston, you know. No, I netted some fat government contracts, and while the main operation's still back home, I need to be closer to my contacts, you know?"

"What's the name of your business?" Mier asked.

"Began Electronics. Ttar here's assistant manager. Never been off-world before, so I'm taking him along this trip. Give him experience, you know?"

"I can imagine." Mier nodded to Hac. "About this smash game . . ."

"Do you play?" Ttar asked.

"Now and then, but—"

"Hey now," Wes interrupted. "You can't turn down a chance for a little fun, now can you?"

Something about the man, something almost desperate in his insistence, caught Mier. "Where and when?"

"How about back here, in about, say, two hours? Nobody will be around, and it will give Ttar time to round up a couple more players. You do want to play, don't you?" This last was addressed to Hac.

"Certainly. Unless Mier is too tired."

"No, I'm fine. We'll meet you back here. Thank you for the brandy."

"Any time."

"What did you think of our new friend?" she asked when they were in the corridor.

"He seemed overly anxious to have us play with him."

"You noticed that?"

"His brother didn't have much to say for himself."

"But he did ask some pointed questions."

"Does that make him suspect?"

"Not necessarily. It could be ordinary business practice for them: the one brother is affable and outgoing, relaxing the quarry, while the other watches and interjects pertinent questions at the right moment."

"Except he wasn't very subtle."

"You have to admit we were on our guard. The game should be interesting." Mier had a thought. "Do you know the rules?"

"Yes. Skill in a number of social games was considered a necessary part of my programming."

"How fortunate." Mier unlocked her cabin, but Hac entered first.

The lights obediently came on, and no one apparently was or had been inside. He carefully checked the bathroom while Mier watched, an amused grin on her face.

"Satisfied?"

"Yes."

"This wasn't necessary, you know. I'm more than able to take care of myself."

"I believe it's part of a partner's duties to assist in these situations."

"I wish you'd stop insisting that we're really partners. We're not. As you pointed out this evening, you're only here to observe."

"You also agreed that I could be of some help."

"I said I'd think about it." Mier dropped into a chair and leaned back, getting comfortable.

"I am curious about something," he ventured.

"I didn't know androids were programmed for curiosity."

"It is important to any information-gathering system. But this doesn't affect the case, except, perhaps, peripherally."

"What is it?"

"I know little about you, except that you have been contracted to the Special Intelligence Agency for the past seventeen years."

"Twenty-three. Six years of school, ten years' training and apprenticeship, seven years' field work. I was fifteen when they bought my contract."

"Very well. Most agents always work with partners. You do not. You resisted strenuously when the Professor assigned me to accompany you. Would you tell me why?"

She frowned. "I haven't worked with a partner for the past four years."

"I realize that. It was in your personnel file."

"Then you should know why I won't work with a partner."

"That information was not in the file I was given."

"I'm surprised. Sit down. You're making me nervous standing there like that." She waited until he complied. "I was born on Tamerin Three."

"Which is the reason you have amplified sight," he told her. "I have heard of the planet. The sun there is quite cool and red. The light reaching the planet is of very low intensity and the original colonists were gene-altered to enable them to see effectively. Thus you were able to spot the mini-spy."

"The Tamerin colonists were given other abilities to survive, too. When they had children, some were born with the new genes while others received only part of them. I was one of those children who didn't get the complete genetic package. I couldn't live on Tamerin."

"You are an exile."

"So was my partner, Karr. We grew up together in a government youth center, and we trained together. For all those years we were partners in every possible way. He was killed while we were on a mission together. Are you certain you want to know all of this?"

"If it is not too painful for you, I believe it would enable me to understand you better."

"And you think that's important?"

"If we are to work together, I should have as much information as possible."

"All right. I can accept that." She took a deep breath.

"Even after four years, you became quite pale when the Professor told you I was going to be your partner. Karr's death, although regrettable, should not have been enough to cause such deep trauma."

"Karr and I had one other Tamerin characteristic. We were resonant to each other's minds."

"Telepathic?"

"You might call it that. But apparently our ability was

limited. It only worked with each other. This made us perfect partners."

"An esper-link would do that," he agreed.

"Now perhaps you will understand. When Karr died, I died. Even now, part of me is still gone. And I don't ever want the responsibility for another partner. No matter how difficult the job, I work alone."

"I understand."

She sighed and sat back in her chair. "That should tell you why I feel the way I do. And, if we intend to play smash, we'd better get going. Before we go . . . Began strikes me as the kind of man who plays for high stakes. Do you have enough credits?"

"Geo-Mining has given me an unlimited expense account."

"I doubt they meant you to use it as a smash stake."

"With my unique abilities, I should be able to turn a profit for them."

"You mean win, don't you?"

"Of course."

"All right. But watch yourself. And," she added as an afterthought, "don't win too outrageously. It won't look right. It might even help if you lost a little."

"I will do my best."

CHAPTER 15

The hologram above the table flickered, displaying Mier's hand—a straight flush of stars.

"That's it for me," David Scott said in disgust, wiping his cards with a slap on the controls.

"Me, too," Ttar agreed.

Hac wore a small smile as he, too, blanked his hand, though more gently.

The chief engineer looked at his three of a kind with a jaundiced eye before canceling it, yawning. "That last hand cleaned me out. I'm heading for my bunk."

Mier totaled her winnings and was pleased to note she had come out ahead. Although she knew there was skill involved in playing the cards, she also recognized that it was luck which gave them to her in the first place. Luck had been with her tonight.

Wes was busy totaling his own winnings. "Broke even," he commented. "How about another round of drinks before we split up? I'll buy."

"Isn't the winner supposed to buy?" Mier asked.

"Not for me," the engineer protested. "I'm on duty in five hours, and the captain will have my skin if I oversleep."

"Me, too," Scott agreed, pushing his chair back. "It's been pleasant—"

"Wes, let's go," Wanda whined, coming to stand behind him, her small hands caressing his broad shoulders. "I'm real sleepy."

"In a minute." He looked across at Hac.

"I'm tired, too," the android told him. "We're still attempting to adjust to ship's time."

"Ttar, why don't you take Lady Wanda back to the cabin. I'll be there in a minute," Began suggested.

"Are you sure?" his brother asked. "You remember what the medic said before we left. You're supposed to get some rest on this trip."

"To hell with the medics. What do they know anyway?"

"Come on, Wes, honey," Wanda whined.

"All right. All right! I'll be right there. Just let me say good night. Go on with Ttar."

"Don't be long," she shot over her shoulder as she followed the shorter brother from the mess.

Mier was on her feet when Began stopped her. "I need to talk to you two," he said, his voice serious, the drawl gone. "It's important."

"Can we talk now?" Mier asked.

"No. It's too risky. I'll meet you in an hour. You know the observation port on the lower deck?"

"Yes."

"Meet me there."

Outside the ship, hyperspace was a glowing sheet streaked with luminescent stars. Mier gazed at it with sleep-blurred eyes, wishing Began would hurry. Hac sprawled in one of the chairs behind her, looking as if he, too, could use some rest. It was a good simulation and she was impressed, although she wondered at the need.

"What time is it now," she asked, not turning around.

"One forty-three."

"He's late."

"Maybe he couldn't get away. How important do you think this information is?"

Mier frowned as she turned her back to the observation port. "Whatever it is, I want to know why he picked us to tell it to."

"Maybe he knows who we are."

"That's exactly what I think."

"Maybe he's the other agent, and he's decided to sell out to us."

"That's a possibility." Mier yawned and rubbed her eyes, trying to push back the need for sleep. "Any more of this and I'll have to go on stimulants. We'll wait ten more minutes."

But Wes Began still didn't come.

CHAPTER 16

The lights outside the passenger cabins shone dimly during the ship's night period. The empty corridors were hushed, except for the muted hum of ventilators, until a shrill scream tore through the air, penetrating even the closed doors. Mier awoke with a start, coming off the bunk in a fluid movement, one hand clasping her pistol, the other hastily pulling on some clothing. Opening the cabin door a crack, she peered, and then cautiously stuck her head outside as a crew member thundered past, going toward the sound of hysterical sobbing.

"What's happening?" she asked one of the people standing indecisively in the passageway.

"Someone's dead," the woman responded, and Mier recognized Harryet Garske. The woman had wrapped herself in a long dressing gown, her hair still disheveled from sleep.

"Who is it?"

"I don't know. The children's cabin is down there," she added vaguely.

"Then what are you doing here!"

The woman turned, her face pale. "I'm afraid. It might be dangerous . . ."

And Mier scornfully realized the fear was for herself rather than the children. Hiding the pistol in her sleeve, she pushed her way into the corridor. The other passengers were standing about, confused and still sleepy, softly discussing the possible reason for such a rude awakening. But apparently no one wanted to be closer to the commotion than necessary.

"What's happening?" Hac asked, appearing at her side.

"I don't know, but I'm going to find out."

The hysterical woman—Wanda, she discovered—was outside of her cabin door. "Dead. He's dead," she wailed in answer to Scott's quiet questions.

"Who?" Mier and the purser asked in unison. Scott gave her a quick glance over his shoulder before returning his attention to the woman who clung, sobbing hysterically, to his arm. Mier pushed the door open and looked into the cabin where Wes Began sprawled on the floor.

"I went in," the companion gasped, "and he was like that. He's dead, isn't he?"

"Stand aside, please," an authoritative voice said as the captain and several more of the crew made their way into the cabin. The purser followed, still supporting the weeping woman.

"Now we know why he was late," Hac commented in her ear.

Mier glanced at the other passengers, who had pressed closer. "We'll talk about it later. Right now . . ."

Scott slipped back into the corridor, closing the door on the grisly scene behind him. "Would everyone please return to their cabins?" he directed. "There is no danger. There has just been a slight accident, nothing to concern yourselves about. But please remain in your cabins," he added, contradicting his previous statement. "The captain may want to speak to you."

"What happened?" one of the passengers asked.

"We're not certain. But I'm sure the captain will tell you all about it as soon as he has the facts. Now, would you please clear the corridor?"

The passengers slowly dispersed, Mier and Hac bringing up the rear. She passed into her cabin, but not before she'd seen a harassed-looking man in healer's blue guiding a grav sled into the passenger section. Leah Roget followed slowly after. The esper caught Mier's eye and nodded, but did not speak.

"So Began's dead. I wonder if this has anything to do with what he had to tell us," Hac commented when they were safely behind the closed door.

"You can bet it does. His neck was broken. Rather efficiently, too, if the angle of his head was any indication. But I didn't really have a chance to see him closely. If they've called an empath in, they're probably going to try a latent probe. It might provide an answer."

"I've heard of that. But it doesn't always work, does it?"

Mier shrugged, busy fastening the pistol sheath to her forearm. "Sometimes it does. It depends on the victim's state of mind when he was killed."

"I don't understand how it works."

She sank down on the side of her bunk. "Neither do I, but evidence from a latent probe has been accepted by the courts, so it must be effective." But why kill Wes Began? she thought. Admittedly the man could be irritating, but if that were an excuse for killing, there would be a lot more dead people.

"Why would anyone kill Began?" Hac asked, echoing her thoughts.

"I have no idea. I wonder if it had anything to do with the game. Did you notice any hard feelings?"

"Not against Wes. He was his usual jolly self. And you were the big winner."

"That's true. Who's there?" she called as a knock sounded on the door.

"The captain's compliments, but we're looking for Hac Andrews and Mier Silver."

"Come in, please."

Scott entered, not meeting her eyes. He was followed by four men and a woman, filling the tiny cabin.

"Ms. Silver, Mr. Andrews," the captain began. "You were playing cards with Wes Began last night?"

"Yes, sir, we were," she answered.

"You are perhaps aware that he was killed sometime early this morning?"

"Yes."

"Can you describe your location and movements between midnight and oh-five-hundred hours this morning?"

"Certainly. We played cards until one-thirty, and then returned to our cabins. When I couldn't sleep, I asked Hac to walk with me to the observation deck."

"And you two were together all that time?" the captain inquired, glancing curiously at the tall android.

"We were."

"I see." Disgust colored the captain's words, for he resented the disruption of his ship's routine, especially with something as sordid as murder.

"If I might speak to you for a moment," Mier asked quietly. "Alone?"

The captain stared hard at her. "If you have something to add you can speak in front of my officers.''

"There are reasons . . ." she began, and then hesitated, not sure how to word her request. Right now she needed the freedom of the ship without the suspicion of murder hanging over her. And she also needed to be a part of this murder investigation. Mier knew she was a catalyst—it was inherent in her job. Wherever she worked, things started happening, and she had to watch for them carefully. One incident might always be coincidence, but two were usually related. With three incidents, however, she could be certain that the pattern of a case was beginning to evolve. Began's death was the third incident since they'd boarded the *Douglas*. There was a very good chance, she reasoned, that his killer was the same person who bugged her cabin and struck her down. And the only person with a motive was their opponent from the Consortium.

Under the circumstances, she decided, she would have to trust the captain with her secret. Since commercial ship's captains were rigorously screened she judged she might safely do this, but she could not be sure about the other officers. She gazed at the crew arranged behind their superior. No, not the others.

"It's important. Please," she added.

"All right, if you insist. But I don't have a lot of time, so please be brief. Scott, the rest of you, please wait outside for me."

When they were alone, Mier willed the ID on her hand into visibility and held it up. "Federal Special Intelligence Agency," she explained as he took her wrist and closely inspected the logo and numbers on her hand. "Mr. Andrews and I are on a confidential mission."

"Just what I need." He released her and stepped back, frowning. "Does your mission have anything to do with this ship or any of my crew?"

"No, sir."

"I see. One of my officers reported that Mr. Andrews has been doing considerable research using the ship's

computer. He even suggested he might be with the
FSA.''

"I'm sorry for the deception, but, as I explained, we
are undercover.''

"Did Began have anything to do with your, ah, mission?''

"I . . .'' She hesitated, but judged candor was the best
policy. "I don't know. We went to the observation deck
to meet him but he never came.''

"Hmm. You security types know a lot of unusual ways
to kill a man.''

"I assure you, sir. We didn't kill Began. He said he
had some information for us. I'd very much like to know
what it was.''

"It died with him.''

"Maybe not. Has the cabin been sealed off?''

"As soon as the medical team is finished, it will be
sealed.''

"I'd like your permission to search the cabin.''

"And what do you expect to find?''

"I won't know until I see it. But, as you said, we
security types are trained to do this sort of thing.
And I'm as anxious as you are to find the killer. I'll
make a complete report to you as soon as we're finished.''

"Hmm. I'd like to cooperate with the government, but
I can't allow things of this nature to go on on board my
ship.''

"No, sir. I understand perfectly. But regardless, it has
happened. Now we have to find the killer, and I'm offering my skill. Will you permit . . . ?''

Mier tried to reassure him, mentally crossing her fingers
and hoping she spoke the truth. But if she discovered
their spy and had to dispose of him while the ship was
still in space, she decided they'd have to shove the body
through an airlock.

"All right.'' But the captain appeared to be unhappy
with his decision.

"Sir, you sent for Leah Roget . . .''

"And if I did?''

"Are you trying a latent reading?''

"You know about that?''

"It's my business."

His frown was formidable, and she was glad she wasn't one of the crew facing his displeasure.

"If the reading works," she ventured to ask, "would you share the information with me?"

"If we find out anything, I suspect the whole ship will know as soon as I do," he said bitterly.

"Yes, sir. And my secret?"

"Oh, it's safe with me. And I don't talk in my sleep—or so I'm told."

She gave a brief laugh. "Thank you."

Scott opened the door just enough to stick his head inside. "Excuse me, sir, but you wanted to be informed as soon as Healer Roget was finished."

"Very well, Ensign. I'll be right with you." He glared one more time at Mier and Hac. "Very well, you can investigate the murder. However, you are to work under my orders. Is that understood?"

"Yes, sir."

"That means if you discover the killer before I do, you are to turn him over. You are not, I repeat *not* to take matters into your own hands. Is this understood?"

"Yes."

CHAPTER 17

Leah Roget waited in the otherwise empty mess room, appearing completely composed even after her experience with the dead man's memories. Captain Getty and Mier took seats opposite her, while First Officer Ava and Hac remained standing. The door was closed after them, a crewman on guard outside.

"First, I want it understood that everything said in this room is completely confidential. I don't want anything to come back to me as chitchat, scuttlebutt, jet wash, or anything like that. Am I being clear?"

"Yes, sir," Ava affirmed. No one else spoke.

"The results of the probe," he continued, looking at Leah. "Do you know the identity of the killer?"

"It isn't that simple," she began, choosing her words carefully. "Began did not have a very disciplined mind . . ."

"Are you trying to say that the probe didn't work? You didn't get a name?"

"Began's last thoughts were chaotic. He was thinking about his work—several new directions he could go with the company—as well as difficulties in the relationship with his companion, and complications with some other people, including Hac.''

''Hac?'' Mier glanced at the android standing impassively behind her.

''An intense need to warn him of some danger.'' She, too, looked at Mier's tall companion. ''Do you have any idea what this might be? If I have background information, I can usually connect the appropriate thoughts.''

''None. I have no idea.''

''His feelings on this matter were very strong. You are certain . . .''

''We had an appointment with Began,'' Mier interjected. ''He asked us to meet him at the observation port early this morning. We waited, but he never came.''

''And he didn't tell you the reason for the meeting?'' Getty asked again.

''No. All he said was that he had some information for us. He seemed nervous. And whatever it was, it was confidential. But back to the identity of the killer: Did you find anything that might give us a place to start?''

''Passive readings of a subject's last moments can be very vivid,'' Leah told her. ''Unfortunately, as in this case, they often do not give enough useful information. In either way, it takes months of careful analysis to construct admissible evidence.'' She closed her eyes a moment as she recalled the probe. ''It is possible the killer was someone Began knew.''

''Why do you say that?'' the captain asked.

''Whoever it was entered Began's cabin without an invitation.''

''Ttar?'' Mier suggested. ''Or Lady Wanda?''

''I have the impression it was male. His thoughts of the Lady Wanda have a distinctly different feeling.''

''Ttar was the man's brother!'' the captain exclaimed, revolted.

''Men have killed their brothers since the beginnings of humankind,'' Leah explained. ''In the fight for survival, to be the strongest required the largest share of nourishment, and siblings, especially male, were unnecessary competition for food. Also in males, there is a deeply ingrained instinct to protect and pass on their own genetic code. Brother killing brother is natural to man.''

"You're discussing people as if they were animals!" Getty was revolted.

Leah closed her eyes on a smile and bowed her head toward him. "I'm sorry if the comparison offends you. I only wished to emphasize the fact that fraternity is not a deterrent for murder."

The captain sighed and looked at First Officer Ava. "What do we know about Ttar Began?"

"Nothing, sir, beyond the fact that he is—or was— Began's brother and assistant manager."

He looked back at Mier. "Who else was at the card game?"

"Ensign Scott and Engineer Gregory."

"Huh. Gregory's been with me the longest, but I think I know both of them pretty well by now. They wouldn't have done it. Still," he added, forestalling Mier's comment, "I'll question them again, too. Ava, send Reese for the three of them—Began, Scott, and Gregory."

"Be careful," Mier added. "Only a trained killer breaks a man's neck in just that way." The first officer nodded and left the mess room.

"I know I said I wouldn't ask about your mission," Getty began. "But, since there is a murderer threatening the safety of my ship, I think I should know more."

Mier shook her head. "I've told you everything I can. Just be careful. The man we're after is dangerous."

"That much is obvious. Are you armed?"

"Oh, yes."

"Huh." He scowled at her. "Carrying arms on a public vessel is against Federal regulations."

"I have a license."

A knock at the door heralded the return of Reese. "We're holding them outside, sir. Do you want them all at once, or one at a time?"

"Question Ttar last," Mier advised him in an undertone.

"One at a time. Send in Gregory."

The engineer stood at attention and answered his captain's questions readily. Scott seemed more nervous and glanced once or twice at Mier and Hac as if wondering why they were present. But both men had gone straight from the game to their bunks, and each had cabin mates who would vouch for their presence. Even more telling was that Mier could sense that they were sincerely horrified by Began's death. No, she told herself, they weren't responsible.

Then it was Ttar Began's turn to be interviewed.

"I don't know why you're subjecting me to this," he began, before anyone could speak to him. "My brother's dead. Not only do I have to deal with the grief of losing my only family, but now I have to get ready to conclude the business deal we have pending on Stonewall by myself. By the Cosmic Creator, you have no idea how difficult all this is for me!"

"I'm sorry to inconvenience you," Getty told him. "I wouldn't do it if it wasn't necessary. Won't you be seated?"

"Thank you." Ttar took a chair and confined his attention to the captain. His eyes were rimmed with red and dark-shadowed, but he leaned back in the chair, seeming completely at ease.

"You and your brother were close?"

"He was all the family I have left. We've worked together ever since I got out of college."

Liar, Mier thought, and wondered that she should have such strong feelings against the man. He was definitely covering up. Suddenly she realized there was something useful she could be doing while Ttar was out of the way.

"Excuse me, please," she said to the captain, and rose to her feet, her hand on Hac's shoulder, preventing him from following her. "Stay here," she whispered. "I'll be right back."

The captain frowned but continued with his interrogation.

Mier went swiftly down the empty corridor, counting doors. Began's door was guarded by a red override lock. She left it alone and went to the next cabin, which she knew was assigned to Ttar. After a moment's work, she got the door open and slipped inside.

The room was a duplicate of her own, except for pieces of clothing scattered on the bunk, and papers and microtapes littering a table that had been pulled out from the wall. Mier glanced through the sheets, but all concerned business matters and bore the Began Electronics logo. She found a reader and checked a couple of the tapes. Business there, too. A locked luggage case stood along the wall. She searched the rest of the cabin for keys without luck, which only proved Ttar carried them with him. She would give anything to know what was in that case. Her sensitive fingers began to work on the lock.

"What are you doing here?" a whining voice inquired.

Wanda stood in the doorway, a robe clutched around her and her hair mussed. Without makeup she presented a less appealing picture.

"Looking around. Did you see Ttar last night?"

Wanda wandered into the cabin, scratching her head and yawning. "I saw him at the smash game. You were there, too."

"And afterward? Did you see him then?"

"He took me back to Wes's cabin." Her face crumpled as if she was about to cry again, but she sneezed instead.

"And that was the last time you saw him?"

"No. He was there when I saw Wes dead. Did he kill him?" Her eyes were wide and curious, and Mier couldn't imagine anyone being that naive.

"You mean Ttar was there when you discovered Wes's body?"

"Oh, yes. He said he was going to get the captain and I should guard the body. But I don't like dead bodies. I was very frightened."

"That's why you were screaming?"

"No. I screamed because Ttar started shaking me."

"He shook you? Why?" It was like trying to get information from a child!

"I said I wouldn't stay there. I don't like Ttar."

"Let me get this straight. You came to Wes's cabin . . ."

"It's my cabin, too. Only now they won't let me stay there because Wes was killed."

"But you went out last night? And left Wes alone?"

"Yes. I went to find Ttar."

"You just said you don't like Ttar. Why did you go looking for him?"

"Oh, I liked him then. I just don't like him now because he frightened me."

"I see."

"I mean, he wasn't really nice to me or anything, but I didn't care because Wes was alive then and he was very nice to me. I wish he wasn't dead." She rubbed her eyes, and her pretty mouth drooped.

"I'm sure you do. But think about last night. You left Wes and went looking for Ttar."

"But he wasn't in his cabin," Wanda explained.

"And when you came back to Wes's cabin, Ttar was there."

"Yes. I thought that was pretty funny. Don't you? I mean, I went to his cabin and he went to my cabin. At the same time. That's funny."

"Very funny. And I think you should share this information with the captain."

CHAPTER 18

"It's inconclusive," Hac commented, continuing an argument he had been having with Mier for most of the morning. He settled into the seat beside her and fastened the webbing with an irritated snap. "Is your job always this confusing?"

"Sometimes."

"How do you accomplish anything?"

"I collect information, and look for patterns," she told him, keeping her voice low because of the people in the seats ahead of them.

"Patterns?"

"Yeah. Patterns. And when I find them, that's usually when things start happening."

"What kind of things?"

She laughed softly. "Usually people start trying to kill me."

"But this time nothing has happened."

"Enjoy it while you can. As we get closer to our destination, life should become more interesting. Although I wouldn't call getting hit on the head and having someone bug my cabin exactly boring."

"We never found out if Ttar was responsible, even if he did kill his brother."

"We can't rule him out. And we still don't know what Began wanted to tell us."

"It could have been anything from corporate espionage to a report of someone cheating at cards. Do you really think his brother killed him?"

"The evidence is pretty conclusive."

"As long as he's in custody we'll never know any more about him."

She knew this wasn't true as long as she had access to Federation computers, but perversely, she neglected to mention the fact. "You sound disappointed."

"He was our main suspect."

"He was our only suspect, though we didn't suspect him until after he murdered Wes. And I'm still not completely convinced he's our man."

"Who else could it have been?"

"I don't know."

Hac was patently dissatisfied with this answer and subsided into a thoughtful silence. Mier gazed through the port beside her, inner visions parading against the flaking gray paint of the launch tube, her mind busy with the case. Now add Stonewall, she thought, another variable, and possibly the most dangerous part of the whole mission. She remembered the information from the intelligence file. Privately owned, and probably one of the largest businesses in the known universe, Stonewall was managed by a board of directors as a gigantic spaceport and tax-free trading center. This was possible only because of its location at the nexus of a dozen interstellar trade routes. There was a saying: "If credits can buy it, it's for sale on Stonewall." Renowned not only because of the variety of goods available there, the lack of taxes and governmental red tape made the center extremely attractive to all kinds of traders. Any and all of whom, she told herself, could be in the pay of the Consortium or another interested party. Which adds considerably to my problems—to our problems, she amended, glancing at Hac's profile. Apparently she was stuck with him.

With the sound of grinding metal the bay doors came open, and the shuttle detached and fell. Mier swayed against the webbing at the abrupt movement, the contour seat hard under her back and legs. The pilot flew with an élan born of familiarity, and the passengers suffered accordingly. Hac moved beside her, his shoulder brushing hers for an instant until he caught his balance. She felt the warm flesh and muscle beneath the thin fabric of his overall. It had become difficult to think of him as a thing of metal and sophisticated programming, and she had to remind herself yet again that he was an android. Brian had been right, but it still didn't make her feel better about working with a partner.

Mier turned her attention to the view beyond the small port. Stonewall rolled between the ship and twin suns. Nightside glowed, lights reflecting off of the interlocked atmosphere domes covering the surface. Did anyone ever sleep? she wondered. Only one hundredth the size of Earth, the planet had been one of the first new worlds settled after the Colonial Revolt, when a corporation formed by four wealthy entrepreneurs claimed the small planet, eager to grab a portion of wealth once held by the Federation of Earth's Ruling Houses. No one else saw any value in an airless planetoid in a system that also included the dreaded anomaly known as the Stone Field. She stared in fascination at the glowing cloud marking the edge of the Field, far beyond the planet. More than a cloud, it recalled the distant fog of her dreams. The shuttle's engine throbbed, vibrating through the cabin, and she could almost hear the drums.

Mier drew a deep breath. This line of thought was nonproductive. Despite Brian's reassurances, she was apprehensive about the Field, but she was curious, too. She held a pilot's license, and on occasion had had to navigate through some tight spots, but she'd never deliberately faced anything like this. There were stories, tales that spacers told in awed voices when they had been drinking too much. It was mostly speculation, since no pilot would go into the Field. Still, they were hard to ignore, especially since more legitimate reports from science probes provided information just as bizarre. It wasn't just the asteroids that gave the Field its name, but the erratic radiation—waves of all sorts, capable of everything from melting a hull to scrambling a pilot's brain. Spacers had even reported hallucinating when skirting certain parts of the boundary, a boundary that constantly changed, shifting, never still, never the same. And yet Brian assured her that there was a way to safely navigate through the Field. She had her doubts. But she had also worked with Brian long enough to know he would never put one of his operatives into an impossible situation. He would definitely send them into danger, but never into a situation where there was no chance of getting them out again. How else would he get his reports, a jaundiced part of her mind added.

As for navigating through the Field, Jarry had done it. He had passed through it twice. Jarry. What had happened to him? Had it been something in the Field, or had it happened on Tori? She wondered about the usefulness of a mining treaty with the native population of a planet hidden in a place that was avoided by any sane spaceman. How would they get workers and equipment in and out?

"What's going to happen to Ttar now?" Hac asked, his voice interrupting another profitless line of thought.

"He'll be turned over to the Federal authorities on Stonewall."

"I thought the planet was neutral."

"It is, but several governments maintain bases there."

"And they'll sentence him?"

"After they have a hearing, and review tapes of the shipboard trial."

Hac shook his head. "And we're back where we started: everyone is a suspect. But now, instead of a ship, we have an entire planet to worry about."

CHAPTER 19

Undaunted by skeptics and prophets of doom, the first settlers on Stonewall had raised an atmosphere dome and set up shop, dispensing basic supplies, offering repairs and refitting with the latest equipment, to any traveler who happened by—all tax-free. Needless to say, this was attractive to spacefarers who, for one reason or another, were reluctant to make use of government-controlled facilities. With such a convenient site, the travelers soon began to lease space in the markets, and the planet also became a place to barter and sell a wide variety of goods. After an initial period of caution, even legitimate traders came to bargain on Stonewall, since a tax-free port allowed them to acquire goods that could, with a standard markup, be sold for much less than the competition charged because it wasn't necessary to add the horrendous cost of port taxes.

Wiser heads in other planetary governments shook in disdain. Such a situation, it was prophesied, would lead to instant anarchy. It would be impossible to maintain order without regulation. But Stonewall remained essentially a peaceful community because of two basic laws, which were stringently enforced. First: No taxes and no off-world interference of any kind was, or would be, tolerated. Second: Anything was permitted as long as it did not interfere with the rights of others.

Outlaws dealt peacefully, side by side, with legitimate traders, since the advantages of such a port far outweighed anything they might gain by using it as a source of plunder. Any trouble, and the offending ship would be impounded, the officers executed, and the crew sold, no mercy given. Peace was maintained by a corporate police, called "the authorities," whose methods were sufficiently harsh to forestall criminal activity—within the sphere of planetary influence, at least.

The naysayers were proved wrong, for Stonewall's system worked, and over decades the trading center grew, a freewheeling, politically neutral post with a reputation for fair dealing. Somehow, Mier decided, such an unconventional outpost seemed an appropriate jumping-off place for Mission: Tori.

Having curved over the terminator and into the fitful sunlight of dayside, the shuttle dropped toward a vast area of docking and maintenance yards. They passed through a permafield and, surprisingly, landed gently on the roof of a four-story terminal, the area of which could have contained an entire spaceport on many other worlds.

Mier and Hac disembarked, and rode an escalator down three levels, joining one of the lines of incoming passengers waiting to be processed.

"The sign said customs," Hac commented. "I didn't think anything was contraband on Stonewall."

"It isn't, except for disease germs. Can you imagine how devastating a germ could be in a closed world like this one?"

"Are we going to be disinfected?"

"They'll probably use a transporter. It's safe for machines, so it shouldn't harm you."

"Oh."

They waited in silence, watching the advertisements, holograms that were beamed throughout the enormous room. Stonewall certainly didn't discriminate, Mier thought. Ads for bawdy houses were side by side with announcements of religious services; offers for new-and-improved navigational modules vied with exotic pets, mercenaries with the latest fashion footwear and cosmetics.

"Identity please," requested an official when they reached the desk.

When these were recorded they stepped into a decontamination chamber. Mier experienced a faint tingling as she and her belongings were molecularly disassociated, every disease-bearing spore, bacterium, and virus instantly zapped. She was never certain how the machines knew to differentiate harmful from beneficial bacteria, but somehow they did.

"Are you all right?" she asked as the retaining field flickered off to allow them to exit through the far doorway, and officially onto the planet.

"Yes, quite well. Thank you," came his placid reply. "As you said, it did me no more harm than it would any other piece of machinery."

"On some other worlds, they do a visual scan. How would you explain yourself then?"

"I have several interesting explanations prepared just in case," he said with a grin.

But Mier wasn't listening. She had spotted a movement, people scattering as a running figure dashed toward the main entrance.

"Mier, that's—" Hac began, but the agent had dropped her shoulder bag, moving as she spoke.

"Stay there!"

Someone cried out as three uniformed figures in pursuit toppled one woman and sent a man tripping over his own baggage. More uniforms set out after Mier, who was closing in on Ttar. One of them reached for her, possibly mistaking her for the fugitive. She grasped his outstretched arm briefly and sent him flying into the wall. Seeing this, most of the other guards went for her, ignoring her shout that they stop the redheaded man. Within seconds it was over, Mier cut off from the entrance by a wary circle of security men, their pistols trained on the agent. Only the original three had given chase outside of the terminal, but Hac knew they were too far behind their quarry to stop him. Only Mier might have done so if she hadn't been detained.

He came slowly toward them, carrying both of their bags.

"You idiots!" Mier shouted. "You let him get away!"

"How were we to know you weren't part of it?"

"She's armed," said the guard she had tossed out of the way. "Watch out."

She raised her empty hands. "I have a permit. Who's in charge here?" she demanded, more calmly.

"I am," said a voice from behind Hac. "Excuse me, please." A tall woman in a security uniform pushed her way into the circle. "Would someone please tell me what has happened here?"

"Escaped prisoner," one of the guards reported. "And this one helped him. Probably an accomplice."

"Hardly," Mier retorted.

"Who are you?" the official inquired. "And what do you know about this?"

"I was a passenger on the *Douglas*, where the prisoner, Ttar Began, was being held for murder. He was supposed to be turned over to the Federation officials for sentencing. I don't know how he managed to escape, but I would have caught him if these goons hadn't interfered."

"Chief Sardo, she slung Wexler against the wall," one of the guards supplied. "Looked to me like she was helping the prisoner escape."

The official looked at her with respect. "Hand over your weapon, please. We'll finish this discussion in my office. Michels, find out if they caught the prisoner yet."

"No," Mier said.

"I beg your pardon?"

"We can certainly go to your office, but I never give up my pistol."

The official hesitated.

"Look," Mier told her, "I'm no danger to you or your men, as long as they don't try to interfere with me again." She glanced at the guard who was rubbing his arm.

"You were really trying to apprehend the fugitive?"

"I was one of the people responsible for his conviction

on board the *Douglas*. You can check it if you don't believe me. And I don't have time to wait around while you do it." She held her hand out toward the security chief, holding it so that only she could see the ID and shielding the action from the guards with her body. The woman came toward her for a closer look.

"Very well, you may go. However, I will certainly check into this more closely. If I need you again, I will know where to find you."

"Thank you."

As the guards dispersed, Mier returned to Hac's side and retrieved her bag.

"I didn't think you'd be able to talk your way out of that," he commented as they once more made their way toward the main entrance.

"You have no faith. I only wish I'd caught Ttar. While he was in custody, he was one less variable for us to worry about. Now he could be anywhere."

They stepped out of the building and into the sunlight that streamed through the dome. Above that, visible through the glare, stretched the black of space, stars obscured by the bright suns. In the absence of a colored sky, some people found the knowledge that nothing but space surrounded the planet easier to endure at night, when the more familiar star-pierced black disguised the lack of atmosphere. Mier gave the curve of plastic a brief glance and, being accustomed to living on an orbiting station, was not discomforted by the obvious void outside.

"Four Star Inn, please," she told the computer as they climbed into a small taxi.

The vehicle moved carefully into traffic, traveling on a narrow roadway beside a lush green park. Trees raised long, slender branches high above grass and walkways lined with carefully pruned shrubs. She could smell them, the humid dark of mulch and decaying leaves underlying the fresh, clean scent of the leaves. Somewhere the fragrance of blossoms spiced the air, faint and tantalizing. She wanted to walk there and scuff her feet in the leaves, give up this crazy job, and spend the rest of her life somewhere green.

"You are riding in a Kay Autocab," the machine suddenly announced. "For a small fee, I can be leased for the duration of your stay on Stonewall. A fascinating tour of the city would fill your idle hours, and for business, I am equipped to see that you arrive at your destination cool, refreshed, and on time."

"No, thank you," Mier said.

"If you would prefer," the machine insisted, "a human guide can be arranged to accompany you, pointing out the sights of interest, as well as the excellent and exciting nightlife Stonewall has to offer."

"Our home office has already arranged for a guide."

"Questions. You must have some questions. I have comprehensive programming and can tell you just about anything you would like to know about our wonderful planet."

Mier laughed.

"Tell me about the trees," Hac interjected.

"Every available space on the planet has been planted with trees and shrubs native to seventeen different worlds. There are even specimens of the giant galobas from Darius Seven, although they cannot achieve the height of their native world due to the difference in gravity and soil on Stonewall. Most important, however, there are ordinances restricting interference with any growing thing. Vegetative plant life is an important part of maintaining a clean atmosphere. Please enjoy the verdure, but do not touch!"

"I thought Stonewall had an atmosphere generator," Mier said under her breath, but the machine heard her.

"You are correct. Stonewall has seven class-five linear atmospheric generators made by the Hataki Company of New Tok-yo. However, verdure supplements the scrub cycle, and helps keep the air smelling clean and fresh, while the carbon dioxide given off by animal respiration benefits the trees. So you see, there are mutual advantages.

"We have arrived at the Four Star Inn, a class-A hostelry run by the Stonewall Company. I hope you enjoy your visit. If Kay Autocabs can be of further assistance, code K into your in-room computer console. Always remember, for the best, fastest service, use Kay Autocabs!"

Their hotel was one of two major hostelries facing the park, across from the terminal. Trees grew here, too, even inside the building, in huge planters. Polished slabs of some light stone paved the floor of what Mier gratefully recognized as a luxury hotel, a relief and a pleasure after some of the places she'd had to stay. And of all unheard-of things, they had been given a suite! What was it about this particular mission that rated them such royal treatment? Mier wasn't sure why this assignment should be so different, unless . . . She glanced at Hac, who was following a floor steward to their suite. Maybe it was the android who earned them the luxuries. Or, the nasty part of her mind intruded, it could be advance compensation for a mission that was going to kill them. She didn't like such thoughts.

As soon as they entered the suite, the vid screen began flashing, signaling an incoming message.

"Our contact is wasting no time, it would seem," Mier commented as she closed the door.

"Welcome to Stonewall," a friendly voice said.

Cool gray eyes looked out of the screen at her, calculating even as the woman smiled, white teeth flashing against dark skin. A crest of black hair rose from a shaved head, longer in the back and intricately braided with beads, the end draped over her shoulder. Glittering silver tattoos swirled over the delicate bones of her skull, arabesques framing cheeks and dark-lashed eyes.

"My name is London, and I am available as your personal guide." As she spoke the woman raised her hand and adjusted one of her heavy silver earrings.

Mier caught a glimpse of a Federation ID among the designs tattooed on her hand.

"Thank you," she replied. "You must be the guide our home base contracted. Where can we meet you?"

"There is a club called the Nightside Palace one block over from your hotel. I will find you there at seventeen hundred this evening. We can plan your itinerary then."

"Thank you. We'll be there." Mier hit the cutoff button.

"Local time is sixteen-oh-seven hundred now," Hac pointed out.

"Then we'd better hurry."

CHAPTER 20

A hodgepodge, the buildings of Stonewall followed no uniform architectural pattern, but were made of native stone, plasticrete, extruded polymers, or anything else that came to hand, in a variety of styles according to the owners' whim. The streets, too, meandered off of a number of main boulevards, the resulting maze a city planner's nightmare. Mier found it intriguing as they walked to their destination. Hac appeared resigned as they backtracked yet again, having taken another wrong turn.

Thick trees almost obscured the Nightside Palace when they finally found it. Not at all pretentious, it was little more than a featureless, low black building sandwiched between a warehouse and a high wall, with a small blue sign flashing the name above the door. The interior, however, was striking. Walls, floor, and ceiling were carpeted in jet black, the main light coming from a glowing dance floor two levels down. Around it spiraled a long, wide ramp where small tables seated the guests. Additional lighting came from tiny crystal stars floating on

mini grav lifts throughout the room. The club was packed
with a variety of individuals—spacers, businesspeople,
toughs, off-duty troopers, garishly dressed natives. Music blared, people laughed and talked and laughed, ice
tinkled against the sides of glasses.

"And how do we find London?" Hac wanted to know,
looking around from their vantage point just inside the
front door.

"Impossible," Mier agreed. "So we'll let her find us.
Is that a bar down there?"

"Looks like it." He started down the ramp behind
her.

Mier was about halfway down, twisting through shadowy figures, when her way was suddenly blocked by a
bulky male dressed in rumpled fatigues. A wide brush
of white hair grew down his back, tangling in the jeweled
rings—at least eight of them—piercing his ears.

"Beautiful one," he rumbled as he swayed, having
trouble with his balance. "I have been waiting for you
all my life. Come with me."

His eyes were completely black, she saw, with no white
at all around the iris, the sign of a heavy soma user. As
he reached for her, Hac stepped between them.

"Thank you, friend, but this lady is with me."

The heavy eyebrows pulled together as the man
frowned, concentrating, his eyes level with Hac's chest.
Slowly, and very carefully, he raised his head, measuring
his tall opponent. "Sorry. Thought she was alone," he
mumbled.

"You are mistaken."

"Yeah." The man turned and staggered away.

Startled by Hac—or, more precisely, by anyone in the
archaic role of the protective male—Mier didn't know
how to respond for a second. It was both an insult and a
sort of backhanded compliment. But from an android?
She continued her descent. "That wasn't necessary.
Soma doesn't usually make people belligerent. Besides,
I can take care of myself."

"Perhaps. But I was here, and you didn't have to."

Still unsure how to take it, she slid without comment
onto a stool in front of the bar.

"Terran beer, if you have it," she ordered as Hac sat beside her.

"Nova, Bud, Coors, Pilsner Gold, Bohemia, you name it," the human bartender responded.

"Nova."

"Me, too."

She turned to watch the dancers drifting across the floor as she sipped the tart brew.

"There," Hac whispered suddenly. He did not point, but Mier looked closely. London, dressed in a silver bodysuit, was seated at a small table with two men in workers' coveralls. "Why doesn't she make contact?"

"Be patient." She sipped her beer.

"I thought time was important."

"It is. The sooner we make contact and get on our way, the less chance we'll have of picking up a tail." Mier had an idea. "Ask her to dance with you."

"What?" The android was startled.

"Dance. Bodies moving to music. Brian said your program included the social . . ."

"I can dance! I am just surprised you would suggest such a thing."

"Is it possible I've offended you? What's the matter? Scared some other love-starved spacer's going to try to steal me away the minute your back's turned?" She grinned wickedly.

"Excuse me. I shall return as soon as possible."

She watched as he approached the trio seated against the wall, back straight, the picture of offended dignity, if it was possible to offend a robot. She grinned. He was undeniably attractive, and she noticed more than one of the patrons admiring him as he moved smoothly across the room. After bowing to London and nodding to her companions, he began to speak. Though she couldn't hear what was said over the music and noise, she could imagine the conversation from body language and gesture: query, comment, rebuff. That was that. London apparently had plans of her own.

Mier's gaze wandered idly over the crowd. She had been on a lot of different worlds, but her favorites were those with the freewheeling social atmosphere, and she was pleased to see that, for all its emphasis on the com-

mercial, there was so much individuality on Stonewall.
Then she noticed a particularly striking woman dressed
in a purple tunic, black-and-white striped hair cresting
in a wild, thick mane over her shoulders. She spoke to a
short man with red hair . . . someone who seemed familiar, although she couldn't see enough of his face to
make a positive identification.

"I'm back," Hac announced from her side.

"No luck?"

"I must be losing my touch."

Except you have no touch to lose, she thought, searching over the rim of her glass for the woman and her intriguing companion. They had gone.

"She did, however, set up a rendezvous. We are to
meet her outside in fifteen minutes."

"Just enough time to finish our drinks."

London and her companions passed them, moving
slowly up the crowded ramp.

Minutes later, Mier and Hac followed. Outside, no
more quiet than the club, the streets were crowded with
people off work and in a noisy carnival mood. There was
no sign of London.

"Did she tell you where we were to meet?" Mier
asked, but as she spoke she saw the redheaded man again,
this time full-face. It was Ttar.

"Damn," she breathed, leaving Hac to follow as she
pushed her way across the street.

"Mier?" he called as he caught up to her. She stood
on tiptoe to see above the heads of the crowd. "What is
it?"

"Ttar. I thought I saw him in the club, but this time I
was sure it was him."

"Where?"

"I don't know. He's disappeared again."

"Could he be following us? Does he know we're
here?"

"I don't know. I don't think so. He didn't seem to be
trying to hide." She shook her head in disgust. "We'll
never find him in this crowd. Or London. Where did she
say she'd meet us?"

"Outside."

"Well, that's where we are. Where is she?"

"I don't know." He looked carefully around, his height giving him an advantage.

"She has to be around here somewhere. She wouldn't set up a meet if she didn't expect to be there. All right, we follow an obvious route."

"What's that?"

"Back to the hotel. It's the only logical direction for us to go."

Pedestrians moved through the streets, a river of bodies, their glittering, nighttime costumes catching every available bit of light and spreading it into the shadows under the trees. But it didn't penetrate the black spaces between buildings. Mier led the way into one of these narrow lanes, remembering it as a shortcut back to the park. Here mutated palmatiers spread their branches overhead, cutting out even more of the illumination, though the high towers of the hotel were visible through the leaves. She paused a moment to push her contacts out of the way, blinking to help clear her sight.

"I hope you know where you're going," Hac muttered as his toe caught on a root.

"Of course," she replied calmly, gazing around. "And if I'm not mistaken, this was the correct choice of route." Her voice dropped to a whisper. "There's London."

To Hac's eyes, a part of the shadow moved, but Mier could clearly see the woman's face beneath the hood of her darkcloak, and the hand beckoning. With a snap, a privacy shield came on around them; if anyone had been watching, they had simply disappeared.

"Palo warned me you would be followed," London commented. "But I didn't know anyone would be on to you so quickly. Or me," she added ruefully.

"Then you weren't able to get us a ship?" Mier demanded.

London smiled, teeth white in the darkness. "Oh, I did that all right. You're set to leave first thing in the morning. Here's the ship's papers and the key."

"Your base has been compromised?"

"Yes, but it's no problem. They searched my shop, but they never reached the basement and the rest of my setup."

" 'They'? Do you know who they are?'' Mier asked, tucking the key and disk away in the top of her boot.

London shook her head. ''I didn't see them . . . and I'm only assuming it was more than one. Whoever did it was good. The first thing they did was set up an induction field and scramble all of my 'eyes. I didn't get a single picture. But since I know they're on to me, I decided to meet you here.''

"You have a backup base?''

"Yes. Unfortunately, you'd never find it alone, and I can't lead you there, so I've arranged a guide. It was the best I could do on short notice.''

"I don't understand,'' Mier told her. ''We've just concluded our business. Hac and I will be off-world first thing in the morning.''

"It's not that simple. Palo tight-beamed a message in yesterday. Says he has to talk to you.''

"Palo? Do you know what it's about?''

"Nope. He said it's urgent, and it would mean my head if you didn't get the message. You know it's got to be important or he wouldn't have risked calling. Headquarters doesn't want you on Stonewall any longer than necessary. And as soon as you're on your way, I'll have to move everything, again,'' she finished with a sigh.

"Why don't you just catch whoever's after you and eliminate them?'' Hac asked.

"It wouldn't work. They might have passed the location of the base on to someone else already.''

"Besides, it's policy to move a base that's been compromised,'' Mier added absently, wondering what Palo could want. ''Keeping it open even long enough for me to call headquarters is dangerous. London, is your computer still connected with the main library?''

"Yes.''

"Good. I need some information.''

"What information?''

"I want to run some idents. I couldn't do any in-depth research on the ship. How do we find your base?''

"There's a twenty-four-hour open-air market down the road back there. Turn right. If you get lost, anyone can show you the way.''

"Open-air?'' Hac tilted his head curiously.

"It's the old market, the one where the smaller businessmen do their dealing . . . and the traders who aren't here long enough to set up a permanent shop. Actually, some of the more interesting business on Stonewall is conducted there," London told him. "It's also where I keep my best informants busy. Anyway, the man you're looking for is a scent dealer named Bezique. He'll be set up in front of a blue pole all evening. It's his regular spot. And don't worry, you'll find it. Ask him for London. 'Perfume from London,' works well if there's anyone around."

"That's all?"

"He'll bring you to me. And try not to be followed. I'd rather not have him compromised. He's my best ear."

"Don't worry about that. Is it all right to use him?" Mier asked, concerned that someone else knew about their mission.

"I've trusted him before. Besides, he's very well paid. And, just in case you're worried, he won't know who you are. I'll tell him you're looking for some special black-market goods." She laughed. "He probably thinks you're running Garan bibles to Ekard, or something like that. And now I have to try to get rid of my tail so I can set everything up for you."

"Is someone watching now?" Hac inquired.

"Possibly. But who can see anything in this pitch black? The shield doesn't even show."

"They'll wonder if we went into the alley and then took so long to emerge," he insisted.

London laughed again. "They'll just think you stopped for a little love play." She smiled up at him. "Under the circumstances, I certainly would. Don't worry about it. Put your arms around each other and look cozy when you come out. Till next time . . ." London looked quickly up and down the alley before she deactivated the shield. In a second she was gone, her darkcloak blending into the night.

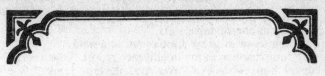

CHAPTER 21

Leaving the alley, Mier and Hac moved into the crowd, walking in a direction that took them deeper and deeper into the maze of twisted streets. Trees lined the middle of the road; glos hung from poles, the light reflecting down from the branches. Here and there, backs to the trunks to keep them out of the foot traffic, buskers played music, open instrument cases on the ground in front of them to catch coins. The sounds blended in a comfortable counterpoint to voices. Before long the street opened into a huge square. More trees provided a roof for this market, and the spaces below sprouted booths where people inspected and haggled over a bewildering variety of goods. More vendors worked their way up and down the aisles, merchandise slung over their shoulders or pushed on grav sleds.

"I'm curious to see this place in the daytime, if this is how they conduct business at night," Hac commented after they had browsed for a while.

"A lot of people who deal on Stonewall prefer unconventional surroundings. But I wouldn't be surprised to find a lot of these traders in modern offices tomorrow, dressed in conservative suits.''

"You seem to know a lot about Stonewall."

"Just what was in the intelligence report." She looked up at him curiously. "You read it, too. Look." She pointed at a red pole decorated with long streamers of the same color. "And there's a green one over there."

"A different color for each row. All we have to do is find the blue pole."

"This way. Let's try to look like we have a reason for being here."

"We could buy something."

"That's what I had in mind." Mier rarely had enough free time to amuse herself, and stolen moments while she was on a job became precious. She had no trouble falling into the role of a giddy shopper, dragging Hac from booth to booth whenever anything caught her fancy. Her eyes sparkled as she flung a gaily embroidered scarf around her neck, standing back as if to get her companion's approval.

"Buy it," he told her.

"Don't be silly." She put it back, fingers lingering unconsciously on the soft fabric before she took her hand away. "There's the blue pole," she said, taking his arm. He turned and started forward, but she held him back. "Let's not be in too much of a hurry. We still have to lose our indiscreet companion."

Hac began to look over his shoulder, then stopped himself. Instead he stepped out of the path, turning at a booth to look over a pile of boots. "I don't see anyone," he whispered.

"She's gone now." Mier took his arm and started him walking again. "Tall woman, purple tunic. She was talking to Ttar earlier this evening in the Nightside Palace. I think she's gone now. Maybe she was just trying to confirm our identities. Or passing the information on to someone else."

"So now we have to look for 'someone else'?"

Mier smiled. "Don't worry. We'll lose them when we have to."

"If they don't kill us first."

She laughed.

A couple more minutes brought them to the next aisle, one marked halfway down with a blue pole. Walking more slowly, they paused to look at the merchandise. Mier admired a caged bird, its feathers colored iridescent red and blue.

Eventually they arrived at a rather large stall and spent a minute sniffing the various scents on display before the owner was free to speak to them.

"I'm looking for something special," Mier said. "Maybe something Terran. Do you have any perfume from London?"

A short man, the proprietor was almost as round as he was tall. Light eyes peered at them from under a thatch of straight white hair. "Yes, indeed I do," he beamed. "But it's very special. I keep it in the back here. If you would be so good as to follow me?" Signaling his assistant to take over, he led them through his display space to a storage area in the back, closed off by a heavy drape. "I think I have what you're looking for, right here." He slid a packing case aside, uncovering a steel-rimmed trapdoor, the standard access to underground utilities. Usually they were kept locked, but this one opened easily. "She said you were being followed, so we'll have to go down here," he whispered. "Quickly. I can't be gone too long."

"You first," Mier insisted.

"Cautious, eh? All right. Hold this, and point it straight down for me. Don't worry about closing the top; it isn't that far." He gave her a handlamp and started down the ladder, following the beam of her light.

"Here." Mier gave the lamp to her partner, preferring to rely on her own eyes. "Stay close."

"Don't worry."

Below, the perfume vendor switched on a second lamp, the light revealing a wide, damp, curving tunnel, the roof buckled here and there where roots tried to force their way through the plastricrete. He led them to the left, nimbly avoiding puddles of dark water. At a fork, he went left again and then paused to unlock what appeared to be a service door set into the curving wall.

"Up the ladder. It will bring you to a courtyard. The door to the house should be open. London is waiting."

Mier nodded. "You first," she told Hac.

He climbed swiftly while she waited below.

"You are cautious," their guide said, "but there is no need. London and I have done business for many years."

Hac reached the top and pushed open the round cover above him. "It's clear," he told her after a quick survey.

"All right, thank—" Mier turned back, but the little man had started back. She could see his light bobbing ahead of him as he quickly made his way through the tunnel, hopping over the puddles.

"What's wrong?" Hac called down in an urgent whisper.

"I don't know. Maybe nothing. Still clear up there?"

"Yes. Are you coming?"

"Be right there. Here, catch." Mier switched off the handlight and tossed it upward before thinking her pistol into her hand. It made climbing awkward, but now she felt ready for anything they might encounter at the top.

After the crowded market and stuffy tunnel, the air in the courtyard was cool and clean. Leaves shrouded the sky, and the dark shadows lay over the twenty-meter square of stone paving.

Mier looked about carefully, but they were completely alone. Two doors pierced the surrounding walls. One was a plastic panel with about a foot of space at the bottom obviously leading to the street. The other, finished to look like wood, probably led to the house. "Check the door," she whispered, jerking her head. "That one."

Hac complied, and it swung silently inward at his touch.

"Wait." She came forward and kicked the door fully open. She swung her pistol to the left and to the right, covering the entrance.

"You can drop the gun, operative," a voice said from the darkness inside the building. London stepped forward.

CHAPTER 22

Mier's heart began to slow its frantic pounding as she straightened up, the pistol retracting into its holster with a faint slap. She could see Hac's muscles relax as he, too, realized that the alarm was false. After all these years, she had to admit she could still be frightened—scared half to death, to be more accurate—but the excitement and even the fear were part of the reason she stuck with the job; adrenaline was addictive.

London took it in stride. "Follow me, please, and be careful. I can't turn on the lights up here since we're trying to keep this base going as long as possible." She led them down the hall and through a low doorway. "Watch the steps."

With a hiss the door behind them slid closed, and a click preceded a flood of illumination. Mier closed her eyes until she could push her contacts down. When she looked again a steep flight lay before them, London almost at the bottom.

"Sorry about all the mystery," she began when they reached her. Before them stretched a surprisingly large room. Shipping cases stood here and there, scraps of wrapping and insulating pellets scattered around them. "We've started packing . . . have to get this stuff out by tomorrow night at the latest, but as usual, headquarters is holding us up."

"It has to be vital if Palo thinks it's necessary to contact me this far into the mission," Mier told her.

"No doubt. This must be a hot case."

"It is, but I don't think you want to know too much about it."

She laughed. "Brian told me to maintain the tightest possible security. And I did, though there's obviously been a leak anyway. You have any idea who I should be looking for? An organization? Or is this an isolated incident?"

"I don't know. I'd hoped to have some kind of a lead by now." She shrugged.

"Nothing?"

"Not quite. Someone put a mini-spy in my cabin aboard the ship."

"You know who it was?"

"No. How long before the call from Palo comes through?"

"Half an hour, at least. I signaled him as soon as you came through the courtyard. Oh, yes, I've got 'eyes all over this place." She gestured to the bank of monitors, some of them still functional while others had been disconnected in preparation for packing.

"If your computer is available, I'd like to use the time to do a little research. I need some IDs."

"Yes. Brian said you might need it. Have a seat and we'll get going. You'd better sit down, too," she added, looking up at Hac. "I'll get a crick in my neck looking up at you. What's your part in all this, or is that top secret, too?"

"Mission observer," he replied, dragging a chair over to the console and folding himself into it.

She shook her head. "My last observer was seventy years old and female. Some people have all the luck." Despite the banter, her fingers were busy at a keyboard, calling up a menu. "All right. What do we have to work with? Name? Address? Ident number? Description?"

"Name, number, and description," Mier supplied. "And I'd like you to run three suspects."

"Very well. Take it from here. Computer, voice on. Ready to receive."

"First subject," the computer requested.

"Ttar Began," Mier said. "ID 289–93–0347 Theta. Terran. Approximately one-point-seven meters. Slender build, reddish-sandy hair, brown eyes, slight scar right side of neck."

"Accepted. Searching," the computer responded. "Second subject."

"Wes Began. Terran ID . . ." She fed in the descriptions of the murder victim and then the Lady Wanda for good measure.

"Fourth subject," the computer asked.

"Finished," Mier replied.

"Searching."

"Voice off. How long," she asked London, "does this usually take?"

"Considering the number of files it has to search, it's fast. About three minutes, maybe less. These are your suspects?"

"They're the most likely. Unfortunately, if their backgrounds check out, I'll have to run the entire passenger list, as well as the crew of the *Regina Douglas*."

"That will take more than thirty minutes."

"Then let's hope it won't be necessary."

London turned to Hac. "What's your evaluation of the suspects?"

"I have had no opportunity to make an evaluation. Your equipment is quite sophisticated."

"You mean for a little back-planet posting like this one?" She grinned, fingers playing with her braid as she looked appreciatively at the handsome android. "Despite appearances, Stonewall is probably one of the most exciting posts around. You wouldn't believe some of the people and goods that get routed through here. My job is to keep track of all of it—and let me tell you, it would be hard without my little toys, such as the Spectra Six."

"I didn't mean to imply . . ."

"I know you didn't." She shrugged. "The job is what you make of it. On Stonewall I have to keep on my toes all the time. That's why I have so many informants working for me."

"How many official agents?" Mier asked.

"There's five of us right now, but sometimes more, and sometimes less. It depends on what's going on. Sometimes we work together, but mostly we're on our own."

"Like now?" Mier wanted to know. "The others don't know we're here, do they?"

"No. Brian told me you were to be my project, and that I was to keep your business here completely confidential. You're going after something big, huh?"

"It looks that way."

A soft bell sounded—the computer calling for attention.

"Computer, voice on," London said.

"Search completed. Third subject, known as Lady Wanda, registered name Wanda Smith Hipp, born Terra, Colorado, Grand Junction Station . . ."

Wanda's background was completely innocent. Employed by a rather expensive service providing companionship and love partners, she was a member of an old profession enjoying a hundred-year stint of acceptability after centuries of social and legal persecution. She was, Mier summed up, precisely what she claimed to be.

Wes Began, to her dismay, was also perfectly legitimate. However, according to the computer, he was the only surviving child of a middle-class Texas family—no brothers or sisters, no cousins, no kin at all. Which left Ttar to be explained. And here the computer drew a blank. There was no Ttar Began. The ID number was as phony as his name.

"Now what?" Hac asked.

"Looks like you got your agent," London commented.

"So we dig deeper," Mier said. "What did they tell you about our mission?"

"Only that you and your observer need transport. As well as any and all support I can give you while you're here."

"Okay. I want you to forget anything I say from here on in."

"I could leave."

"No. Brian said you could be trusted. And the fact that you call him Brian instead of Inspector Palo tells me he should know."

London burst into laughter. "Don't assume what I think you're assuming," she said when she could speak again. "I know Brian too well to get caught up in his sexual fantasies!"

Mier smiled. "If you know him that well, I don't think you can blame me for jumping to conclusions."

"And I could say the same for you! How did you manage to keep out of his silken web?"

"Diligence. And someday when we have the time, maybe we can compare notes."

"It's a date. We finished just in time, it seems. If I'm not mistaken, this should be Palo."

The computer signaled with a symbol that flashed until Mier pressed the accept button.

ALPHA PRIORITY, the screen read.

SILVER 2207, ALPHA ACCEPT, Mier typed. DECODE, ON; SCRAMBLE, ON.

The symbol faded, and the screen opened to show Inspector Palo, the image somewhat fuzzy due to the distance the tight beam had to travel.

"Hello, Silver. I see you managed to get this far. Who's with you?"

"Hac and London. Do you want them to leave?"

"That won't be necessary. You're going to need London's help. There's been a new development. Let's make this fast; budget'll be all over my ass when they get the bill for this call."

"We're listening."

"There should have been a class-one empath on the *Douglas*. Name Leah Roget."

"I met her," Mier acknowledged, a sudden tight feeling in her gut. Was this a suspect she had overlooked? She had liked the woman. Had she allowed emotion to cloud her judgment?

"She was called to Stonewall by the parent company. Seems an independent salvage operation picked up a derelict ship. There was a survivor on board, more dead than alive. The salvage people brought the ship to the

nearest inhabited planet. The local medical staff couldn't
handle the survivor and called the authorities for help.''

"Let me guess: the survivor shows the same symptoms
as Jarry. Do you think he came from Tori?''

"It looks that way. I want you to check it out. I want
to know who it is, where he's been, and what the hell he
was doing there. More important, I want to know who
financed the trip. Get the information to me through London, and then get on with your mission.''

"I understand. Do you have anything else for me about
our, uh, opponents?''

The image of Brian ran a hand through his already
disheveled hair. "Nothing. No one's reported in, and as
for our little domestic problem, I'm no further along than
I was when you left. But then I haven't had a lot of time
to work on it, either. With the Professor gone, I'm han-
dling all of his business as well as my own. Haven't you
come up with anything?''

"I have a suspect, Ttar Began. The computer here has
no information on the name or the ID number he used
on board ship.''

"Hmm . . .''

"Plus, he was traveling with a businessman, Wes Began, listed as brother and assistant manager of their firm.
Information confirms that Began had no brother.''

"Have you questioned him?'' Brian asked.

"Impossible. Ttar killed him on board ship.''

"Which would tend to confirm your suspicions. All
right, I'll run him through the Cosmostater.''

"Fine. Ttar Began, Terran ID 289-93-0347. Maybe
you should know he escaped from custody and is somewhere on Stonewall. I've caught sight of him a couple of
times, and I don't think it was coincidence.''

"Keep on your toes, Silver. This sounds like it's gonna
be tight.''

"Even tighter if we have to hang around here checking
into Leah Roget and her patient. Are you sure London
can't handle it?''

"She could, but if it concerns Tori, I have a feeling it
might be something you'd better handle.''

"A feeling? Isn't that a little nebulous?''

"Not this time, Babe. The whole case's a 'little nebulous.' Do you have any idea how you're going to get in to see Roget?''

''I met her on the *Douglas*. I think there's something I can use.''

''Then get on it. You can leave as soon as that's finished. How's the android working out?''

''No problems'' was her noncommittal reply.

''All right. Take care of yourself, Babe.''

The screen dissolved to a circle of light, which shrank to a pinpoint and then to black.

CHAPTER 23

''After I talk to Leah Roget, how will I contact you?'' Mier asked as London led them back up the stairs and through the dark hallway to the street door. ''I want to leave Stonewall as soon as possible, and it's going to be tight.''

''Code anything you want me to know, I'll have someone waiting at the port to pick up the recorder. When do you think you'll be there?''

''If everything goes well, and I get in to see Leah Roget, probably around noon.''

''I have someone there all day, just in case.''

''An agent?''

''Short man, dark hair.'' She paused, hand on the door latch, and turned back. ''I hate these sneaky assignments, when you never really know what's going on. They're the worst kind. You'd best be careful.''

''And you.''

''Are you sure you don't want a cab? Or an escort?''

''On the map you showed me, the hotel's not far. I don't think we'll have any problems.''

London grinned as she opened the door and, after

making sure the courtyard was clear, watched as they passed through. The door closed behind them.

Mier looked up and down the street. A gentle glow reflected off of the atmosphere dome far overhead, laying dark shadows under the trees. Her unique vision penetrated the gloom: no one was there. "It's clear," she whispered.

Silence weighted the night, broken only by a distant rumble—voices and other sounds from the part of the city where people were still awake. The still air felt strange to Mier as she walked under the trees. She expected a breeze or a rustle, but there was no sound except the soft pad of their feet on plasticrete. She focused, her awareness growing until the footsteps echoed in her ears. Two sets of footsteps . . . or were there more? She listened, and the short hairs on the back of her neck rose.

"Do you hear it?" Hac whispered, his breath warm on her cheek.

"Yes." She looked for a hiding place and settled on a recessed gateway, deeply shadowed by an overhanging tree limb. A hand on Hac's arm urged him swiftly forward beside her. The gate swung wide, revealing an empty courtyard, the house beyond untenanted, windows hanging, stripped of any removable hardware. "Watch my back," she directed as she willed the pistol into her hand.

Standing with her back flat against the wall, she swung the gate almost closed, leaving an opening just wide enough to give a view of the street. Whoever had been following them was still coming, light steps barely discernible, hesitating now as the quarry was missed. Suddenly the steps accelerated and a figure dashed past the opening, running almost silently on tiptoe, a dark, hooded cloak obscuring features, defeating even Mier's enhanced vision.

Hac moved closer to her. "Did you see who . . ."

"Shsss," she hissed, swinging around into the gateway. The street was empty in both directions.

"Who was it?" he insisted.

"I don't know." The pistol retracted with a faint click. "Let's find out."

Peering around a corner of the wall, Mier discovered

that the next street opened up onto a lighted boulevard lined with bars and shops, still enjoying the late-night trade. A shadowy figure moved against the light, hood still in place. She sprinted forward, Hac at her side, but by the time they arrived at the street, the dark cloak was nowhere to be seen.

"Why did she run?" Hac wanted to know.

"Realized we were on to him. Why did you say she?"

"I don't know. Just a feeling. The figure was short— not even as tall as you are, so I assumed it was a woman."

"There are men shorter than I am. Ttar for one. The hotel's just a block over."

"Don't you want to know who was following us?"

"In this crowd? We'll never find him now. Come on. Let's get back to the hotel. Even if you don't, I could use some sleep."

Hac wandered restlessly through the main room of their suite, while Mier adjusted the lights and dialed a drink from the small synthesizer. She tasted it and then sprawled in a chair, legs out, head back.

"I didn't know androids were prone to repressed emotion," she commented, watching the tall male from beneath heavy eyelids. "You'd better tell me what's troubling you before you blow a fuse or something."

He came to a stop, back to the window. "I am having misgivings . . ."

"Sorry you came? You can still back out."

"No. I don't want to do that. But London was right; there are too many variables, too many unknowns. We have nothing to work with. It's like trying to fight with a pile of feathers."

"Vivid analogy. But you're wrong. We have a lot to work with. Ttar Began . . ."

"Who is hiding somewhere on this planet. Who may or may not have murdered Wes Began, who may or may not be his brother. Who may or may not be working for the Consortium. You have to admit, that's thin."

"I don't think so. There's enough evidence identifying Ttar as Wes Began's murderer. We're certain they weren't brothers. Therefore, both Wes and Ttar were lying about the relationship. Why?''

"There could be a perfectly good reason, completely unrelated to our assignment.''

"All right, I'll give you that. But what if . . .''

"You're speculating.''

Mier sat up straight. "Give me a chance! What if Ttar was using Wes Began as cover in order to get on board the *Douglas*?''

"Because he knew we were going to be there?''

"Right.''

"Then how do you explain the fact that Began and party had reserved their tickets a month before departure?''

"The reservation was for Began party of three. Originally he might have intended to bring his real assistant manager, or a secretary . . . who knows? There were no names except Began on the reservation.''

"All right. You've made a point. But it still doesn't prove that Ttar is interested in Tori.''

"You're right. It doesn't as long as you isolate the incidents. Put them together, and you have something else again. For instance: Ttar wasn't in the mess the morning someone broke into my cabin.''

"He could have been anywhere in the ship.''

"Which includes my cabin.''

"Where he planted the mini-spy and then struck you.''
Hac came closer and rested a hip on the edge of a table.
"And the next thing you're going to say is that Wes was going to sell him out, so Ttar killed him.''

"I would put money on it.'' Mier finished her drink and went to get another.

"I still say it's thin.''

"It's all we have and we have to use it. But none of this matters anymore. Ttar—or whoever—can spy all they want. We'll be gone by noon tomorrow.''

"That's another thing that bothers me. How are you going to get in to see the empath, Leah Roget? If she's working for the Stonewall Company, they'll have her somewhere in the government complex. From what I know of Stonewall, they're not just going to let you waltz in. And besides, we don't need to call any attention to ourselves or our assignment.''

"I have a good enough reason to see Leah. Let me worry about what will or won't call attention to us or our assignment.''

Hac raised an eyebrow at her.

"When we were talking on board the *Douglas*, Leah was recruiting for her guild,'' Mier explained.

"But you said you don't have talent.''

"I know I don't. Except there's a good chance that I'm an amplifier. Leah seemed to think that has possibilities. Anyway, I can use her invitation to get in to see her. After that . . .'' She shrugged and took a deep swallow of the amber liquid in her glass.

"Do you always drink when you're working?''

"No. Not unless I'm tired and keyed-up. I'm still full of adrenaline from that episode in the street. A drink helps me come down enough to sleep.''

"There are pills . . .''

"And there's alcohol. They do the same thing. I prefer the one with a taste.''

"Hedonist?''

She shrugged. "It reminds me I'm still alive. And I believe people take too much for granted. I get a lot of pleasure from simple things—a meal prepared from real food, nice clothes, music, a glass of good wine . . .''

"Does this include friends, interesting conversations?''

"Yeah, it does. Does that make me a hedonist?''

"No. But there are other ways to unwind.''

"I know. Right now, this—'' she hefted the glass, ''—is a substitute. When I'm home, I usually work out in the gym.''

"A massage might help.''

She cocked her head, and her voice took on a distinct edge. "What kind of an offer is that? You're beginning to sound like Brian Palo.''

"I'm sorry if I offended you. I didn't mean to.''

"No. Sorry. You didn't offend me. I told you, I'm on edge. And I guess I tend to take things too personally.''

He stood and walked around behind her, hands folding over her shoulders. "Relax,'' he said when she stiffened. As he kneaded the tight muscles, they slowly loosened. "They say women carry their tension in their neck and shoulders.''

"Umm," she replied, eyes almost closed.

"Men, however," he continued, his voice as soothing as his hands, "carry theirs in their lower back. It's a fact."

"Trust you to know it," she mumbled.

"Is this working as well as the drink?"

"I'm almost asleep."

"Good. Don't move." He removed the glass from her slack hand and set it aside before scooping her up in his arms.

"What—?"

"Relax. You'll undo all my hard work." Carrying her effortlessly, he went into the bedroom and placed her carefully on the bed.

Mier stared up at him as best she could with her eyes trying to close. "Brian said you were programmed to duplicate all human functions. Does that mean you have a working libido?"

"A machine does not depend on glands. However, sex is also a good way to relax."

"It takes more than a need to relax to get me into bed."

"I know. Most women want emotional reinforcement."

"What's that?" she muttered.

"You want a commitment. It's a biological necessity."

"If this is a pickup, then I'm sorry I had the second drink. I can't . . ." The rest of the sentence trailed off. Eyes closed, body completely limp, she was more than half-asleep.

Hac smiled and pulled off her boots. She stirred, then curled up on her side, breathing deeply. He watched for a second, but she didn't move again. Silently, he went back into the main room to resume his thoughtful pacing.

CHAPTER 24

Sunlight streamed through the windows of the empath's suite, warming despite the cold black of space beyond the great dome. Mier stood at the window, looking out, not sure how to word her request.

"Sit down and be comfortable," Leah invited.

"I didn't come because I've changed my mind about opting for the guild," Mier admitted when she finally settled into one of the chairs. "I used that as an excuse so I would be allowed to see you."

"I know," the empath replied. "You're in some kind of trouble. Part of it stems from your companion. Who is he? And why did you insist that he wait outside?"

"Hac? He's not really a problem. He's working with me, but I thought it would be easier to talk to you alone."

"I see." Leah folded her hands in her lap, the picture of patience. "How can I help you?"

Mier hesitated, rapidly deciding how much she could tell the guild member. "I know what brought you to Stonewall. I need to know more about the case. How much can you tell me?"

"I can't imagine how you would get such information, unless . . ." Her words trailed off in a question.

"There are a lot of things I can't tell you. I work for the government."

"The government? Of Stonewall? Or the Federation?" The empath's voice held a distinct edge.

"The Federation," Mier responded calmly.

"And I suppose I shouldn't ask what office you represent."

"It would be best."

"But, trusting me so little, you still expect me to reveal the details of my business for the Parent Company of Stonewall."

"I know it sounds—"

"It sounds very bad."

Mier sighed and looked out the window, searching for inspiration in the featureless black.

"Let me read you." Leah's voice cut into the lengthening silence.

"What?"

"Let me read your emotions. If what I feel is right, I may give you the information you request."

"You said 'may.' Can't you give me more of a guarantee than that?"

"No." Leah stared at her, blue eyes serene and implacable. The only sound in the room was a barely audible hiss from the air vent.

"All right," Mier capitulated. "How do you work?"

Leah rose and pulled her chair closer to the agent. "Give me your hand," she instructed, reseating herself.

The empath's clasp was warm and dry. Minutes fled, and surprisingly soon, Leah broke the contact.

"Is that all? Can you work so quickly?" Mier wanted to know.

"I only needed to skim your emotions to learn all I needed."

"And you'll help me?"

"You gamble, young woman. You came in here wanting something from me and yet you were unwilling to give me anything in return."

"It isn't that I'm unwilling. I can't. There are others—"

Her words were cut off by Leah's upraised hand. "I don't need to know more than I do. And, yes, I will help you as much as I can. The man you are interested in is dead, so I cannot take you to see him."

"Dead? So you weren't able to read him after all." Mier couldn't help the disappointment that colored her tone.

"Not quite. He was still alive when I arrived here. I had two sessions with him before he died."

"Who was he?"

"I can't tell you that."

"But . . ."

"As a guild member I owe certain loyalties to my employer. If they wish to divulge this information that is another matter. Without their permission, however, I cannot."

"All right. What can you tell me about him?"

"He was in extreme mental confusion—terror greater than anything I have ever experienced. His mind was total chaos during my first reading. And all of this was reflected on his encephalograph. But the second set—"

"Let me guess," Mier interrupted. "His mind was a total blank. Beta waves suppressed—something that looked like *flexibilitas cerea*."

Leah's eyes widened in surprise. "How could you know this?"

"I've seen something similar." Mier suppressed her sad memories of Jarry. "Can you tell me anything else?"

"Where did you see this before? Someone you know? A friend? Your feelings were very strong just now."

"Yes. A friend," the agent admitted. "He's dead, too. I'm trying to find out what killed him."

Leah drew a deep breath. "Very well. Let me see what I can do for you."

She got up and went to a wall unit to key a call. With the screen blanked, she spoke low-voiced for a couple of minutes. There was a wait, and then she spoke some more. When she returned to her seat, her face was stern.

"I can tell you everything you wish to know, but," Leah added, "only if you help me. I told them I could get more information about what killed the patient, but only if I divulged everything I know. In all honor, I cannot go back to my employers empty-handed."

"What do you need from me?"

"Who was your friend? Where did he contact whatever it was that killed him? And what is this thing?"

Mier deliberated and then spoke. "My friend was called Jarry Jackson. He was traveling . . . attempting to explore in the Stone Field. Something found him there, destroyed his ship. He managed to get away in an escape pod. He was picked up, routed to a hospital on Terra Three, where he eventually died. Tests were inconclusive; they didn't have much luck finding out what was wrong with him either. And that's the whole of it."

"Except that you have been sent to find out what killed him. Am I right?"

"In part, yes."

"I'll accept that. This patient was Bright Woburn. His ship was not disabled, but for some reason he was incapacitated. The ship was found drifting on the fringes of the Stone Field, badly battered, they presume by asteroids."

"And the ship's log?"

"There wasn't one. At least that's what they tell me."

"Bright Woburn: who was he? Who did he work for?"

"He was an independent miner. He had a number of small claims on various asteroids throughout this sector. That's what we think he was doing in the Field, prospecting."

"Prospecting." One of the jack miners Palo had warned her about. "That's all you know?"

"It's not very much, I'm afraid. Does this help at all?"

"A little. When you read Woburn, what did you see?"

Leah broke eye contact. "Frightening. It's hard . . . when I try to put it into words." She shook her head. "There's no way to describe it . . . a mind stripped piece by piece. And then the pieces put back, but out of order. Total chaos. I said that before, did I? And the fog . . ."

"Fog?"

"I know it doesn't sound like much, but the experience was terrifying. I can't describe it. We're trained to protect ourselves—we'd go crazy otherwise—but this—this was something I'd never encountered before, as if . . . I know this is going to sound crazy, but it was as if whatever got to Woburn was trying to move from him to me.''

Mier sat up straighter. ''That might be important. You actually felt something?''

''An invasion. The fog, trying to get into my mind.''

''The fog,'' Mier whispered, the memory of her dreams coming back.

''You've felt it, too?'' Leah asked, looking at her curiously.

Mier drew a slow, deep breath. ''I thank you for all your information, and hope what I told you will help. Are you returning to Terra immediately?''

''I don't think so,'' Leah said slowly. ''I have a feeling I may be needed here.''

''You expect more . . .'' Then Mier realized what Leah alluded to. ''Let's hope not.''

''But you're leaving Stonewall very soon?''

''Yes.''

''Be careful. Be very careful.''

Mier smiled. ''I'm always careful.''

''One other thing—your partner.''

''Hac?''

''I get very strange feelings from him.''

''Don't worry about Hac. There's a good reason for that.''

''You know then?''

''Yes, I know.''

''Then I need say no more.'' Leah walked her to the door. ''Once again, take care.''

''Thank you.''

CHAPTER 25

Leah Roget had had nothing new to add to Mier's knowledge, beyond confirming her gut feelings about the fate

of anyone who went to Tori. And it was obvious that
Woburn had been there. What took him, what glimmer
of prospector's intuition, rumor, or leaked information
still had to be discovered. But not by Mier. With the
competitors for the treaty so close, her early departure
was now more vital than ever.

As for Leah's comments about Hac, Mier promptly
relegated them to the back of her mind. It was curious
that an android should have any emotions for the empath
to read, but, in the increasing urgency of the mission, it
didn't justify immediate attention.

He moved beside her as they rode the grav tube from
the fifth floor of the government hostel. Mier whispered
into a minicorder, rapidly dictating a report and instructions to London. Woburn would be her problem from
here on out. Finished, she pocketed the machine and
followed Hac to the pavement outside.

"There's a cab," she directed, moving swiftly forward.

"The hotel's not that far."

"We're not going back to the hotel."

"Where . . ."

"Later. Let's get out of here. Main space field," she
told the computer when the door had sealed them into
the two-seater. "Step on it."

"Mier . . ." Hac tried again.

"No. I said we'd talk about it later." She fished inside
her pocket for the ship's key. Attached was a disk im-
printed with the Port Authority logo, which would allow
them entrance.

Minutes later found them at their destination. A small
cargo train, grav lifters hissing, stood nearby while two
workers wrestled a freight cube onto one of the trailers
and lashed it in place. Mier left the cab and approached
them.

"We're looking for slot thirty-four."

"Level six?" a sandy-haired woman asked, curiously
looking them over.

"Yes."

She obviously decided they were all right. "We're going that way. Hop on board," she invited with a jerk of
her head.

The cab was crowded with four of them, and Hac stood on the step, clinging to the back of Mier's seat.

"So you bought the old Slipstream, huh?" the woman continued, driving the train skillfully through the pylons, ships, and stacked cargo.

"It's a nice ship," her companion added, head bent to light the butt of a small cigar that sent acrid smoke curling through the cab. "Been around awhile, but still got some klicks left in her. That's it over there." He pointed, an SIA ID glowing briefly on his hand.

Mier squinted through the fumes at the streaked, dull silver sides of the craft. The Slipstream had seen many years, and action, too. She hoped it would be up to the trip ahead of them.

"Thanks for the lift," she said, climbing to the plasticrete. "Did you drop this?" she added, bending and then rising to hand the minicorder to the cigar smoker.

"Yeah. That's mine. Thanks." He slipped it into his pocket as the train hissed forward.

"That's our ship?" Hac asked, staring.

"Don't let appearances fool you. The Slipstream was a good line."

"I think 'was' is the operative word. The design's ten years out of date. The *Corsair*," he read. "Exotic name for an old tub."

"Not a tub. This ship was top of the line a couple of years back. If it's been refitted, we couldn't do better. It has excellent range and speed for a one-man ship. Plus it can maneuver." Mier used the remote to open the hatch, releasing a breath of stale air. Lights blinked and, reluctantly, it seemed, came on.

"At least we know no one's been on board for a while," her companion commented sourly.

"London did say it was stocked."

Hac went past, stepping inside, and she followed. They checked fuel and provisions: everything was full and ready. "Have you ever flown this model?" he asked.

"Once. The controls are standard. And the nav computer's new. Look at this, it's a Locus Two."

"I hope they put in more than just a new nav computer."

"What did you expect, a Blessard Nova? Come on,

stop complaining and strap in. The quicker we get out of here, the more we'll confuse everyone following us. I'm beginning to feel like a pack leader.'' She slipped on a headset, and punched buttons. ''Port Control, this is the *Corsair*, level six, slot thirty-four.''

''We hear you, *Corsair*. What can I do for you?''

''We'd like clearance for a test flight.''

''No problems, *Corsair*. Elevator engaging. Sit tight until you're topside. Want to file a flight plan?''

''No thanks. I'm just going to take this one as it comes.''

''Orbit's pretty crowded until about fifty thousand klicks. Keep it out beyond that, all right?''

''Data loaded and saved.'' As the elevator engaged, the ship rocked once and then steadied while the inside of the spaceport began to descend past them.

''Lift path clear in seventeen minutes,'' the Port Controller said.

The atmosphere dome appeared above them as the *Corsair* rose to the top level. ''Hold your engines until we can get the blast shields in place. And watch out for the electrostatic barrier. But you'll remember it from when you came in.''

''Loaded and saved,'' Mier repeated. Her fingers were busy readying the engines, while her eyes searched fuel-mix and systems-status readouts.

''Everything's set,'' Hac announced from beside her. ''Hatch is dogged tight. Systems all check. You were right; this ship has been refitted. I was fooled by appearances.''

''Mix?''

''Hot and ready to go. Just push the right button.''

''*Corsair*,'' the Port Controller said. ''Ready for countdown?''

''We're set. Proceed.''

''Mark. Fifteen, fourteen . . .''

Mier activated automatic ignition sequence and watched as numbers flicked by on the monitor. Control of the ship would remain with Port Control until they had achieved orbital altitude. After that, the nav computer would kick in. All she had to do was set their destination. She choose coordinates away from the Stone Field.

"Confusion?" Hac asked.

She grinned.

"Five, four, three . . ." the speaker counted. When it reached "one" the ship shuddered, drive coming on. On "zero" they began to lift, moving with infinite slowness at first, and then with breathtaking swiftness.

"Bon voyage," the voice of Port Control from the speaker said, crackling with static as the *Corsair* burst through the dome and the black of space embraced them.

The angles of her face brought into sharp relief by the glow of the control panel, Mier ran a complete systems check, taking the *Corsair* through its entire repertoire. The ship responded well, a little raggedness in one engine, perhaps, but as she fiddled with the controls, bringing speed down and then up again, it steadied. Everything was in the green from converter mix to life support.

Satisfied at last, she sat back and took time to look around. The wide viewscreen above the console reflected the stars surrounding them, naked space colored like a scattering of jewels. She played with the keys, scanning through 360 degrees. Off the rear port side of the *Corsair*, the Stone Field glowed with its own luminescence, malevolence palpable even at this distance, or so she thought. But avoiding it, even for another hour, wouldn't make a difference. Entering the Field was something she had to do.

Maybe I'm getting too old for this, she thought. Once she would have eagerly faced such a challenge. Time, however, had bred caution . . . or was it fear, now that she had enough experience to anticipate what might happen in there? Whatever it was, the anticipation made her edgy. You're getting to be a coward in your old age, she chided herself.

"Are you going to tell me about it?" Hac's voice interrupted, surprising her out of her mental wanderings.

"What?"

"Your meeting with Leah Roget. I might complain that, as your partner, I shouldn't have been excluded."

"There are some things you don't need to know."

"I could argue with that. In order to function properly—"

"I know, I know. You need access to any and all information related to the mission. All right. Leah's patient was Bright Woburn, an independent prospector who was picked up with his ship by salvage operators on the edge of the Stone Field. No other information available on him at this time.''

''You said 'was.' He's dead?''

''He died after displaying more or less the same symptoms as Jarry.''

''And you assume he had been to Tori?''

''It's a logical inference.''

''How did he know about the planet?''

''That is something London will have to find out. We know there's been a leak, so someone either sent him there, or he himself has, or had, access to classified information.''

''He might have followed one of the supply ships.''

''That's a possibility, too.''

Hac spent a silent moment digesting her words. ''I see no reason to withhold this information from me. There is nothing overly sensitive about it.''

''I know that now. I couldn't know it ahead of time.'' She spoke with most of her attention on the viewscreen. The Stone Field wouldn't go away no matter how long she procrastinated. ''All right,'' she said suddenly, sitting forward in the pilot's chair. ''Now that we've gotten our test flight out of the way, let's see what this machine can do. Slow to quarter speed.'' Her fingers picked out the commands on the keys. ''Nav computer, display locator map.'' A grid marked with star names overlaid the view through the forward screen.

The *Corsair* swung, obedient to the controls, until the Stone Field lay dead ahead. The nav grid changed with the movement, identifying the new star coordinates as they appeared.

''What do you think, Hac? Ready to face the ultimate challenge?''

''The computer seems to have an extensive listing for the Field. London was thorough.''

''Yeah.''

He looked at her curiously. ''You don't seem pleased.''

''Nor would you be if you had the ability to imagine what could happen in there.'' She worked the controls for a moment, her attention seeming fixed until she spoke again, words carefully casual. "How does one go about altering your programming?"

"I beg your pardon?" His eyes widened in surprise at her abrupt change of subject.

"Programming. How would I, for instance, go about adding to it or changing something?"

"Is there something you don't like?"

She had to smile. "You look so dismayed."

"The input of information is constant. I adapt, and my programming alters itself as necessary to utilize the new data. That is the way I was designed. Is this what you wanted to know?"

"Sort of. So if I wanted you to pilot this ship, for instance . . ."

"Oh, if that's the problem, don't let it worry you. I am familiar with all of the systems here. I can fly this ship."

"You've answered my question then. We're about three hours away from the Field, but we can't go directly. We have to swing around and make a more gradual approach, looking as if we're planning to skirt it and head out beyond. It will add about two hours to our time, but I think it's necessary. If I leave you with the conn and get some sleep, do you think you can handle that kind of maneuver?"

"I have no doubt of it."

"And you'll wake me if anything even the least bit unusual happens?"

"Such as?"

"Anything!"

"Very well."

"The controls are yours then." Mier yawned hugely and stretched her arms over her head. "Thank providence androids don't need to sleep."

"Amen," Hac replied, his head bent over the console as he planned their course.

Mier unstrapped and wandered through an interior hatch in the back bulkhead. The *Corsair*'s designer's main concern had been to produce a small ship, capable of being handled by one person, with range, speed and maneuverability. This meant most of the ship was engine,

computer, and sensory apparatus, with little space left
for cargo or accommodations. The single cabin tucked
behind the bridge contained a fresher, water dispenser
and basin, and a built-in bunk—top and bottom sleeping
space for two. Mier was in no mood to be choosy: she
flopped down on the bottom mattress, curled up on her
side, and was fast asleep.

Dreams floated through her mind, but none of them
had enough substance to impress themselves on her consciousness. It seemed like only minutes had passed when
Hac's voice intruded, calling her back. Yawning, she
swung her legs over the side and hurried to the bridge.

Patterns of dust and cosmic debris filled the screen,
colored like a picture in a physicist's handbook.

"The Stone Field," Mier said, settling into the pilot's
seat, eyes never leaving the view.

"We're about a hundred klicks out. Thought you'd
want to be here when we take the plunge."

"How long did I sleep?"

"Five hours. I checked on you once; you were completely gone."

"Any problems with the ship?"

"None. London chose well. The *Corsair* might look a
little worn on the outside, but everything that counts is
up-to-date and in perfect working order."

"For which we can be grateful. I'd hate to get halfway
to our destination and have something critical fail."

Hac watched the board in front of him and didn't reply.

"What's wrong?"

"I don't know. I've been running periodic scans of the
surrounding area of space. Can't get a reading from the
Field, of course, but there's something . . ." The words
trailed off as his fingers began punching for magnifica-
tion.

"Main screen," Mier instructed. "Switch to rear view,
wide scan."

They watched as the Field faded, revealing a new area
of space.

"I don't see it now," Hac complained.

"This is a wide view. Where did you see . . . whatever
it was?"

"There, between those two clusters of stars. It was a light spot, moving fast."

Mier magnified that section of space. "I don't see anything unusual." She searched for another couple of heartbeats. "No. There's nothing. Are you sure?"

"I'm positive. It moved from what would be right to left across the screen, from that star cluster to this one . . ." His words trailed off. "There. Do you see it?"

One of the stars had detached itself and hung suspended far out from the cluster.

"Computer: grid on. Look at that."

Measured against the lines that bisected the port, the point of light could be seen to move.

"Not a meteor," she commented, mostly to herself. "In fact, I doubt it's anything natural."

"What is it then?" Hac asked.

"A ship. The way it's angled, the light of Stonewall's sun is shining right on it."

"We're still being followed!"

Her mouth was grim. "Looks that way."

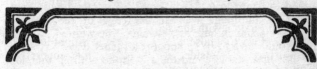

CHAPTER 26

"We lose him," Mier said in answer to Hac's unspoken question.

"In there?" He indicated the Stone Field, filling the forward screen. "Our nav program describes a safe passage through the Field. If we use it now, we will lead him straight to Tori. If we deviate from the program, we will be putting ourselves into danger."

Mier grinned. "Afraid of a little risk?"

"I would not define creative navigation through a known hazard as a little risk."

"Creative navigation. I like that." Now that she was committed, Mier would go all the way, former fears held back by a superficial glitter of excitement. "Into the Field, my friend."

Obedient to the commands of the navigational computer, the *Corsair* entered the Field, although there was nothing to indicate a boundary. Proximity sensors registered an increase in mass outside of the ship—asteroids making their presence known. A cloud grew at the edge of the screen.

"External radiation increasing," Hac reported. "The ship's shielding is taking care of it—so far."

"The voice of doom has spoken." Mier watched the cloud come closer. "Switch to rear view."

"Rad figures show density, mass, and a constant energy emission," her partner quoted from the monitors in front of him. "The ship's following us into the Field. And it's definitely a ship—one of the Cheque line, a one-man flyer."

"Screen to forward view."

"Outside interference is building. We won't be able to use our instruments much longer. Are you still determined to try to lose him in here?" The cloud had come closer, a luminous web at the edge of the screen. "There's a star in here somewhere," he warned.

"Would have to be to support a planet like Tori."

"But how stable could the system be with all this debris? The asteroids could be remnants of other planets. What happened to them?"

"I'd leave that to the astronomers if I were you. Or does your programming include astrophysics?"

"No. I just can't help but be curious. Nothing exists without a reason."

"Maybe the answer's on Tori. Scan the cloud."

"Not easy. There's a lot of background radiation. It looks nasty."

"Good. That's what I hoped. Project our course in relation to the cloud."

"We skirt it with a forty-degree alteration in eleven thousand klicks."

"Perfect," she breathed. "Record course correction: initiate forty-degree alteration in one thousand klicks. Feed it into the nav computer and tie it into the flight plan."

"We can't do that, Mier. The preset course is safe. You're taking us into . . ."

"Into the cloud. That's where we lose our tail. Now do as I say, or do you want to lead him to Tori?" Their eyes met for a moment, hers determined, his bewildered and not a little apprehensive. "Trust me. I know what I'm doing. Besides," she added with a quick grin, "we have no alternative."

Space folded, twisted, distorted out of all sync with itself roiled around them as the *Corsair* entered the cloud. Blue became purple, faded to ultraviolet that hummed a visual chord in Mier's augmented sight. Hac, effectively blind, had no references for what he saw.

The *Corsair* forged ahead, shuddering now and then as something interfered with its existence in this dimension.

"I'm glad I wasn't on the ship that discovered Tori," the android commented dryly. "This is a very nasty place. Our friend, by the way, is still following us."

"There's a theory," Mier told him, her face much paler than usual, "that the ship is actually quite still, while space moves outside us."

Infrared moved up to microwave, blinding the forward sensors.

"If the ship can't see, how will the nav computer operate?" Hac inquired.

"Chronology. So many minutes at this coordinate, turn, so many at another—I hope." By now Mier felt disoriented with all the visual input on top of stress, and had to call on all of her self-control to resist the urge to be ill.

The radio crackled to life, hissing with static and barely audible words. ". . . know what you're . . ."

Hac's fingers worked as he tried to find and amplify the signal. The *Corsair* dropped from beneath them as the proximity sensors belatedly picked up mass and rapidly compensated. Dark shapes moved through the cloud, and they had just barely avoided hitting one of them.

"This was not a good idea," Hac informed her emphatically.

"Twenty-twenty hindsight is a rather common gift.

Unfortunately there's nothing we can do about our situation right now.''

''. . . damn,'' the radio crackled, quite appropriately. ''Suicidal maniacs!'' came through clearly.

The *Corsair* lurched again.

''We're not losing him,'' Hac said. ''He's almost close enough for visual—if it's possible to see anything in this soup.''

''All right, my friends,'' the voice said, volume undulating and words peppered with static. ''I guess you win.''

''What's happening?'' Mier wondered out loud, switching the screen to rear view again. The other ship, a distinctive needle shape, came through faintly, a darker shape in the light. As she watched, it tossed, oscillating wildly, one anterior engine flaring brightly. If its navigator held it on course manually, he had to have nerves of steel and a constitution to match.

''Thank . . . for the ride,'' the voice came again. ''Sorry I couldn't make . . . whole trip, but my ship seems to . . . breaking up. Shit!'' The expletive came in loud and clear, obviously in response to something happening in the other control room.

''We have to do something,'' Hac said.

''Are you crazy?''

''The ship is breaking up.''

''Good! That will discourage him from following us.''

''You'd leave him here after what happened to Jarry and Woburn?''

''What happened to them, happened on Tori. He won't be going to Tori. That's the whole point of this exercise.''

''But we know he's the other agent. If we lose him here, we'll never know who's responsible for leaking SIA information.''

Mier glared at her partner. ''Oh, damn.'' Her gaze went from the screen to the bewildering readouts on her console. Some of the data had to be registering truly, but how was she to sort it from the false traces caused by interference? Nothing made sense. Visual, too, was chaotic. As they watched, apparently the fluctuating engine on the following ship flared and went dead. ''All right,

Hac. We'll do what we can. Match our speed to his. There's a chance. It's slim, but . . ."

Her hand went to the radio and she keyed the mike open. "This is the *Corsair*. Who in hell are you, and what are you doing following us?"

"Nice to . . . you, too, *Corsair*," came the voice. "Sorry . . . dropping in unannounced, but . . . how it is. Too bad I can't . . . longer, but my ship's . . . to fall apart."

"So we noticed. Would you like to come aboard? So far we're managing to hold together."

"Thanks for . . . invitation, but I don't see how . . . in this mess."

"Get suited up. Your other engine's about to go, and when it does we're going to lose you."

"Match locks and scoot across?"

"That's it."

". . . in this?"

"Say again, I couldn't hear you."

"I said, I can't see . . . ship . . . coordinates?"

She glanced at Hac, who reeled off a string of coordinates, ending his recital with a fervent, "I hope."

"Did you get that?" Mier inquired into the mike.

Most of the numbers were repeated to her.

In the eerily lit darkness the other ship began to maneuver, but Mier didn't stay to see. "Handle the bridge," she instructed. "I'll work from the hatch."

Pulling a suit from the locker, she shoved her feet into the legs and pulled the bulky pack over her shoulders. Stumbling as the ship avoided yet another collision, she caught herself on the doorsill and didn't notice as Hac cast one concerned look her way before turning his attention back to the board. With a low moan the hatch came open, and Mier went inside, dogging it tightly closed after her. Sealed in, she pulled on her helmet and punched the buttons that evacuated air from the chamber.

"Hac, can you hear me?" she called, voice muffled in the enclosed helmet.

"You're clear. Please be careful. Brian will be furious if anything happens to you now."

"It wouldn't please me very much, either. Let me know when our guest is ready for transfer."

A thin cable unreeled from her utility belt, and she fastened the end to an eyebolt beside the wall. Secured, Mier opened the outer hatch and let the cloud into the ship.

Space is vacuum, but far from empty. Gas atoms interacting with free electrons glowed, their light reflecting off of the dust from which the cloud was formed. Breathtakingly beautiful, it appeared solid enough to walk on, though Mier had no real desire to step through the doorway. At that moment the dark bulk of the other ship intruded, slicing through the crystal landscape. Within moments a hatch opened, precious oxygen blowing and instantly freezing, the ice refracting light and adding another dimension of magic to the beauty of the cloud.

The *Corsair* lurched, throwing Mier forward, snapping her hold on the door. She spun dizzily from the hatch, moving swiftly away from the ship until she had presence of mind enough to catch the cable and pull against its brake. All around her dust transformed, scintillating, a whiteness that proved that the color was indeed all colors collected in one. She gazed in awe, stunned by the immensity of it all.

"Mier? Mier, can you hear me?" Hac's voice called her back to her danger.

"I'm here."

"You all right? Can you . . ." Static burst, obscuring his words.

"Hac? I can't hear you."

"Get back to the ship! Hurry. If it maneuvers again, your line will snap."

"On my way."

She didn't bother pulling on the line, but after orienting herself with the doorway, fired the jet pack. In seconds the hatch loomed before her. Across from the *Corsair* another bulky, suited figure stood, outlined against the opening in his ship. As she reached home, he kicked himself clear and drifted toward her.

At first no more than a misty silhouette, the figure took on size and substance as it came closer, impelled by a suit pack. A long tether, fine enough to be almost invisible, snaked out behind him. Mier swung into the safety of the hatch.

"Are you in?" Hac's voice demanded.

"I'm in. Our uninvited guest is almost across. I'll start cycling as soon as he's—"

Her words cut off as the figure reached the doorway, his jet still firing. He collided with her, the shock driving her backward into the inner door. Honed reflexes saved her as the vibroknife he held flashed toward her helmet. Grabbing his wrist, she struggled to hold the vibrating blade away while she twisted, getting space behind her.

"Hac!" she yelled frantically. "Close the hatch! Hurry!"

Mier managed to evade his left hand, using his momentum to push them both into a bulkhead. Rebounding, she twisted, forcing him toward the closing hatch. The vibroknife hit the edge of the door, bathing them both in a shower of sparks. Her weight against him was just enough that he had a choice; let go of the knife or risk having his hand caught. The weapon floated away as the door closed the last inches.

As the pump began cycling air back into the chamber, Mier swept her opponent's feet out from under him and dropped him, facedown, to the deck. Breathless, he lay still, and she sat on him until the gauge inside her helmet indicated that the atmosphere was fit to breathe. Struggling out of helmet and sleeves, she aimed her pistol before climbing to her feet. Kicking the figure over, she bent and ripped his faceplate open.

Ttar gazed up at her.

"Just the man I wanted to see," she said through gritted teeth. "Welcome aboard the *Corsair*."

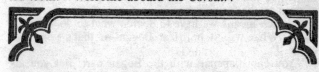

CHAPTER 27

Under Mier's watchful eye and the unwavering mouth of her pistol, Ttar climbed sulkily out of his suit.

"What are you going to do with me?" he asked.

"After going through all the trouble of rescuing you, it would seem a shame to have to kill you."

He didn't respond.

"On the other hand, I would imagine you might feel some kind of gratitude . . ." She let the words trail off suggestively.

"What do you want?"

"Information, of course."

"I don't know what you're talking about. I don't have any information."

She grinned and shook her head. "Ingratitude. I should have expected as much."

"It wouldn't do you any good anyway. None of us are going to get out of here alive." The ship lurched and then shuddered, punctuating his statement.

"Pessimist. You can't . . ."

"Mier, get out here," Hac interrupted, his voice metallic through the speaker grille.

"I'm cycling now," she told him, pushing the buttons with her free hand. A lithe wiggle dropped her suit over her hips, and she kicked her feet from the legs, eyes all the while fixed on their prisoner. "Pick up the suits. Both of them." As the door opened, she left the lock backward, motioning for Ttar to follow.

"What's the problem?" she asked Hac.

"The cloud's expanding. We should be coming up on the original course projection about now, but we're still in the cloud. All our outside sensors are good as dead: too much interference. I need your help here. Two pair of eyes are better than one."

"Which means we have to decide what to do with our guest. What will it be, Ttar Began—if that's your real name."

"You can dispense with the Began part, but you already know that. Do you mind if I put these suits down?"

"Hang on to them. We realized Began wasn't your name after we learned Wes didn't have a brother. But we'll argue your antecedents another time. What I have to decide now is what to do with you. I can't sit here, covering you with a pistol, and help fly this ship. At the same time, we can't have you running around trying to

kill us. So what will it be? I could ask for your parole—
at least until we're out of this—but can you be trusted?''

"Not bloody likely," the little man snarled. "You got
me into this . . ."

"And I'd think you'd want to give us the chance to get
you out of it.''

The ship lurched again.

"Mier," Hac warned. "Time's running out."

"So I'll have to put you up somewhere." Her eyes
took swift inventory. "The air lock."

"What?" His eyes opened wide with surprise.

"Put the suits down, and back into the lock."

"But . . ."

"Do it!''

Her hard eyes and the pistol persuaded him. Dropping
the suits in an untidy pile, he backed carefully to the
hatch, apprehension visible on his face. "You could at
least let me take my suit."

"Sorry. The knowledge that we can space you anytime
we want should guarantee your good behavior. Oh, we'll
override the lock controls from here. You won't be able
to use them.''

"Bitch!" Ttar snarled.

"In the hatch!"

The door slid closed on his curses.

Mier buckled herself in beside Hac. "What's happening? What can I do?''

"There are things in the cloud. With external scanners
as good as useless, I can't identify them. We're avoiding
them, just, and that's only because of the proximity sensors, and they're about crippled, too." The ship dropped
beneath them as he spoke, lights flickering and fans hesitating before coming back on again. "See what I mean?
The ship can't take much more of this."

"They're asteroids, they've got to be."

He glanced at her, having heard the edge of fear in her
voice. But if she was frightened, she hid it very well,
precise fingers working the keys in front of her as she
tried to coax the ship's blind eyes into seeing again.

Dust, minutely faceted into the gleam of a million
rainbows, filled the viewscreen. It was as if they had
flown into an icy sun, beautiful and terrifying at the same

time. Something dark swam off to the port side and the ship avoided it, again just in time.

"According to the chronometer, we should be intersecting with our original path about now," Hac announced.

And, obedient to the nav computer, the ship maneuvered.

"There," Mier said. "There's black ahead. We're coming out of the cloud."

And with her words the ship struck something with a crash that reverberated throughout its length. The lights flickered again and went out. Fans stopped, their muted hum replaced with silence. The engine roar died, the console black and dead. The harsh rasp of breathing filled the cabin.

CHAPTER 28

"Can you fix it?" Mier asked, on her hands and knees behind Hac in the narrow chute that connected the engines with the control room.

Hac examined the shorted link by the light of a flash. "I think so."

"I don't understand why the backups didn't come on."

"Because they were damaged earlier. We're lucky we got this far."

"Well, let's hope we're luckier still and this crate gets us to Tori."

"And home again." He grunted as he pulled one end of the burned wire loose.

"That would be nice. Can I get you anything?"

"Shove the toolbox closer. Yeah, thanks. Go into the stores and see if anyone thought to provide us with a spare optic bundle. We'll need some connectors, too," he called after her retreating figure.

Muted thuds came from the other side of the hatch as she came into the bridge, but she ignored them, taking a second to stretch her aching back.

"Ttar's still raising a fuss," she commented when she crawled back into the chute, handing the required materials to her partner.

"He should know better. He has less air than we do and he's using it faster."

"Speaking of time running out, how long do we have?"

"Enough, I hope."

"I wish you hadn't added a qualifier." She squinted, trying to see, but his shoulders were in the way.

"That should do it," Hac grunted. "Go back to the controls and see if you can get the computer up."

Ttar had subsided somewhat, limiting himself to intermittent bangs on the door. We're doing all we can, she told him mentally. Hang on. She pressed the reset button. One of the idiot lights flashed once, and a feeble bleep sounded from the panel.

"Nothing!" she shouted to Hac.

"Damn. Try it now!"

A second bleep, flash, and then a steady light as the computer whirred into life. A clicking began somewhere within the console and then the hum of ventilators as the fans came back. Cool, dry air wafted into the cabin, followed by light, dim at first, then more intense.

Hac emerged and took his place at her side.

"What I don't understand is why we haven't had any more collisions while we were floating," she commented as she ran a systems check.

"Because we were floating," the android replied. "Anything that might have collided with us, just pushed the ship aside. And now we're off course as well."

"Pull in the nav computer. Find out where we are. We need to get back on ASAP."

Numbers paraded across the small screen in front of him. "Could be worse. A slight correction and we'll be all right, barring any more collisions."

"How far are we from Tori?"

"About eight hours at a safe speed."

"What's considered safe in this soup?"

"Slow."

"Once we're back on course, I think one of us should try to repair the backups. We might need them before we're out of here."

"I'll take care of it. There's a large dent in the hull; fortunately the skin didn't rupture. Lots of other stuff was jarred loose. We've lost some computer functions."

"Whose bright idea was it to put a computer against the outer hull?"

"It wasn't against the outer hull. As I said, it's a large dent."

"Oh."

"Our guest is quiet."

"Probably glad to be breathing again."

"I wonder if he's all right."

"Do you really care?" she asked.

"He hasn't told us anything yet."

"And I doubt if he will. A lot depends on his silence. Systems are all up. Everything looks all right."

"Good." Hac flipped a switch. "Ttar? Can you hear me?"

"Yeah. I hear you."

"You all right in there?"

"Am now. What the hell happened?"

"Little problem with an asteroid."

"Is that all. Hey, you going to keep me locked up the whole trip?"

"Are you reconsidering our offer for a temporary truce?"

"Looks like we're stuck in this thing together . . . and it looks like a pretty tight place. I might be able to help."

"Might." He looked at Mier, who shook her head. He switched off the intercom. "We could use him."

"For what?" she demanded. "Target practice? With us on the receiving end?"

"He can't go anywhere."

"Without us he'd have the nav computer and a programmed course in to and out of Tori. That's what he came here for."

"So we lock the program away. He wouldn't be able to get to it."

"I still don't think it's a good idea."

Hac shrugged and opened the link again. "Sorry. My partner doesn't trust you."

"Hey, I'll give my word," Ttar replied, his voice a little panicked. "Hell, man, it's cold in here. Can you imagine what it's like locked up for hours in a box? And then the light and air gets shut off? Where are we going anyway? How long before we get there? I'm hungry and I have to use the bathroom."

"Complaining won't get you anywhere. You had your chance," Mier told him.

"Yeah, and I made the wrong choice. So now I've seen the error of my ways. Won't you give me a break?"

"I'd love to," she said with subtle emphasis. "Where would you like it?"

Hac glanced at her in surprise.

"You really want out?" she continued.

"Hell, yes!"

"And you'll swear not to interfere with us in any way."

"Until you set me down on a friendly planet, you won't have a single problem with me."

She sighed. "I wish I could believe you."

"You can! How can I convince you? Hell, you scared me out of my wits back there. I thought I was dead."

"You almost were. The situation is dangerous enough without having you creating complications."

"No complications. I promise. Hell, we're in the Stone Field. I wouldn't do anything that might keep us from getting out again—in one piece. Or three, as the case may be. You gonna let me out?"

"In a minute." She closed the link. "All right, encode the nav program. And double lock it. I don't trust Ttar any more than I would a theeta rat."

Hac worked intently at the computer for a couple of minutes before he sat back and looked at her. "Code's Jarry Woburn."

She started. "Why did you pick that?"

"Ttar should have no way of knowing it."

She nodded. "Let him out, then."

CHAPTER 29

The rest of the journey to Tori passed uneventfully, despite the harrowing nature of their route. Ttar seemed content just to be out and remained webbed in a seat against the bulkhead. Mier could feel him sitting there, at the periphery of her vision, his presence a constant prickle in the back of her neck that did nothing for the state of her nerves. Still, having promised to cooperate, he made no threatening moves. Apparently having spent his aggression on embarking, he was now determined to make himself more or less agreeable.

The screen showed static, dancing dots of color that occasionally coalesced into a shape, a curl of radiation, or something very like a segment of a kaleidoscope slowly playing through its repertoire. Despite the aesthetic appeal, Mier would have preferred something a little more informative.

"What's our destination, anyway?" Ttar asked when nothing untoward had happened for a while.

"You mean for me to believe your employer didn't tell you?" she returned.

"By the blue moons of Festus Three, I told you, I'm doing this on my own," he persisted.

"You went through an awful lot of trouble to set up your cover. What hold did you have on Began to make him pass you off as his brother?"

"A big one."

"But he was still going to expose you in the end."

Ttar shrugged, the movement registering on Mier's oversensitized nerves even though she couldn't see it. "There's no accounting for loyalties."

"Why don't you take a nap or something," she snapped, irritated at his lack of candor.

"Good idea, but I'd rest better if I had something to eat first."

"I'll feed you in a little while."

"Don't bother. I can work the synthesizer. Want me to bring you something?"

"Stay where you are!" She swung her seat around, glaring, the pistol in her hand. "Sit down, and stay there until I tell you it's all right to move. Do you understand me?"

"Yeah." He subsided in a huff. "I thought you were going to trust me. I mean, we're in this together now, aren't we?"

"We're in it. You're just tagging along until we decide what to do with you. If you're not careful, we just might drop you off on a rock somewhere."

Hac glanced over at her, but Mier was intent on their prisoner.

"All right! All right. I'll sit here. I'll go to sleep if that's what you want. Geee-sh."

"Geee-sh?" Hac inquired sotto voce when Mier had resumed her position at the control panel.

"Look it up in your data bank." She glared at him, daring him to pursue it.

"An archaic Terran colloquial expression, in this context denoting acquiescence when faced with an unacceptable alternative."

Mier closed her eyes, but opened them the instant she realized how good it felt. Wearily she blinked a couple of times, wishing for sleep, but in Ttar's presence she didn't dare. "What's our ETA?"

"Any time in the next hour," her copilot replied.

"That's not very precise."

"Sorry. Our little detour threw everything off. Our route appears to be correct . . ."

"Appears to be?"

"We haven't collided with anything major in the past four hours."

"Sensors are still limited."

"Better than they were. There's a definite pattern to a large portion of the radiation, so I'm able to compensate more and more as we proceed."

"What kind of pattern?" Mier's fingers called up a grid on one of the small screens backing her console. "When did this pattern become apparent?"

"About an hour ago. We seem to be approaching the source."

"A planet?"

"Could be."

"Why didn't you say something before this?"

"There was no opportunity."

"You should have made one." Her hand raked through her hair and she sighed. "I wish we could see."

"I've been trying to discover a way to translate these colors. I think we can identify the radiation, and then use the computer to build us a visual model of this space."

"Does it work?"

"Marginally. Watch."

The pointillistic patterns left the main screen, replaced by a three-dimensional display of geometric shapes, each one a different color. The shapes weren't static, but shifted, flowing, stretching, and contracting.

"We're here," Hac told her, keying in a moving dot to represent the *Corsair*. Their flight path took them through the shapes, avoiding them by microns, it seemed.

"Can you project what's ahead?"

Hac worked as Mier watched the ship's progress.

Suddenly she leaned forward, intent. "I think I can see your pattern. The radiation is in a loose spiral, out from . . ."

"Here," he supplied. A red globe appeared in the construct. It lay directly in the path of the *Corsair*.

"Tori?"

"A good guess." Hac continued to work as he spoke. "Punching in figures, I would estimate our time of arrival at pre-cise-ly oh-two-thirty-four. That's one hour and twenty-two minutes from now."

"Tori? Is that the name of the planet?" Ttar interjected. A very interested observer to the preceding events, he leaned forward, speaking into the lull of voices.

"I suggest you forget you heard that," Mier warned.

"You can't pretend I'm not here."

"No, I can't, no matter how I wish it. How do we let them know we're coming?" she asked Hac. "Radio's out of the question as long as this interference holds. And we can't just try to find a clear spot to set down and then hope someone notices."

"That would appear to be our only alternative. Radiation's thick all the way to the planet."

"What about atmosphere?" Ttar asked. "By Saturn's rocky rings! We've got to be able to breathe!"

"You won't have to worry about breathing much longer unless you shut up," she warned.

"Under ordinary circumstances we would be able to see the planet by now." Hac switched the screen from the computer-generated image back to forward view.

Ttar forgotten, Mier sat forward in her seat, eyes wide with astonishment. Black space, studded with stars, surrounded them. Floating dead center on the screen was a blue-green world, clouds curving over the surface. Seas stretched from the north to south poles, divided by what they could see of two major continents.

". . . be damned," Ttar intoned, for once unchastised for speaking.

Mier's hackles rose in alarm as the radio crackled, and a strangely echoing voice insinuated itself into the cockpit.

"Welcome, travelers. Welcome to Tori," it said breathlessly, eagerly.

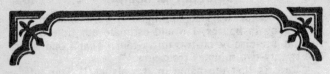

CHAPTER 30

Landing coordinates having been given, the *Corsair* banked into the atmosphere surrounding a planet that looked remarkably like Earth. As the ship dropped lower, the oceans receded and green patches became meadows bordered by trees, leaves dancing in the wind. Feathery clouds traced their way across a blue sky, muting the glow of Tori's primary. Mountains lined the horizon, completing a backdrop to the small city, which Mier assumed was their destination. The landing field to which they were directed lay just outside the buildings. It was little more than a stretch of dirt, burned in a couple of places where other ships had been, but understandable for a civilization that didn't have spaceflight.

The sensors rated the atmosphere breathable, and the hatch slid open, admitting light, sweet-smelling air and a cool, gentle breeze. Mier stepped out first, apprehensive, her fingers itching for the feel of her pistol. Ttar followed, a watchful Hac behind him. She paused, looking at the stone buildings and the group of white-gowned figures coming slowly toward them.

"Our hosts?" Hac suggested.

"I hope so."

"By the tail of Sigma Draconis, they look more like a religious delegation!" Ttar added. "I hope we're not going to have to listen to a sermon. What do you know about these aliens, anyway?"

Mier glanced at him, but didn't answer. Full of questions, Ttar fished constantly for information, and she was determined not to give him more than she had to.

A wide grav step lowered them from the *Corsair* and settled softly on the ground, where she went forward to meet the four Torians. Eight water-colored eyes gazed politely at them, but no expression was visible on their faces. They were distinctly humanoid, uniformly slender within the flowing gowns as far as Mier could see, but with smooth, less well defined features. They looked enough alike to be blood relatives, if Tori had such things—their long, pale hair lifted on the breeze, gently drifting around their shoulders, catching sunlight.

"Greetings," said one of them, standing a little in advance of the others. A leader? He spoke Terran Standard clearly with only a slight accent. His voice had the same strange hollow overtone she remembered from the radio transmission. "I am Daw. My companions are Galan, Sor, and Dree. You are welcome to Tori."

So the planet's name was their own, she noted. "I am Mier Silver. My companions are Hac and Ttar."

The slender, white-clad figures bowed, hands tucked out of sight within their sleeves.

Mier's hands hung at her sides, and she reflexively stretched her fingers wide, more than a little apprehensive at her inability to see if they were hiding something. Weapons? And yet, in the delicate situation of a first meeting with an essentially unknown, and possibly hostile—dangerous?—alien race, she didn't know if she should inquire. Damn, she thought, I'm trained to dig out the bad guys, not to initiate diplomatic relations.

"Will you come with us?" Daw invited. As if he was able to read her mind, he removed his hands and gestured toward the city.

His slender fingers were empty, she noted with relief. But

the others? "We've come to see the Diplomatic Group our
government sent here. Could you direct us to them?"

"We would be pleased to do so. However, they are
some distance from here. Perhaps you would like to rest
and refresh yourselves first?"

"Some distance? How far?"

"They are making a geological survey in the extreme
northern latitudes of this planet. I am afraid it will take
several days to reach them."

"We could go in our ship."

"Indeed you could, if you wished to travel more quickly.
If this is so, we will happily supply you with a guide."

"Thank you. We'd appreciate that."

"Then please come with us. You can rest in your people's headquarters until the guide arrives."

"You don't know where they are?"

"I am sorry to say that I, myself, do not. However, a
guide will be provided in a very short time." He moved
toward the city as he spoke, and the landing party was
drawn with him.

"Is there no one left at the headquarters?" Hac inquired.

"No. Every one of the Group has gone to the northern
base. We are not in touch with them at this time or we
would have directed you there instead of to this city. I
hope this does not inconvenience you too greatly?"

"Apparently it couldn't be helped," Mier reassured him.

Made of stone, the city had a primitive and oddly un-
finished look to it, as if work was still in progress. There
were numerous vacant lots, rich with plant life between
the structures. The buildings themselves had a nebulous
quality; they could have had any purpose, been shops,
houses, hostels—anything. There were no signs, no advertisements, no writings of any kind.

Mier gazed around her as they proceeded, memorizing
their route. Nothing felt right here; there was no overt
danger, but underneath—her nerves alive, warning her,
but of what? She looked again at one of the buildings; it
said nothing to her, had no message, no content, like
something glimpsed out of the corner of an eye and that
can't quite be identified. All that she'd seen of Tori so
far had that same look. And she found it disquieting.

Their footsteps echoed through the cobbled streets.

"Where are the people?" Ttar asked.

People? Yes, Mier thought, that was it. They hadn't seen any people other than their hosts. The city was empty.

"The people are here," Daw told him. "They are occupied with what I believe you call tasks. There is one now."

A white-gowned figure crossed the street ahead of them, disappearing into a building without even a glance at the strangers.

Ttar subsided into silence, looking curiously around him.

Mier grew more edgy with every second. One of the larger plastisteel prefab buildings loomed before them as they rounded a corner. Standard government issue, its pedestrian appearance reassured her as she went to the door. Daw and his companions stood aside as she tried the handle. The lock defeated her for a second, and then the door recessed and slid aside. Stale air indicated the building hadn't been used in some time.

"We will leave you here," Daw told them, seemingly reluctant to enter. "You may rest and refresh yourselves until the guide arrives."

"When will that be?" Mier asked.

"He will come soon." They departed, melting away into the streets.

Soon? How long would that be? And what could she do about it in the face of Daw's polite implacability? Mier wandered into the building, followed by Ttar. Hac thoughtfully closed the door. The generator was apparently in working order: the lights came on immediately, revealing a shambles. Furniture overturned and smashed, unidentifiable bits and pieces of machinery mixed with personal belongings scattered throughout the room.

"They can't fool me," Ttar said irritably, gazing around him. "This place's deserted. Nobody's been here in a long time. Looks like they left in a hurry, too."

"See if the synthesizer still works," Hac suggested. "Maybe some food will make you feel better."

"A drink is what I need." Ttar obediently made his way around an upended table to the wall unit.

"What do you think happened?"

"I don't know," she told her partner. "But I think Ttar's right; no one's been here in a while."

"Do you think Daw knew about this when he brought us here?"

"Of course. What's your impression of him?"

"Spooky."

"Spooky? That's all your analytical mind can come up with?"

"Sorry. It's difficult to define. And I think that's what's wrong with the whole planet. Have you noticed? Everything's dreamlike. All the edges are blurred, like something you can't quite remember."

"That's a good way to describe it." She took a deep breath and let it out, looking at the mess. "I wish I knew what happened here. If I can find the mainframe . . ."

"There. Is that it?"

She looked into an alcove off the main room. "Yes, that's it. Why don't you have a look around. See if you can find anything else that might help us."

"Shit! Damn them!" The words exploded from Ttar. Mier whirled to see him yanking at the door. "The sons of bitches have locked us in!"

She hurried to his side and tried for herself. The door was locked. She punched a priority override on the keypad, but still nothing happened.

"There's got to be another door," Hac said. "Or windows, skylights."

They scattered, checking every opening, but all of them had been sealed behind plastisteel, welded closed.

They were locked in, no way out.

CHAPTER 31

"Who put this building up, anyway?" Ttar demanded. "You're not going to make me believe it's native."

"It was built by a Federation Diplomatic Group," Hac responded, his eyes exploring the walls, ceilings for likely-looking vents. Still searching, he wandered into one of the other rooms.

"Government issue. By the pockmarked sands of Luna, I should have guessed. But I still don't understand," he complained to Mier. "Looks like they were preparing to withstand a siege. But against who? The Torians? And why? They didn't look particularly harmful to me."

"Nothing ever looks harmful—until it tries to bite," she replied, pistol in hand. She switched the setting to laser and began to cut the shield away from one of the windows.

"That's going to take forever."

"Would you prefer that we do nothing?" she asked over the hiss of heated metal.

"So let me help. I'll work on the main door."

"I don't have another laser."

"I've had some experience picking locks."

"Not that kind."

The steel over the window was three centimeters thick, and the work went slowly. Ttar watched for a couple of minutes, and then went to the front door, determined—despite her warning—to attempt to dismantle the locking mechanism.

Alone with the improvised laser, she tried to imagine why anyone had felt the need for such precautions. The shields, on the inside, were meant to keep something out. Had they been on the outside, the opposite would have been true. But the absence of the mission tended to prove that even these drastic measures had been ineffective.

What did they fear?

Hac returned and checked her progress. "It's going to take a bigger laser to cut that off. Whoever put it up did a thorough job."

Mier stepped back, turning off the pistol with a sigh. "I know. And the charge is more than half-gone already. Ttar's trying to get the main door open."

"Without luck. Our hosts were thorough. Guess they want us to stay put."

"Why do you think the Torians did this? It could have been the first mission."

"To keep something out? What?" Hac looked around at the vandalism. "But why trash the place? And why are we confined?"

"I don't know. The destruction seems so meaningless. But we could have been locked in for protection."

"Whose? Ours? Or theirs?"

"I don't know. We need some answers. I'm going back to the computer."

Seated on the edge of a chair, she activated the machine. It responded sluggishly at first, for someone had yanked the keyboard loose and smashed some of the keys. She had no way to tell if there was any mechanical damage and set it to run a self-diagnostic program

"What's the rest of the building like?" she asked.

"It's a mess. But I did find a lab of some sort."

"Probably for assay work."

"Mier, do you think they're still alive?"

She slowly shook her head. "Do you?"

"The evidence would seem to be against it. And if the team were the ones who sealed this building, they were afraid of something coming in from the outside. The only thing out there are the Torians."

"And, as Ttar pointed out, they may be spooky, but they don't look particularly harmful."

"Except they did lock us in."

"Yes, they did do that."

"Is it possible that there's something here that they're afraid of, too? Some kind of life . . . a life-form we don't know about? And they didn't want it to harm us?"

"Then why didn't they warn us about it?" she argued.

"I know it's slim. But according to the reports, the Torians are the only inhabitants of this planet."

"Which in itself is strange. Did you notice, there is no mention of any other fauna. No birds, snakes, dinosaurs, webstars, nothing like that. It would make you wonder—a planet with only one species. Doesn't fit with evolutionary theory."

The computer finished its program and announced that it was up to ninety percent capability.

"I hope we don't need that last ten percent," Mier

commented as she began to search for any reports or personal papers left by the team.

"I'm going back to the lab," Hac told her when it appeared her task would take some time. "There's another terminal there. Maybe I can find something there."

Mier nodded absently, for she had found a log of the original Group's landing on Tori. At first the reports were dry, detailed facts, no recording of the team's personal experiences. The natives had been helpful, selecting a site and assisting while the Group erected its headquarters. But if anything strange had happened, or if anyone had had any initial reservations, it wasn't recorded here.

"I'm going to find a bed," Ttar said, interrupting her reading. "I'm a little tired. Think I'll lay down for a while."

"Right," she responded, her eyes never leaving the screen.

Once the team was settled, however, the problems began. They had had trouble getting ore samples. Then the team geologist went out and didn't come back. A search party was organized, and it didn't return. The original Group of fifteen was down to eleven when a thread of panic started creeping into the report.

"Mier? Where's Ttar?" Hac asked.

"What?" Brought suddenly back to their situation, she didn't at first remember the redhead speaking to her. "He was here just a minute ago. Said something about taking a nap."

"He's not in the bunk room. I just looked."

"Damn." She shoved the chair back from the terminal and got to her feet. "Do you think he got out?"

"I don't know. Unless you are doing something you can't leave, you'd better help me look for him. Anything interesting?" he asked as they made their way to the back of the building.

"Members of the original team began to disappear about a week after they got here. First a geologist, then the people who went out looking for him."

"Which would tend to substantiate my suggestion that there is something dangerous out there. Any clues to what it might be?"

"No. What did you find?"

"Mostly chemistry notes. Someone was working with radioactive compounds. I thought the main purpose of this mission was to establish diplomatic relations, and do a geological survey."

"It was. He's not in the bunk room," she corroborated. "Did you check the showers?" She pulled the door open as she spoke.

They found Ttar crouched in the back corner, shivering violently.

"I'm cold," he said, teeth chattering. "Can't see too good. Dizzy."

Mier sat down on her heels and reached her hand out to him, but he pulled further back, eyes enormous in his white face. Sweat beaded his upper lip and darkened his hair.

"No! Don't touch me! Leave me alone," he babbled. "You're in on this. You did it to me! You're responsible. *Get out of my mind!*"

CHAPTER 32

Ttar fought them, mad with terror from something they couldn't see or hear. Finally Mier managed to subdue him with careful pressure on the carotid artery, and Hac carried the limp body into the bunk room.

Here they made a startling discovery: several of the cots to one side of the bunk room were already fitted with restraints. After helping strap the unconscious redhead down, Hac stepped back and looked at his partner.

"What's wrong with him?"

"I don't know . . . or I'm afraid I do." Visions of Jarry came back to her, the mindless body sitting on the edge of the bed.

"Is this what the original team was afraid of?" Hac persisted.

"Bet on it."

"And it's the same thing that got Jarry and the man Leah Roget tried to save?"

"Woburn. Yes."

"And it's going to get us now, isn't it?"

Mier looked up at him, startled. "Me. Just me. It can't affect you, you're mechanical. We have to get out of here, off this planet!"

"At the moment, that's impossible. Mier, don't you start to panic on me now!"

"I'm not panicking!" And she wasn't, but, as the sum of all this became clear to her, she began to realize what they were up against. "It's invisible. That's the only answer."

"What's invisible? What answer?"

"The life-form, or whatever it is. It's an invisible menace."

"Or it could be too small for us to see. A microbe, virus, bacteria, something like that."

"That's invisible." Mier raked her hair with her fingers. "Can nothing ever be simple?"

"The computer in the lab might be able to help us. If the radioactive compounds they were working on had nothing to do with geological analysis, they might be a cure."

"How can we tell? I don't know anything about geology."

"But I do."

Despite her apprehension, she grinned. "Right. I keep forgetting you belong to Geo-Mining. Will he be all right if we leave him?"

"He won't go anywhere for a while. Until we have more information, we won't be able to do anything for him anyway." Hac led the way to the lab, which appeared to have been damaged even more thoroughly than the rest of the building . . . except, fortunately, the computer. It came on at a touch. "The information I found was still in active memory, so someone was working on it when . . ." He looked around at the wreckage, and didn't finish the sentence.

"Yeah. I wonder what happened to the bodies."

"Maybe the Torians buried them."

"Maybe they ate them." She shuddered. "What do you see? All of this's incomprehensible to me."

"As I said before, it's a low-grade radioactive solution."

"Solution? A liquid?"

"That's right. And as far as I can determine, it has nothing to do with geological assay."

"So it's medical?" Mier asked hopefully.

"Could be. Superficially it looks like some kind of an antigen. But I'll have to dig further; we'll need more information before we can use something so potentially dangerous on a human subject."

"Can we hope they included something as simple as instructions? Or even notes?"

"There should be notes . . . unless there wasn't enough time." He scrolled through formulas and diagrams, equally incomprehensible to Mier. "Here's something . . . no, this won't help."

"You keep looking. I'm going to check on Ttar."

He didn't answer.

The redheaded agent lay in the same position, still unconscious. Mier checked his bonds and, satisfied, straightened up. There had to be something she could do, she thought. Even if he was the enemy, common decency demanded it. And, another part of her mind added, they couldn't afford to lose even one member of their small party. She recognized the old herding instinct: three were even better than two in a tight situation, and this one was tight.

Finding a rest for her hip on the edge of the cot, Mier gently placed the palm of her hand on the side of Ttar's head and closed her eyes.

Nothing.

She mentally went through her body, finding tense muscles and forcing them to relax, willing her mind to be still, open, receptive.

With a startled cry, she jerked her hand away and leapt from the bed. Standing there shaking, she swallowed convulsively, trying to understand what she had felt. It had been faint, but enough to reach her, an impression of extreme turmoil, fear—terror greater than anything she had ever experienced. Taking a deep breath and trying to

JOHANNA M. BOLTON 163

regain her equilibrium, she watched Ttar. How could anyone live with something like that going on in his head?

But they didn't live, her mind replied. They went mad, it seemed, and then they died. And you will, too, unless you find a way to defeat this menace.

"Damn," she muttered, and headed back to the lab. This was too much for her, and she could see it had already influenced her work. Mind stuff, phantoms—she was an agent, not an exorcist! But that's what Tori needed, someone to nullify this evil. She felt helpless: no matter how hard she tried to counter its effect on her, the dreams and now this—this *thing* in Ttar's mind—were corroding her efficiency. The signs were everywhere. So far this trip, her work had been sloppy.

She stepped into the wrecked lab, putting her chaotic thoughts behind her. Thank the Goddess for Hac! At least there was one member of the party who couldn't be influenced by spooks.

He still sat in front of the computer, reviewing some three-dimensional models. Mier left him to it and began to pick through the debris littering the floor. She righted a counter and collected the unbroken bits and pieces there. In the end, there was a lot that could be salvaged, and finding a sweeper, she swept the rest against the wall, where a disposal received it. There were some larger machines, which she also righted, although she doubted some of them could be made to work again.

"I think I've found something," Hac announced suddenly. "I was right. Whoever was working on this was trying to find a cure for the Torian parasite."

"Is that what they called it."

"Good a name as any. The compound I told you about destroys it. Simple."

"Side effects?"

"They don't mention any."

"So why didn't they use it on themselves?"

"I don't know. Maybe there wasn't time."

"Or maybe the cure killed them."

"Maybe it did. What would you rather do? Try the antidote and risk death, or get the parasite and know you're going to die? And die badly?"

"I'm not at risk here . . ."

"Yet."

"Yet," she conceded. "But do we have the right to experiment on Ttar?"

"I don't know. How would you feel if you were in his place?"

Mier remembered the terror. "All right. We'll try it. Where is it? And how is it administered?"

"Good questions. Unfortunately we have to make our own batch."

"How long will that take?"

"It might not be possible, if we don't have the ingredients. Did you clean this place up?" he asked, surveying her work.

"I guessed we'd need it."

"What we need is the waldo box and a synthesizer. A couple of hypodermics, too, if you can find them." He went to a wall unit and examined the broken plexi window. "We can scavenge another cover for this."

"And hypos are here. But there are only twelve ampules left, I'm afraid."

"Should be more than enough. To be sure, we'll fill them all. Look at this." He pointed to the waldo box, which fitted against the wall, covering the synthesizer. "Looks like someone started to make the serum."

Mier flipped a switch. "The synthesizer's broken. Now what do we do?"

"Fix it?"

"Beyond my capabilities. If you can't do it, ask the computer."

Hac shunted his work into a file and requested the result of the last self-diagnostic run. After a minute, he grimaced and sat back. "Looks like the synthesizer is the inoperative ten percent."

"Wonderful."

"See if there's anything else we can use." He started going through the materials Mier had salvaged when a horrific scream rang through the building.

"Ttar." Mier dashed for the door.

"Get it *out of me!*" the man screamed, struggling against his bonds. "Help me! Damn, get—it—out!" He fell back panting, his head thrashing from side to side. "I can't see! I can't see!"

But his eyes were wide open.

She sat at the side of the cot, trying to quiet him with her hands and her voice. "Ttar, calm down. It's me. It's Mier Silver. We'll help you."

"No! Let me go! Get out! Get away! *No!*"

"Hac, get back in the lab. We've got to have that serum."

"You're sure you can handle him?"

"There was a first aid kit. Get it. I'll try a sedative."

"No! Get out! Get out!" He screamed.

Hac fled and returned in seconds with the kit. Fortunately undamaged, its contents were almost complete. Mier found the sedative and swiftly pressed a patch against the artery on Ttar's throat. Slowly his thrashing stilled and his cries diminished to incoherent mumbling.

"I can handle him now," Mier said, turning to her partner. But Hac had gone.

CHAPTER 33

Mier was asleep, her back against the wall, knees drawn up and her head dropped on her crossed arms, when Hac returned. Ttar was still, eyes wide, staring at nothing.

"Silver?"

She raised her head, face still sleepy, and brushed a lock of hair back.

"I've got it. The serum. According to the notes, it will take two injections at two-hour intervals."

She pushed herself upright. "Have you ever done this before?"

"Given an injection? No. Have you?"

"Once. Let me try. In the muscle, under the skin? What?"

"It didn't say. I've set the hypo for maximum penetration."

"All right." She took the device, checked the gauge, and then bent and swiftly pressed it against Ttar's neck.

The hypo hissed, and the little man screamed, his body arching in one almost impossible spasm against the bonds. As suddenly he subsided, limp, his eyes closed.

Mier checked his pulse: it was weak. "Now what?"

"We wait," Hac told her. He checked his chronometer. "Two hours. Here's the second dose. I color-coded them: first one's green, the second blue."

Mier snapped the ampule into the hypo. "I could use something to eat. Will you watch him?"

"I'll be here."

There were the remains of a meal on the table in the main room, Ttar's meal. Mier hesitated; he was the only one who got sick, and he was also the only one of them to eat anything. Was the plague carried in the food synthesizer? That would make things even more difficult. She wandered over to the door. Still locked, it resisted her efforts. And the lock itself was intact, although gouges around the case showed where Ttar had tried to force the cover off.

A packet of protein tabs rested in the bottom of her pocket, and she took them, wishing for something to wash them down with. Maybe there was some distilled water in the lab. Mier went that way and found an unbroken jug. Rinsing her mouth with a small sip, she looked over the collection of equipment Hac had assembled to prepare the serum. For the first time on the mission, she felt grateful to have him along. She couldn't have done this alone.

Back in the bunk room, Ttar lay still and silent. Hac had brought a chair to the bedside and watched him closely, although he looked up when his partner arrived.

"You still look tired. Why don't you sleep for a while? I'll wake you when it's time for the second injection."

Wearily she nodded. "I took some protein tablets. Ttar ate, and I'm not sure if he didn't get this thing from the food."

"You're sure he ate?"

"His dishes were still on the table."

Hac nodded and turned back to the patient.

Mier chose a cot, rolled onto it, and slipped into an exhausted sleep.

Fog rolled in, knee deep, surrounding her, and covering an empty plain that stretched in all directions. Somewhere a faint keening noise began, high and shrill. She turned but couldn't find the source. Walking forward, fog swirling with every step, she headed toward the source of the sound. It lay under the mist. Closer she came, careful of her steps . . . closer.

"Mier?" Hac called, gently shaking her by the shoulder. "Wake up. It's time."

She lay for a second gazing up into his blue eyes before she sat up. He straightened.

"You want to give the injection?" He held out the hypo.

"You do it. Just hold it against his neck and press the button."

Ttar didn't move immediately this time. For a couple of minutes he lay completely still; then his eyes blinked open.

"Ttar?" she called softly.

He stared at the ceiling and then turned to Mier and Hac. "What happened?" he whispered from a sore throat.

"You don't remember?" she asked.

"I . . . Oh, God. It was too unreal."

"How do you feel?" Hac wanted to know.

"Tired. You wouldn't believe how tired."

"Sleep, then. The bad part's over."

"But what happened to me?"

"You were ill. Some kind of a parasite, I think. We believe it wiped out the original mission."

"A parasite?" His brow furrowed.

"What was it like? Can you try to tell us?" Mier coaxed. "You kept screaming, 'Get out. Get out.' "

"It was inside me," he said hesitantly. "It was . . . something trying to take over." Eyes closed, he shook his head. "I don't want to think about it any more."

"But it's gone now?"

He looked at her. "Yeah. It's gone. And if we have any brains, we'll get ourselves gone, too. Whatever you think you'll find on this godforsaken planet, it's not worth it."

"We agree with you. And we're going, as soon as we figure out how to get out of here. We're locked in, remember?"

"So build a bomb. Blow the wall out. Do anything, but get us off this planet before it comes back."

Ttar closed his eyes, and his breathing deepened into sleep.

"We could unstrap him," Hac suggested. When she nodded he did so. "And in the meantime?"

"We find a way out of here. I like Ttar's bomb idea."

"You're not going to wait for confirmation of the original mission's deaths?"

"We'll take all the records back with us. Let someone else decide what really happened here. After seeing what Ttar went through, I don't want to stay here any longer than necessary. Do you?"

"No."

"And I doubt the Torians are going to tell us anything. Do you know how to build a bomb?"

"Explosives? I . . ." Hac shook his head. "I'm having trouble thinking. I'm dizzy." He grabbed at the doorway for support as his knees sagged.

Mier stood frozen, staring at him, her mouth open in shock. "Hac!"

"Help me over to a cot. You'd better strap me in. I'm afraid . . ."

She rushed to his side and supported him a few steps until he collapsed.

"What are you doing? What's wrong?"

He didn't answer, his jaw muscles tight as he fought his internal battle.

"Hac! You're a machine! The parasite can't affect you!"

"Yes," he hissed, "it can. I'm not . . . not . . ."

And she realized what he was not. "You son of a bitch!" she screamed, tightening the restraining web with

a furious yank. "You fucking bastard! Brian lied to me!
You're human!"

CHAPTER 34

Her face wet, but unaware that she cried, Mier stood at
the side of the cot, gazing down at Hac, her emotions in
turmoil, rage warring with blinding terror. After the initial spate of invective, she was paralyzed, her throat
closed, unable to speak or move, sick from the feelings
that boiled within her—thoughts in chaos, an image here,
a fragment there. The Professor and Brian were responsible. They knew, they *knew* why she couldn't work with
a partner! And yet they did this to her! She remembered
the agonizing months in rehab after Karr died, his mind
ripped from hers . . . living in the pain, always fresh.
And then nightmares for years afterward, replaying the
same scene, over and over again. Her stomach rebelling
suddenly, she bolted into the bathroom and bent forward,
retching. The spasm over, she leaned against the wall,
eyes closed, breath shuddering.

All right, Mier, the voice of reason told her sternly.
You've had your little bout of hysteria. Now pull yourself
together. With the other two members of the party inva-
lids, someone has to be responsible. You've got to handle
everything.

Everything. First things first—she had to help Hac.
Damn him! Damn him! How could he go along with such
a deception!

She pushed herself away from the wall and went back
into the bunk room.

He lay trembling, lips pressed tightly together, sweat
beading his skin. As she watched he stiffened, his head
thrashing violently from one side to the other, muscles
in his neck and jaw rigid with strain as he fought what-

ever had hold of him. The hypo and ampules rested in the box on the floor where he had left them. She quickly fixed a dose, pressed it against his neck, and pulled the trigger.

"No!" he screamed, rearing up against the webbing. She took an involuntary step backward as his eyes snapped wide open, staring into hers.

"You don't know what you're doing!" he yelled, voice hoarse and distinctly overlaid with the echoing tones of the Torian. Despite her surprise, she didn't question how it came to be there, but started forward, her intention to soothe him, although she didn't know how to do this. She didn't want to touch him, to risk entering the terrifying world she had experienced in Ttar's mind.

In an instant the paroxysm was over, and Hac went limp, head back, eyes staring blindly, and jaw relaxed, mouth slightly open. It was the face of death, something she had seen many times.

"Oh, no," she whispered, terrified anew. "Don't you dare die on me!" Mier dropped the hypo and placed her hand on his neck. Beneath her fingers a thready pulse beat. Shock, he was going into shock, she realized. Whirling, she looked frantically through the litter, finding a thermal sheet. Tucking it gingerly around him, she hoped the sensors were still adequate to the job of warming him.

"By the lava pools of the Eiger plain, what in hell's going on over there?" Ttar called weakly from his bed. "Too much noise. By the nebulas of Orion, I'm a sick man."

"You're not the only one," Mier replied.

He lifted his head. "Hac's sick? Oh, great." He subsided. "So you get to run this show all by yourself now."

"No, not all by myself. Since you're back among the living, I expect you to do your part."

"I can't. Gods of Chaos but I'm exhausted! You don't know what it was like."

"And I don't intend to find out. You get some rest. In about two hours I have to give Hac another shot. By then you should be on your feet. We have to get out of here."

"That's the only good thing you said all day," he mumbled, eyes closing.

Mier watched the two of them for a second and then

went back to the lab. Ttar's suggestion about the bomb, even if it was said in jest, now seemed to be the only solution to their problem. If she could only find something, or rig something to blow out the door.

She sifted through the remnants of the chemicals—without a working synthesizer, she was helpless to get more. Nothing struck her as useful. She didn't want to consider her one remaining option: her pistol could be set to overload and explode. But she'd be as good as naked without it.

Don't be a fool, her inner voice reprimanded. Better naked and free than well-armed and stuck here, waiting to die.

She went to the main door, trying the lock one more time. It remained stubbornly closed. Taking a survey, she realized the blast would take out most of the front wall, but that didn't matter; they wouldn't be coming back.

She directed the pistol to her hand and looked down at it. All right, she conceded. She brought adhesive from the lab and, unlacing the gun from the sheath, attached it firmly to the door. Now all I have to do is depress the firing stud and we have a way out, she told herself. So the next thing is to get Ttar and Hac back on their feet.

She began to feel heat then, warmth covering her . . . coming through the ventilators? What happened to the cool air?

Not now, she complained silently. This wasn't the time for the generator to go out! The warmth quickly turned her bones leaden, and she dropped into a chair, intending to rest for a moment. Tired. She was so tired! She hadn't had but a couple of hours' sleep in the past two days. It wasn't enough. While she waited, maybe she should try to get some more.

That was her last coherent thought for a very long time.

CHAPTER 35

Ttar stared stupidly at the ceiling for quite some time before his mind cleared enough for him to remember where he was. Pushing himself up to a sitting position, he gazed around the room, locking on Hac's recumbent form.

"Hey," he ventured.

The lack of a response made him curious, and he dragged his legs over the side of the bed. Weakness made him dizzy at first, but as he stood and moved carefully, he steadied.

The man in the bed lay breathing deeply, asleep. Ttar remembered Mier telling him that she would give him another injection in two hours. Had she done so? Were the two hours up yet? Where was Mier? Busy elsewhere, obviously.

What was this injection business anyway? The same thing they used on him? He eyed the hypo and box of ampules on the floor, but didn't touch them.

Ttar cursed his fate. Here he was, alone, unwatched—an excellent opportunity to escape. But he would never get out of the building without help, which meant no matter what his long-term goals, he had to assume a temporary loyalty to Hac and Mier. At least until he reached the ship. After that . . . well, he'd do whatever was necessary to get back to Stonewall and the people who hired him.

The people who hired him. They wouldn't be pleased with what he had to tell them. Which was exactly nothing.

Then a nasty thought struck. Nova stars, would they? No, they couldn't! After everything that happened, they couldn't expect him to try to make contact with the natives on his own. That would be impossible! Besides, after everything he had been through, he wasn't about to stick his neck out enough to try. No matter how much he was threatened. They had no idea what Tori was like. No one in his right mind would come here.

But then, his employers were a nasty bunch—mean enough even for Tori. And he didn't like the idea of coming back to them without something useful.

Blazing comets, he was caught in a vacuum with no suit handy!

He made his way to the shower room, where he rinsed his face, rubbing his gritty eyes and washing the foul taste from his mouth. Which reminded him of food. Something to eat would be nice right about now.

And where was Mier?

What time was it, anyway?

The bulky attachment to the door caught his attention as he entered the main room. Rapidly assessing the improvised bomb, he nodded with approval. Crude, but it would be effective. Could he risk detonating it now and try to reach the ship on his own? Abandoning his companions didn't bother his conscience, but after his recent, terrible experience, he shrank from the thought of leaving even the dubious comfort of the building alone. No, he'd have to take them with him . . . or at least Hac, who seemed to him the most reasonable of the pair. Mier meant trouble—she was too suspicious. But he didn't see how they could get away without her. No, it looked like all three of them would have to leave . . . or none.

The wall unit in the main room delivered a steaming

plate of synthetic goulash, soy bread, and coffee. Ttar activated the computer. Mier had left the first mission's log in memory, and he read it as he ate.

Torian parasite. Yeah, he had firsthand experience with that. Nasty business, best forgotten as quickly as possible.

The time was oh-four-hundred Stonewall, three days after they'd left!

Where was Mier?

He finished his meal and went to find her. Unsuccessful, he went back into the bunk room. Hac lay in the same position.

"Wake up." Ttar shook the sleeping man's shoulder. "Hac! Get up. I can't find Mier."

There was no response.

Damn.

His eyes fell on the hypo. Suppose, he thought, Mier never gave the second shot? Suppose . . . ? By the novas of Herculis, what did he have to lose?

He picked up an ampule and, after fitting it into the slot, uncovered Hac's shoulder and gave the injection.

Okay, he thought, now you can live or die.

Ttar sat on the side of the cot for a couple of minutes, watching. Nothing happened until he got to his feet and started away.

"What . . . ?" came a sleepy whisper from behind him.

"Thank the hairy gods of Orlan! You've got to get up."

A dead weight at first, Hac sagged against Ttar, who tried to get him to his feet.

"Give me a minute. I can't think. My mind's fuzzy."

"Don't think," the redheaded agent suggested. "It's better you don't try to remember anything. Just get up. You'll feel much better after you've had something to eat. I did."

"I don't think I can. Not just yet. Where's Mier?"

"I was afraid you'd notice. She's gone."

This caught Hac's attention. "Gone? How could she? How did she get out of the building?"

"I don't know. The door's still locked, none of the

windows have been opened, but I looked everywhere and she's not here.''

"Damn." Hac closed his eyes, gathering his strength before he pushed himself to his feet. "We have to find her.''

"What we have to do is get out of here." Then a thought struck him with dismay. He grabbed Hac's arm. "You don't think . . . ? No, she couldn't have!''

"Now what are you talking about?"

"If she's out, I mean out of the building . . . if she got to the ship. She wouldn't leave us here, would she?''

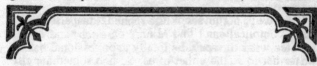

CHAPTER 36

"She's got to be in here somewhere." Hac sighed, sinking into a chair, more tired than he wanted to admit even after a brief search of the building. His strength—mental and physical—wasn't up to normal, and that frustrated him. With so much to do, he needed every advantage he could get, especially with an ally who was also an enemy.

"Unless she's outside. Maybe the Torians came for her," Ttar suggested, flopping into the other chair. He, too, was nearing exhaustion.

"For what purpose? And why did they leave us?"

"I don't know. Unless . . ." Ttar swallowed in acute discomfort, remembering his brief but thoroughly unpleasant experience. "We were infected by the parasite. Maybe that scared them off," he managed with artificial bravado.

Hac's answer was noncommittal, his mind elsewhere occupied, trying to find a solution to this impossible dilemma. Where could she be?

Ttar, ruled by his gut instinct—apprehension fueled by his acute dislike of Tori—tried to be his most persuasive, wanting more than anything to get as far away as possible, and as quickly as possible. "Look, forget Mier. The two of us—together, we have a chance of escaping. All I want to do is get to the ship and blast my way off this freaking planet." The thought intruded that this might not be so simple. Apprehension blossomed into fear. "That is, if she hasn't already taken it. You don't think she's taken the ship, do you?"

"She wouldn't leave us. And I'm not about to go without her."

"You keep saying that. By the fourteen moons of Jupiter, what hold does she have on you? You're not lovers, are you?"

"No, we're not lovers," Hac replied, exasperated with Ttar's complications. "We're here on a job, and Mier's a professional. It would be totally unprofessional behavior for her to strand either of us. So find something else to occupy your mind."

"I'm a professional, too, and in her place, I'd leave us."

"So why didn't you go when you had the chance?"

Ttar cast a frightened glance at the door, seeing in his mind what lay beyond. "I'm not sure how to get back to the ship," he lied.

"I think," Hac told him, with more understanding than he showed, "we'll all need each other to get out of here alive. Come on. Let's make another search—a thorough one this time."

They started in the showers and proceeded to the bunk room, where Hac busied himself pulling open lockers while Ttar looked under beds and sorted through the litter whenever something interesting caught his eye.

"What's in these, anyway?" he asked, picking up the hypo and box of ampules. "Is this what you used on me?"

"It's a compound, a serum that someone in the first mission was working on. Unfortunately it wasn't ready in time to save them."

"But it did save us?"

Hac nodded. "Green ampule, followed at a two-hour interval by a blue one."

"Now that's the only good thing that's happened since we got here."

"Perhaps not," said Mier, coming into the room.

She looked drunk, her hair disheveled, eyes glazed, movements overly precise. She advanced into the room and stood leaning slightly to one side, despite her body's obvious strain at holding such an unnatural position.

"Where in Fornia's seven hells have you been? We've been looking all over for you!" Ttar started toward her when Hac caught his arm, holding him back.

It wasn't so much Mier's appearance that made him cautious as her voice. He had heard that hollow overtone before. "Mier, are you all right?"

"Yes, Hac. I am fine. Are you well?"

"As you can see, I've recovered completely."

"That is good. Now you and Ttar can come with me. The Torians are waiting."

"By the seven moons of Gaea, you're an icy one!" Ttar interrupted, not understanding where any of this was leading. "Where have you been? What's going on? How come they want to see us now? And how do you know what they want all of a sudden?"

"Because I have been outside. I have spoken with them. We were wrong. The first mission was wrong. There is nothing to fear. Nothing will harm us. Come with me. I will take you to them now."

Hac turned his back to Mier, screening his actions from her sight as he took one of the green ampules from the box Ttar still held. "Put this in the hypo. As soon as I have her, inject it," he whispered.

"Wha— Oh." Enlightenment struck the redheaded agent, and he glanced at Mier as he would at some dangerous animal, not sure he wanted to have anything to do with her. He shoved his burden in his pocket and prepared the hypo. Why not just kill her and be on their way? He was about to say as much to Hac when she started forward.

"Why are you waiting? What are you doing? We must go now."

"We're coming." Hac turned and approached her calmly. "Mier?" He cautiously reached out a hand.

Her eyes widened and she pulled back. "No, you must not touch me."

Hac leapt, his weight bearing her into the corridor and

down, all the while hoping his diminished strength would
be great enough, that whatever possessed her had weak-
ened her enough, so he could hold her. They fought, she
with all the cunning viciousness her body could invent,
and he with desperate need to immobilize her without
doing irreparable harm. Ttar stood stunned by the battle
that raged at his feet. He never even thought of trying to
use the hypo, although he held it ready.

Beyond the battling figures, the main door flew open,
admitting something like a great wind that whipped up
dust and litter. Two of the Torians stood in the opening,
white gowns blowing around them, their howling added
to the sounds that came from Mier's throat. Hac, in a last
effort, sent his fist crashing into her jaw, snapping her
head back. As she lost consciousness, the Torians rushed
forward, seeming to sail on the wind, their howls never
abating.

"Come on," Hac roared at Ttar, who stood as if paralyzed. He lifted Mier's unconscious form to his shoulder
and started toward the main door. If they didn't move,
he fully intended to run over any of the natives who stood
in his way. Desperate not to be left alone, Ttar scrambled
after him.

The Torians' strange flowing motion brought them
straight on. Hac broke into a run, angling his body so
that Mier would be protected from the impact. If he could
knock them aside, if he could get through them, the open
door lay just beyond.

The anticipated collision never happened, and Hac
staggered, tingling from something like an electrical
shock as he passed right through the white-gowned figures. Holo projections? He didn't take the time to be
amazed, but continued through the door and onto the
street.

Black night enveloped them; black night, but not complete darkness, for the buildings shimmered, giving off
an eerie light. The light glittered in the fog that rose from
the ground, swirling around their knees, obscuring pavement and foundations both. If Mier was awake, she would
have recognized the fog, but fortunately, she lay still,
limp over her partner's shoulder. Neither he nor Ttar had

her memories, nor the time to analyze the illogic that assaulted their senses.

Stone buildings do not move, the mind insisted. But these did, going from solidity to transparency and back again with the regularity of a heartbeat. The ground, hidden in the mist, lifted and fell beneath their running feet, fighting them, slowing them. And the noise! The howling could be wind, although the same sound had come from the enraged Torians as he fought with Mier. By now, however, it had increased in volume, growing to the scream of a hive, an entire planet protesting their escape.

"Wait! Wait!" Ttar was yelling. "Where are we going!?"

"Ship!" he managed between breaths. "This way!" His ears rang with the noise, adding to his confusion. Mier, a dead weight over his shoulder, began to wear him down, but he wasn't about to leave her. The ship should be just ahead . . . just around the corner . . .

But the corner loomed over him, the building expanding into a glowing, amorphous shape, occupying the space that had once been a street.

"Hac! Hac! Spaceshit! They're right behind us!"

He risked a glance over his shoulder to see the white shapes of the Torians sailing after them, making no pretense of running or in any way touching the ground. Their speed was unreal.

Lungs burning, he denied what his eyes told him, and continued on where the road had once been. He ignored the electric tingle as he passed through the transparent, undulating walls of the building. Ttar, cursing steadily, followed close behind, reluctant to be left alone in the sensory maelstrom.

And the ship . . . The ship, half-covered with mist, sat where they had left it, the sight spurring them on to even greater speed. The fog rose higher, as if to add its mite of inconvenience. If it continued to rise at this speed, it would soon be over their heads. But the ship was closer every second.

"Take her!" Hac called, shifting Mier into his arms.

"What? No! I can't . . ."

"*Take her!*" Hac transferred the weight and reached in his pocket for a remote key. In obedience to the elec-

tronic signal, a black rectangle slowly spread over the
vessel's side, and a faint crackling through the mist indicated that the grav lift was operational.

Hac once more swung Mier to his shoulder. Freed from
the burden, Ttar darted forward, his only thought to reach
the ship.

"Hurry," he urged, wishing he had the remote control. "Get us out of here!" But Hac already had the lift
in motion, and within seconds they were within the *Corsair*, surrounded by the familiar solid bulkheads. The
hatch closed and locked.

Hac dropped Mier in the bunk, swiftly fastening a web
around her. When he reentered the control room, Ttar
occupied the copilot's seat, staring in desperation at the
controls.

"Is this the mix?"

"Allow me." Hac opened the chambers to each other
and alerted the computer of their intentions. The lift-off
sequence began, the engines of the *Corsair* trembling in
their eagerness to be gone.

Ttar found the controls for the sensors, and the viewscreen came to life.

"Zue!" he intoned. "Look at that!"

Around them the planet continued to dissolve, signs of
it visible even through the darkness. The mountains were
a silhouette in the distance, black against black, their
outline suddenly more harsh, jagged. Trees vanished, replaced by stone spears piercing the fog. The city was
gone. Nothing replaced it. Even the fog diminished, as
if sucked back into the ground. And the ground . . .
Littered with rocks, it looked like ash—barren, sterile,
distinctly inhospitable.

Something flitted across the screen, something diaph-
anous and glowing. Another streamed after it, like
animated fog.

"Shit! The Torians!" Ttar exclaimed. "Let's *go*!"

Hac complied, giving the ship the order. The *Corsair*
shuddered but did not move.

"Now what?" Ttar screamed.

"They're holding us somehow."

"Shit! Damn! No! *Do something!*"

Hac increased thrust and the ship shuddered again . . .

and then broke free, streaking out of control and somewhat unsteadily into the atmosphere.

Ttar sagged back in his seat, eyes closed.

Hac waited until the *Corsair* steadied and it looked as if they were indeed free of Tori before he, too, allowed himself to relax somewhat. Still there was much to do. He ran a belated preflight check before setting the nav computer to do its work. Now all they had to do was get through the Stone Field—again.

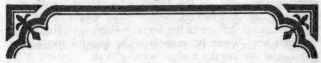

CHAPTER 37

Ttar jerked his head toward the small cabin. "What do we do with her?"

Hac glanced up from his work. "I'll take care of Mier as soon as it's safe to leave the controls."

"It that what happened to us . . . to me?"

"Something similar."

"So the Torian parasite isn't something like a plague, is it? It's some kind of possession, right?"

"I don't know. Would you care to describe your symptoms?"

The redhead went pale.

"I didn't think so. Nor would I. I don't want to think about it at all. But we're going to have to."

"What do you mean 'have to'?"

"There will be an investigation. You do realize that we'll both be questioned about it."

"If there's going to be an investigation, it won't involve me. Which brings up another point: what do you intend to do with me when we get back to Stonewall?"

"The authorities are looking for you. There's the matter of Wes Began's murder to consider."

"Zue! I'm no killer! That was self-defense."

"Can you prove it?"

''No, but . . .''

''Tell it to the authorities.''

''They won't believe me. Look, I could make it worth your while if you could lose me . . .''

Hac directed the computer to run the program he had selected and sat back, turning toward the agent. ''What do you mean by that?''

''The company that hired me is powerful . . . rich . . . generous.'' His lips wore an ingratiating smile below his watchful eyes.

''I'd have to think about it. Think you can fly this ship?''

''Don't know. I thought the nav computer handled everything.''

''It does, but someone still has to keep a eye on it . . . and the screen.''

''What are we looking for?''

''Anything. Everything. The Stone Field's supposed to be impossible to navigate, remember?''

''It's supposed to be a lot of things, but we seem to have made it . . . at least once.''

''And if you remember, you almost didn't make it. We had to come back for you.''

''Yeah. But then I didn't have a nav computer like this one.'' Ttar reached out his hand to caress the gleaming case, but Hac caught his wrist, steely strength in his fingers causing the smaller man to wince.

''The computer's only as good as the program. This one's special. Best leave it alone. Right now it's all that stands between us and certain destruction in those asteroids out there.''

His fingers opened, and Ttar reclaimed his arm, rubbing the red marks on his wrist. ''Didn't mean to interfere.''

Silence fell, amplifying the clicks and chirps from the panels, overlaid on the almost subsonic engine rumble of a busy ship. It was hard to tell what thoughts occupied Ttar's ratlike mind as he stared at the viewscreen. Once again the curtain of interference drew in tight, blinding the sensors. Obedient to instructions from the nav computer, the *Corsair* thrust forward, but while this specialized computer could calculate the position of major fields, it couldn't anticipate the position of each and every asteroid. This job had been left to the drive computer, which depended on the sensors, and the sensors were all but blind. It made for an exciting trip, the ship frantically dodging each obstacle as it came within its limited range.

Hac sat poised over the controls, ready to assist, even though he knew his reflexes weren't nearly as fast as the computer's. If only he really were an android. Which thought brought him to Mier: would she ever forgive him for participating in such a deception? It had been Palo's idea of a perfect cover, and he had agreed at the time, though now he wasn't so sure it was the right decision. Still, it allowed him to go along on the mission.

No, he didn't think she'd ever forget or forgive; she had too many good reasons for insisting on the conditions that Brian had so ruthlessly ignored. And since Brian wasn't available, Hac supposed he would have to bear the brunt of her anger. But not until he gave her the injection. He wondered how she was doing alone, back in the cabin. The web would both protect her from the rough ride and keep her immobilized when she regained consciousness. But, if her symptoms were anything like his had been, her mind would be in turmoil. Which raised yet another question: while he didn't know about himself, Ttar had exhibited signs of paranoia, had been almost hysterical with it, but Mier had been almost calm, speaking in the voice of a Torian.

"I need to know something," he said suddenly.

"Yeah?"

"When . . . when you and Mier decided I had the parasite . . . how did I act? Can you remember?"

"I was still kinda groggy."

"But you were there, in the room?"

"Yeah. I was there. You said you felt sick, and then she started screeching. That's when I started paying attention. Stars but she was mad!"

"I can imagine." And he could. It didn't sound good. "What happened to piss her off like that?"

"Something between us, private."

"I knew there was something like that going on when you didn't want to leave her. And the way you used to watch her."

Let him think what he wants, Hac decided. "But when she took sick, it wasn't anything like that, was it?"

"I dunno. I did think it was kinda strange the way she was talking. But how do I know? Maybe she really was possessed by one of the Torians. I know that's how I felt, like something was trying to get into my mind. And this is something I still don't want to talk about. How much longer till we're out of the Field?"

"It's a total of twenty-two hours."

"Zue! If you don't need me right now, I'd like to get something to eat and maybe some sleep."

"All right."

"What about you? Want me to bring you something from the chef?"

Hac shook his head. "I'll eat later. But you could check on Mier for me."

"Sure."

His attention divided between the control panel and the screen, Hac didn't notice how long Ttar was gone. When he turned around, Mier stood in the hatchway, a very efficient-looking dart gun in her hand.

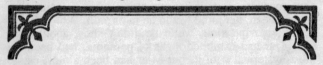

CHAPTER 38

Ttar cursed as he rubbed his sore head, pushing himself up from the floor where he'd landed when Mier slugged him. Who would have suspected a woman to hit so hard! Especially a sick one! By the black hole of Delta Arani, this whole thing was a mess!

"You will turn the ship around," Mier said, her voice coming from the control room.

"I can't," Hac replied gently. "Think, Mier. You know why that's impossible."

That's it, friend, you tell her, Ttar thought, walking softly to the doorway. Ain't nothing going to get me back to that planet-size hell! Mier's back was to him, but he could see she held some kind of a weapon leveled at her partner. Now where did she get that? Damned woman was trickier than a Caspard monkoid.

He looked around for something to use against her, and his eyes lit on the discarded web. Last time I do a favor for anyone, he promised himself. He picked up the web, holding it in both outstretched hands. If he could get her tangled in it . . .

He cast the net and jumped after it, hoping the weapon wouldn't go off, hoping Hac wasn't standing in the line of fire. Mier screamed, rolling as she hit the floor, and Ttar discovered he had caught more than he anticipated.

"Shit! Help me!" he yelled.

But Hac was there, wrenching the dart gun away and hanging on to Mier's arms. Ttar had the legs even though they threatened to come free and send him flying any second.

The larger man took over, pulling Mier to her feet and almost flinging her into a seat. The web followed, and he jerked it tight around her.

"What in hell happened? I asked you to check on her!" he blazed.

"I did," Ttar replied. "She was awake. Said she couldn't breathe and would I fix the net so she could sit up. How was I to know she was planning something? Zue, but she whacked me a good one! My head'll be ringing for a week."

"You deserve it! Where's the hypo?"

"Hypo?"

"I gave it to you on Tori."

"I must have dropped it."

"You what?"

"It's lost. Hey, don't blame me! I can't think of every-thing."

"You can't think of anything, it would seem. Damn." Hac drew a breath, trying to control his anger, trying to think. "I can make more of the serum, but not now and not here. Get the med chest. It's in the storage locker."

Ttar went, glad to be out of the way even for an in-stant.

"What are you going to do?" Mier asked, still panting

from her exertions. Her voice, Hac noted, still had the eerie overtones.

"Give you a sedative. Don't worry; no one's going to hurt you."

"But there are things you could do to this envelope that would kill me. It has knowledge of such a substance."

"What are you talking about? What envelope?"

"This one. This being you name Mier."

Shocked, he sat down on his heels to be at eye level. "You're not Mier?"

"What's she trying to get you to do now?" Ttar asked, coming back. "Whatever it is, don't listen. She's tricky." He steadied himself with one hand against the ship's roll; a blue box was held in the other. He set it down and rummaged through the contents. "I don't know what the—ah, here it is."

He gave the multipurpose hypo to Hac, who dialed up past the mild soother to a stronger dose. It might be risky to use it, but they'd all be dead if he had to spend too much time away from the controls. "I don't know who or what you are, and I don't have time to find out. This," he punctuated his words by giving her the injection, "will keep you out of trouble for now."

"But you do not understand!"

Desperation spoke not only from her words, but every line of her body, but Hac steeled himself. He couldn't spare time for feelings right now, not hers or his own. "Later. Watch her," he instructed Ttar. "And remember what happened before; don't believe anything she has to say."

"Hey! You don't have to tell me. I've learned my lesson."

Hac returned to the control panel as Ttar settled himself in a seat. Mier—or whoever she was now—slumped within the web, eyes almost closed, but watchful still.

Ttar fidgeted. His body wanted food and other comforts. He glanced at Hac's broad back. Necessity, he realized, made strange partners. His enemy sat, vulnerable, for once, and he couldn't do a damned thing about it. Life was full of frustrations, and this job was turning out to have more than its share. He'd better be well compensated at the end! And he would be. Ttar Quinn might not be on top of the situation at the moment, but he would be . . . he would be soon. He'd have a chance sometime before they got back to Stonewall, and he was ready to take advantage of it.

"I can help you get what you want," Mier said sleepily.

"You're in no position to help anyone," he retorted. "And don't think you can trick me again. You can't."

"I know that now. I know what you're thinking."

"Hah!"

"It is true. This envelope has interesting capabilities. Not all have been fully realized, but they are there nonetheless."

Ttar's interest piqued, despite his apprehension. "What are you?"

"You know that. I am of Tori. I am Tori."

"You're a Torian, and you have taken over the body of Mier?"

"Such a definition is not precise, but if it satisfies you, it will suffice."

"And you say you can help me?"

"I can read the thoughts of this envelope . . ."

"Mier."

"If you will: Mier. These thoughts inform me that you seek a mineral called tridenite which is common to my home world."

"And?"

"I can enable you to obtain that mineral."

Hope, sudden and intense, flared in Ttar's mind. If he could only believe that this creature possessing Mier told the truth. "Why would you do such a thing?"

"A very simple reason: I wish to live. This env—Mier," it corrected itself quickly, "believes that you, or the other called Hac, will kill me as soon as you reach a place called Stonewall."

"And you think I'll save you?"

"You could do this if you wished. And in return I will enable you and your employers to obtain this tridenite."

Ttar glanced at Hac's back once again; the man was intent on the viewscreen. Still, he might be listening. "I don't believe you."

"But . . ."

"No. Shut up." He jerked his head toward the pilot's back and shook his head.

Then he closed his eyes, trying to figure ways to take advantage of this new development. His employers weren't going to be content until they had a treaty with the natives on Tori, and now he had the means to give it to them—more than one means! He had lied; the rest of the ampules, the serum that Hac had synthesized back in the ruined lab, rested in his pocket. It represented a way to deal with the parasite, or whatever it was that afflicted humans on Tori. Although he didn't intend to go back to that hell-planet himself—no chance of that, no chance at all! Someone else would, though, and they'd pay dearly for what he had to sell them. Plus the nav program to get them through the Field, if and when he got the ship away from Hac. And there was Mier, and her "guest." That might prove to be worth more than all the rest.

By the twin suns of Greater Orion! When this job was over, he was going to retire a very, very rich man. Ttar gave himself over to these gratifying thoughts, unaware that Mier watched him and smiled.

CHAPTER 39

Everyone but Mier felt grateful when the *Corsair* finally left the fringes of the Stone Field behind and reentered normal space, flying much more smoothly. Leaving the ship to the nav computer, Hac stretched his arms above his head until his shoulders cracked. Weariness rode him like a heavy weight, but he couldn't afford to relax—the tricky parts of the mission weren't over yet. He unsnapped the seat's restraints and rose to his feet.

"How's our patient?" he asked Ttar, who dozed on his seat.

"Huh? What?" Red-rimmed eyes regarded him, then opened wide as they discovered the small stunner in the tall man's hand. "What's this all about?"

"We're out of the Field. By past agreement, all treaties are now null and void."

"You've got to be kidding. I'm no threat to you, Captain!"

"I'm precisely aware of the manner and degree of threat you represent. On your feet."

"What are you going to do to me?"

"Nothing drastic. Into the cabin. You'll be perfectly comfortable in there until the authorities come for you."

"Hey! I thought we had an agreement."

"I wasn't aware of it. Now, do you go willingly, or do I have to use force?"

"No, I'll go. I'll go." He cast a hopeful glance at Mier as he went past, but her eyes were closed and she appeared to be asleep. "I could make it worth your while to let me go," he tried one last time. "I had quite a little chat with your girlfriend . . ."

But Hac wasn't interested. "I heard it. And you'd be a bigger fool than I think you are if you believed anything that it said."

"Are you kidding? Great stars, Captain! She could give us the whole planet. Think of it, a monopoly on tridenite! We'd be rich!"

"I'm already rich. Besides, there's no tridenite on Tori."

"What are you saying? How could you know?"

"I'm a geologist. And I read the lab records." Hac shook his head, losing patience at Ttar's folly. "Just about everything on Tori was a projection. Do you understand what I'm saying? There is no tridenite. The city, the natives—hell, probably even the atmosphere—was created specifically for us. Do you remember what we saw just before we took off? That was the real planet. That blasted rock was the real Tori."

Ttar went pale, visions of untold wealth fleeing from his mind. But then he understood: Hac was trying to trick him. He would do anything to keep Tori for himself.

"Enough. Into the cabin."

The redheaded man went slowly. This was just another

complication. But he would find a solution. He wasn't beaten yet.

Hac locked the door on him, and, having satisfied himself that Mier was still secure, stretched out in his seat in front of the control panel, and went to sleep. A buzzer woke him five hours later. Stonewall lay dead ahead.

The *Corsair*, identified to the satisfaction of the port authority, landed under remote control. While this happened, Hac tried to reach London.

"I'm sorry," a disembodied and patently disinterested female voice told him. "There is no listing for anyone with that name."

"Then give me the local Federation representative."

"Stonewall does not have a Federation rep. But," she added when he was about to give vent to his frustration, "we do have a representative from the Terran Ruling Houses."

"That will do. Please connect me."

"One moment, please."

Two receptionists, one rude secretary, and a lower-level bureaucrat later, he spoke to someone who refused to admit he belonged to SIA and insisted on a visual connection with his caller. Hac sighed and keyed the sequence.

"Very well," the man's voice said then. Though he could see Hac, he didn't return the courtesy of projecting his own image. "We'll be in touch."

Static indicated that the connection had been terminated. Hac growled. The bastard didn't even give him a chance to speak.

By then the *Corsair* had been locked onto an elevator and lowered into the port. Hac shut down everything but the automatic systems and went to check Mier. The last sedative he'd given her would remain in effect another couple of hours. Even though, he realized by now, the drug didn't affect the Torian parasite, it did immobilize the host body. Even without the web—which he checked again—Mier wouldn't be going anywhere.

Ttar answered his knock and query with a curse. It didn't bother Hac. Ttar could be as angry as he pleased, but he was still a prisoner.

The ship lurched once and then settled, ventilation fans

humming audibly in the silence left by the lack of engine rumble. Hac made one last check of the control board before he stepped to the hatch. Locking the *Corsair* behind him, he set out, determined to find help on his own, since SIA seemed disinterested. A checklist ran through his mind: first of all he needed a lab to synthesize some more of the serum for Mier. Second, while she was recovering, he would turn Ttar over to the authorities. Third . . . Third never received consideration.

"Mr. Andrews?" a familiar voice called over the sound of a motor. The same man who had given them a ride to the ship appeared, driving what appeared to be the same tractor. "Hop in. They're waiting for you." He held out his hand, flashing an SIA ident tattoo at him, before he shoved the machine into gear.

CHAPTER 40

"Please go over it one more time, Mr. Cary," the gray-haired man asked, his quiet voice backed with the certainty that he would be obeyed.

"You've already heard it twice!" Hac replied harshly, reaching the end of both endurance and patience. He had been sitting without a break in a small, bare room for the past three hours, answering the same questions over and over again. "If you'll excuse me, I'm leaving now. I have better things to do with my time." He pushed himself up from the hard chair, ignoring the steely stares from the two men on either side of the door. If he had to, he would go through them . . . or certainly try.

"That's enough, Beta," Brian Palo's voice said, projected eerily from a hidden speaker as if from out of the air. "I'll take over now. Bring him up to the suite."

"Brian?" Hac called. "What in hell's going on?"

"I'll explain when you get here. I just arrived, or your

little question-and-answer session wouldn't have gone on so long."

Hac heaved a sigh of exasperated weariness and followed his erstwhile interrogator through the halls and up a lift. He and Brian had been close friends in school, and had kept in touch afterward, despite the inconvenience of distance and time. But friendship was only one of the reasons why Hac had been allowed to involve himself in an SIA mission. The other, even more persuasive reason was that he worked as head of security for the Gemsbuck mines, a company owned and operated by his family for the past nine generations.

Brian greeted him with his customary grin and a friendly clap on the shoulder before escorting him to a comfortable chair. "How'd it go?"

Hac remained standing. "Terrible. Look, Brian, there's no time to waste. I have to get help for Mier. And then there's Ttar."

"Don't worry. We'll take care of everything. Your part's finished. You can relax now."

"It isn't finished. I'm the only one who knows the formula for the serum."

"I know that. And you can give it to us later."

"Later? Brian, you don't understand . . ."

"But I do! Come on, sit down and relax. How about a drink? You look like you could use one." He moved toward the wall dispenser.

Hac stared. He didn't remember his friend as being so insensitive. Mier was back on the *Corsair* dying, for all anyone knew, her mind negated by the Torian parasite. And Brian wanted him to relax and have a drink? No, this wasn't right. Something, some nasty undercurrent was at work here.

"By the way," his friend was saying over his shoulder as he punched up two beers, "we'll need the ship's key."

"Brian, are you going to do anything for Mier?"

"Of course! But you should understand there is more at stake here than just one agent's life. Here, take one."

Hac set his untasted glass on a table. "More at stake? You mean the Torian parasite?"

"Hac! Would you please sit down. Word's come down from the Families. They want Silver to continue to act as

host for the Torian until we can talk to it, find out what's
going on. It's a unique opportunity."

" 'A unique opportunity,' " Hac repeated, his tone
deceptively bland. "You're willing to risk Mier's life just
so someone can have a chat with an alien?"

"She'll be very well taken care of. You don't imagine
we'd do anything to hurt her, do you? The medics have
been briefed and they're preparing a complete life-support
unit even as we speak. She will be attended by the best
physicians and monitored round the clock. Things
couldn't have worked out better."

"I don't think Mier feels that way."

"She's a professional, contracted to SIA. If she had a
say in matters, I'm sure she'd agree. Look at it from our
point of view. You were sent to get the truth about Tori,
and you succeeded far beyond our expectations. You actually managed to bring one of the natives back with
you."

"In Mier Silver's body."

"And it's a great body. Just between you and me, I
couldn't imagine a better place to be."

"Cut it out!" Hac yelled. "You're talking about Mier!
Someone you worked with—someone who has risked her
life time and time again for you and your department!"

"And I appreciate that. But is what she's doing now
any different?"

"Hosting an alien parasite? You consider that part of
her job? You saw what happened to Jarry, and the other
man . . . Woburn? They died! They died, stripped of
their identity, their personality . . . Good gods, Brian!
How could you ask that of anyone?"

"This time it's different. This time the alien's trying
to communicate with us. Don't you understand? That's
why Mier's perfect. Her altered genes have made all this
possible. There isn't anyone else in the universe who
could do this for us. We can't risk losing a chance to
make a connection, find out what the Torians want. Just
think, we can get our treaty after all. We'll have access
to the tridenite, and Gemsbuck will mine it for us! Hac,
this is the opportunity of a lifetime."

"Not for her. If you know this much, then you know
I've had a firsthand taste of what it's like to host a Torian

parasite. In all humanity, you can't ask that of her or of anyone. And there's no reason for it—there is no tridenite on Tori! What do I have to do to get you to believe me?''

Brian dismissed this with a wave of his hand. ''You can't know that for sure. We need to go in and make an extensive survey. A treaty will give us that opportunity. Damn it, Hac, what's gotten into you? I thought this new source of ore was important. You risked your life to get it, and now you want to throw it away.''

''I have a right to risk my life, but not the right to risk someone else's. And especially not Mier's.''

Brian cocked his head, looking down his nose at his old friend, the grin still in place. ''She got to you, eh? She always seemed a little cold to me, more of a challenge than anything else. I prefer a more willing armful, but if it's the silver princess that turns you on . . .''

Hac hit him, fist connecting with his jaw, propelling him backward over the sofa, beer and glass flying. A guard from outside the door tried to stop him, but Hac wasn't in the mood to be subtle. The heel of his hand and a kick sent the man spinning into a corner, and then he was into the lift. A rooftop ramp connected to the spaceport, a drop down a utility grav shaft brought him to the right level, and a fast walk to the base of the *Corsair*. Strangely, no one was in sight, no guards, nothing. Maybe the SIA hadn't dispatched them yet.

Hac never hesitated, but used the remote key to get into the ship. He started cursing softly when he saw the damage. The hinges had been blown off the cabin door, and both Ttar and Mier were gone.

CHAPTER 41

"We're sorry," the computerized voice announced, "but no one at this number is available right now. If you will . . ."

"Damn," Hac breathed.

". . . call you back as soon as possible." A chime sounded and silence waited to be filled with a message.

"This is Hac Cary. I need a priority link with the home office, and I need it immediately. Tell them to call out the troops; there's major trouble, and I need help. I'll be moving around, so you won't be able to reach me, but, since there's supposed to be someone monitoring this line constantly, I'd better be able to speak to a human when I call back! End of message."

The computer came back on the line. "Your message will be referred to the proper office for processing. Thank you for calling Gemsbuck Mining."

So much for family support! Now he'd have to try to do it alone, whatever "it" turned out to be. Hac had no ideas, and concern for Mier began to make him frantic.

The Nightside Palace stayed open for business twenty-

one hours a day. Hac sat at the bar, the blackness of his
mind welcoming the dark interior. But the twisting of his
gut found no solace in the Crystal Clear he drank. Neither drunk nor sober, he sat, watching, waiting . . . for
what he didn't know, but London had been here once and
might be again. And the woman in the purple tunic who
had worked with Ttar might also show up. The chances
of any of this happening were slim to the point of impossible, but just now he had no other options.

"Again?" the bartender asked, noticing the empty
glass.

Hac nodded, and then took the refilled drink across
the dance floor to where the woman in purple had just
seated herself, alone.

She looked up, startled, as he sat down opposite her.
"Sorry, friend, but this is a private table."

"Good. My business with you is private, so it should
be all right for me to sit here."

"Who are you?"

"It doesn't matter. We have a mutual friend."

She took in his stained and wrinkled jumpsuit with a
look of disdain. "Unlikely."

"Sorry if I'm not dressed for the occasion, but I assure
you, we do have important business to discuss."

"Important to you, maybe, but not to me. I could care
less what you're into. So now, I suggest you leave before
I—" And then she saw the stunner pointed at her over
the edge of the table.

"Willingly or otherwise, you are going to help me. If
you do, you'll be well compensated. If you resist, I'll
hurt you. Make a decision, and make it fast."

Something in his eyes let her know he was serious,
and yet, despite her inner qualms, she managed a show
of bravado. "What's in it for me?"

"Name your price." Which could have been considered an unwise statement, for it let her know how important it was to him.

"What do I have to do?"

"Find someone for me."

"That's all? Easy. A thousand credits, and I'll do what
I can."

"Two thousand if you succeed."

"Two . . ." Her eyes widened and then she smiled. "Done. Put the gun away."

"If you insist, but it can be back in a second. I want to find someone named Ttar."

"Don't know him."

"Short. Redheaded. You were with him here seven days ago."

"What do you want with him? You with the authorities?"

"No. Quit stalling. I thought you agreed to help me."

"He's at the spaceport. A ship called the *Stellar Drake*. I spoke to him less than an hour ago. Where's my money?"

"Take me there. You'll get it then."

"Half now."

"All or nothing. Take me to him."

"You're a real bastard, you know that? All right. Let's go."

A scooter took them to the port and up seven levels before she stopped. "You'll need a pass to get inside. Have you thought of that?"

"Don't worry about it. Where's the *Drake*?"

"Right in front of you."

The Consortium's logo decorated the yacht's side, under the name and registration number. A robot-controlled grav train brought provisions to an access hatch, while two uniformed guards watched, rifles in hand.

"Ttar's on board. Now do I get paid?"

"I'll take your word for it. And, yes, you get paid." Hac spoke into the message chip she grumblingly provided, stating the amount and a voiceprint authorization for the credit transfer.

"Good luck," she said before the scooter rose on its lifters and took her back down to the street.

"Yeah, good luck," he muttered, walking back down one flight. He'd spotted a busy workshop on the way up, indicating the maintenance level. He needed a reason for being at the port, and techs were rarely questioned. Judging from the activity, the *Drake* wouldn't be going anywhere for at least a couple of hours, enough time for an inventive mind to find something to use as a disguise.

Back on the flight deck, with all the preflight activity,

the guards didn't question another tech in a rumpled jumpsuit complete with a pass and a well-worn tool kit. Hac wormed his way into the access hatch between a case of Terran wine and a freezer of Orlan humpsteaks. He removed his stunner from the kit before making his way to the passenger section. The yacht was spacious and luxuriously appointed, a marked contrast to the battered *Corsair*, but he didn't notice the furnishing as he carefully checked the storage and then the staterooms.

The lock on the second one yielded to the keypunch thoughtfully provided among the stolen tools. Behind the door Ttar lay, stunned or dead, he didn't care; all his attention focused on Mier, prone on the bunk, a tragically familiar, blank stare on her face.

"Mier?" he whispered, kneeling beside her and taking her slack hand. He had no way of knowing what nightmares filled her mind, or the extent of the damage from leaving the parasite with her for so long. He cursed himself for being so careless as to leave the hypo and serum back on Tori. If it was too late to save her, it would be no one's fault but his own. The thought, and accompanying grief, surprised him in its intensity.

A groan from Ttar halted the self-recrimination and brought him back to the necessities of the present. Stunner in one hand, he used the other to slap the man to startled wakefulness.

"Zue!" Ttar pushed himself to a sitting position, blinking rapidly as he cleared his sight. "Hac? Am I glad to see you."

"Not for long, my friend. You have a lot to answer for."

"No! You have it all wrong." Ttar protested. "Look. I can't explain now. It's too dangerous. We have to get out of here."

"Not before I have some answers. You were working for the Consortium all along."

"Great blazing comets, man, of course I was. But they tricked me. They had no intention of paying me. I've been betrayed."

"Now you know what it feels like. What did they do to Mier?"

"Nothing. But they're taking her back to Tori."

"Back? Why?"

"To make her deal with the Torians, of course. They want the tridenite."

"But there isn't any tridenite. How many times do I have to say it?"

"Right now I don't care whether there is or not. They insist that I go along, but they took the ampules away from me. That's the worst part."

"What ampules? The ones I made?"

"Yeah. The serum."

"You had it all the time?" Rage blazed in Hac's blue eyes and the smaller man cowered.

"But they didn't get all of it!" he stammered. "They didn't get the hypo! Look!" He produced the device from a pocket down by his shipboot.

Hac snatched it up and checked the ampule; a green one, the first dose of the series, the one that would kill the parasite. And it was intact. He didn't know what it would do to Mier without the second shot, but he wasn't about to risk losing this chance to save her, no matter now slim it might be. Ttar forgotten, Hac went to her side and pressed the nozzle against her shoulder. As the hypo hissed, her eyes widened in shock, and she screamed. The sound cut off abruptly as his hand covered her mouth. A second later she went limp. He caught her, easing her down on the bed.

But the brief sound had been enough to betray them. Footsteps pounded down the corridor, and the door slammed open, admitting rifles, guards, two suited men, and a very familiar figure, following more slowly.

"Good afternoon, Hac," the Professor said pleasantly.

CHAPTER 42

"A man named Balzac once wrote that 'bureaucracy is a giant mechanism operated by pigmies,' " the Professor told them, his manner, despite the situation, completely relaxed, smug, and thoroughly pompous. "The government is amazingly easy to fool if you have intestinal fortitude. I doubt you've heard of Balzac, but then, the standards of education have dropped steadily in the past years. Which, *pro tanto*, is interesting, but aside from the point." He smiled, enjoying himself hugely.

Success within reach, nothing could stop him now that the last member of the mission was in his hands. And by an act of fortune, too, proving the gods did indeed smile. He felt witty, warm, wise . . . even loving toward those who had provided him with such opportunity. They deserved an explanation, to be allowed to appreciate the genius confronting them.

"The bureaucratic machinery that we call the Federation is a bloated monster, a Gargantua feeding on the populace it supposedly regulates. And that size is its weakness." There was no change in the bland stares confronting him. "Are you with me so far?" No one replied, and he suspected they still didn't understand. "I realized early in my association with the department that one office is usually completely ignorant of what the other is doing. Because of this I was able to operate openly, even in the midst of the Special Intelligence Agency, a section whose modus operandi is raging paranoia. And this, my children, even you should appreciate, took considerable skill, as well as precise timing. On the whole, it was a *coup de maitre*!"

Leaning against the wall, Ttar listened, his eyes never wavering from the guns. Having already experienced the Professor's perfidy, he wasn't about to be impressed. Words were words, and couldn't hurt him. Firepower, now that was something else.

Hac stood protectively in front of Mier, aware that he was in the presence of a mad genius and wondering what tri-vee drama he'd wandered out of. "Why did you do it?" he asked.

"Mine was the most obvious of reasons, my ignorant one: credit! I was about to retire on a government pension. Do you know what that means?" He laughed, the grating sound of derision filling the cabin. "It means enough, or barely enough, to live on for the rest of my life. Plus an assignment to a squalid, little apartment set in the bowels of one of the megacities, where I could idle away my hours with other Golden Citizens, waiting to die. Was this worthy of me, a future *infra dignitatem*? The Professor? The man who virtually made the SIA?" His face, tinged with an angry red flush, scowled, and then smiled again. "When I realized the Consortium was making overtures to a couple of the agents, I saw my chance for a better future. So I took it. And I have no regrets. None, whatsoever."

"Are you trying to convince me? Or yourself?" Hac demanded.

"Like all the others, you have no appreciation of excellence. But then, what can one expect from a machine?"

What indeed. They had no conception, no wit to understand what he had achieved. The realization depressed him, grating on overwrought nerves. These were commoners, not worth his effort. The blue eyes narrowed, and his words snapped out, the subject changed as abruptly as his manner. "What have you done to Mier?"

Hac glanced down and realized the Professor hadn't seen the hypo hidden by her body. "She was being difficult. I had to put her out." His eyes met Ttar's, willing the smaller man to silence.

"Out? What did you do?"

"I hit her."

"For nothing more than an overly dressed-up robot, you are proving to be extremely tiresome. Oh, yes," he added for the benefit of Ttar, who started, looking from one man to the other, confusion obvious from his face. "Didn't you know that your companion was nothing more than a glorified machine? A robot, mannequin, homunculus? You admired him, perhaps? He is something to admire: tall, well featured, capable, and even, at times, quick of wit. So he fooled you, who spent so much time with him! My dear friend, meet H.A.C., a Human Analog Computer."

"You're a computer? You're not real?" the redheaded agent stammered.

"As the Professor says." Once again his eyes flashed a warning.

"But you . . . back on Tori. The parasite!"

"I faked the whole thing," Hac interrupted quickly. "For Mier's benefit."

A commotion in the corridor signaled the arrival of a uniformed crewman, who handed something to the Professor. "Thank you." He returned his attention to his prisoners. "But *satis verborum*, though I'm sorry to end this pleasurable intercourse, time grows short. Hac, it has been interesting knowing you. After major alterations in your programming, you may once again prove your worth, although not to the same master. Or mistress." He aimed a small device.

"What's that?" Hac tensed, though at this point there was no place for him to go.

"A universal control . . . of a sort. A very clever young man was obliging enough to find it for me. It will turn you off, Hac. And when you awake, it will be with a new personality and a new purpose."

"You don't know what you're going to be up against on Tori—I could help . . ."

"I'm sure you could, but, as you are, I very much doubt you would override your programming enough to switch loyalties. No, this way is best."

He depressed a stud and the device sent out a beam of ruby-colored light. A laser, Hac realized, although there was no pain, no sensation at all. He obediently closed his eyes and collapsed, hoping this was the correct response.

"It is a pity," the Professor intoned, turning away.

"What about him?" one of the guards asked, gesturing toward Ttar with his rifle barrel.

"No. We will need him when we get to the planet." He gazed around the cabin. "I don't imagine he can get into any trouble in here. Lock them up."

"And the android?"

"He isn't going anywhere." The Professor turned away.

The last guard backed out and swung the door closed. The sound of the lock put a period to the episode.

Ttar let his breath out in relief. The madman was gone and he was still alive. That was something to be glad about. And if the android . . . He looked down at Hac's prone form and saw the eyes come open.

Ttar gasped and took a hasty step backward. "But you're—"

His words broke off as Hac shook his head and whispered, "We can't assume the cabin isn't being monitored. I don't see anything. What about you?"

"No visual. But there's a mike in the light above the bed."

"Bath?"

"Nothing."

"Good. We'll talk in there." Hac pushed himself to his feet and made for the narrow door.

"So you're not an android? Or are you? What's this all about?"

"I'm not."

"So why did the professor think—"

"It's a long story. Only one person at the agency knew the truth. He had his suspicions, and they were obviously right."

"Did she know you were . . . I mean that you weren't . . ." He got tangled in words.

"Mier didn't know the truth, until I caught the parasite."

"No wonder she was so mad."

"Yes." Hac's lips thinned to a line at the reminder. But right now he had other things to worry about. "How big is the ship?"

"Don't know exactly. It's one of the largest atmospherics, but I'm not familiar with the specifications. Why?"

"We have to find where they've stashed the rest of the serum."

Ttar had a sudden suspicion, and knew his were different priorities. "What for?"

"We're not leaving without Mier."

"Again?" He rolled his brown eyes in exasperation. "This is Tori all over!"

"Then you know it will be useless to argue with me. Do you have any suggestions of where we should start looking?"

"Are you crazy? We have to get out of here. We can't risk searching for the serum."

Hac didn't bother to answer.

Ttar sighed. "All right. It's in a box in the Professor's cabin. What's left of it, that is. He sent samples off to be analyzed."

"Do you know which cabin?"

"Yeah." He jerked his head. "Up one level. Maybe over one. But you can't get to it. The corridors are full of guards."

"Damn." Hac gazed at the overhead, deep in thought. "Do you have any idea when they plan to leave for Tori?"

"Not until morning. They're waiting for some big geologist from the main office."

"Morning? Why wait so long? Isn't that risky?"

"The Professor was as mad as a new nova, but stars, you don't know what the Consortium is like. When they say wait, you wait."

"You work for them long?"

"Little jobs, on and off for the past couple years. But no more. No one gets a chance to double-cross Ttar Quinn more than once."

Hac watched the smaller man, weighing his words. "I gather from what you've said that they didn't live up to their promises to you?"

Ttar gave a snort of disgust. "To put it simply, yes. They wouldn't pay me. After all I've been through. And then the Professor insists—insists that I return to Tori with them. He's got to be crazy."

"I think he is. And not just a babbling fool, either. The man's dangerous. I wonder if the Consortium is aware of his aberrant behavior."

"That's why the ship has to wait for the geologist. I got the feeling they were sending a couple of big-time troubleshooters as well."

"All right. There's a lot I need to know from you, but we don't have the time. I have to get help."

"Armed help. Like the authorities. Or the Feds. That's who you work for, isn't it?"

"Not me. Mier."

"Oh." He digested this. "You aren't going to try to

make me believe you came along to Tori just for the fun of it. I mean, it wasn't exactly a pleasure trip."

"No, it wasn't. I work for Geo-Mining."

"Why not call in the Feds?"

"I may. First I have to get off the ship. You'll stay with Mier until I get back?"

"Are you sure you don't want me to come with you?"

"I'm pretty sure I can get out alone, but two of us will never make it. I have to trust you. You'll stay with her?"

"As long as they let me—and I hope that isn't all the way back to Tori. I have a feeling it's going to be a one-way trip for both of us this time."

"I'll be back long before the ship leaves. That much I can promise."

CHAPTER 43

Boredom with his post slowed the guard in the corridor enough that Hac was able to take him out with a minimum of fuss.

"They'll look for him eventually," Ttar warned, helping drag the unconscious body into the cabin. He used the man's own cuffs to secure his hands, and then gagged him with a towel.

"I hope to be back before then."

"Promises are easier to make than keep." Ttar straightened up from the prisoner. "Just don't stop for lunch on the way."

Hac nodded and, after one last look at Mier, set off in the direction of the access hatch. This time it was fastened shut, and he silently cursed the wasted time while he worked the lock. He had to be fast—as soon as the door came open, he knew it would register on the bridge monitor. Well, that couldn't be helped.

The guards outside were another matter. "What are

you doing there?'' an authoritative voice asked as he dropped to the 'crete beside the ship. Two flex rifles, held by determined-looking men, aimed at the largest part of him.

"Came to fix the warp dubber. Who locked me in?" Hac replied, trying to look properly indignant.

"Where's your work order?"

"Work order? Musta left it inside. You don't want me to go back an' get it, cause I can't. Gotta get back. Got another job waiting. We're busy."

"Bren," one of the riflemen called to someone on the other side of the ship.

"Yo?" A slender blond woman dressed in the Consortium uniform jogged into sight.

"Caught this guy climbing out the aft cargo hatch. Says he was working on the warp dubber."

"I saw him go in earlier. I think he's okay."

Hac mentally blessed the woman's generosity, as well as her laxity.

"I should let him go?" the first guard insisted.

"Yeah. We got better things to do than harass the techs. Let him go."

"Don't forget your work order next time." An ungentle shove sent Hac on his way, while underscoring the guard's displeasure.

He moved as quickly as possible without running, the tool kit bouncing against his leg.

"Hey! Stop him!" shouted a new voice, the words having the opposite effect on the fleeing figure.

Hac sprinted toward the big doorway, sky and open air beckoning. His chance for freedom was seconds away.

"Halt! Or I'll fire!"

A sharp slap on Hac's arm, and then something like a burning needle pierced his side, the force of it slamming him into a pile of cargo cubes. He dropped to the plasticrete, but quickly pushed up to his knees, searching for cover. A large number of shipping crates were piled beside him, and pushing breathlessly from knees to feet, he staggered into their sheltered maze. Staccato footsteps marked pursuit and drove him onward, although the warm wet trail down his side reminded him that he wouldn't last very much longer. Fortunately the pain hadn't had time to penetrate the mixture of desperation and adrenaline that kept him moving.

"Here!" came a hiss from up ahead.

Hac blinked sweat from his eyes and spotted a blue-suited tech just beyond the last of the crates. Vaguely he remembered the woman who had driven the tractor so long ago. Was she another one of London's agents?

"This way. Hurry!" She beckoned, and he moved.

She lifted the cover from a maintenance well and motioned him inside, following and dogging the hatch. A tight fit, they crouched, knee to knee, gazing up through the grid.

Footsteps pounded as shadows moved swiftly overhead, and then were gone.

"You hurt bad?" she whispered in his ear.

"Don't know. Didn't have time to check."

"Hope you didn't bleed all over everything up there. All we need is a trail. I'm Kaya, by the way. SIA. But you knew that."

"I guessed. Yes."

She nodded, the motion more felt than visible in the dim light. "Come on, let's get out of here."

Her handlight guided them through a dark, claustrophobic tunnel. They moved straight for a number of yards before coming to a shaft, rungs leading both up and down.

"Hope you can climb. I've got a car, but you'll have to get to it on your own."

He flexed the fingers of his left arm. The skin was torn and frame slightly bent, but the fingers still moved. "I can climb." And he did.

Breathing was about all he could manage as he followed the flashing blue-clad legs. Thankfully the car wasn't far, and he leaned heavily against its side as she unlocked the door. "Where are you taking me?"

"To London."

"What if I suggest an alternate destination?"

She looked at him askance. "You're in no position to argue. You need help. London can get it for you."

"So can a lot of other people." He carefully slid into the two-seater, while Kaya activated the dash and punched in their destination. "Can I call out from this thing?"

The car lurched into motion as she shook her head. "It isn't shielded. How's your side?"

"I don't want to think about it."

She leaned over, but didn't touch. "Looks like they used a slug. Nasty. You're lucky they didn't aim better."

"I don't think they wanted to kill me," he managed, beginning to feel very sick.

"Couldn't prove it by this. Hold your arm against it. It might slow the bleeding."

"Good idea," he replied faintly, already too weak to follow the suggestion.

"London will take care of it when we get to base."

Eyes closed, he rested his head on the back of the seat. He didn't see the car pull into a parking garage, nor did he open his eyes until hands tried to lift him from the seat. "I can walk," he protested, trying to focus. Blurred faces became silhouettes, and silhouettes fuzzy shapes. His fingers rested desperately on the shoulders supporting him on either side.

"Then walk," London retorted. "You're no light weight."

With Kaya's help she guided his staggering steps into an elevator. Somehow enduring those nauseating moments, he was grateful when they finally stopped, and he was pressed down onto something soft. A bed?

Hands pulled at his suit, hurting him, but he didn't have the strength to protest. He felt tired and wanted to sleep . . . if only they'd leave him alone and go away. But the voices continued, following his consciousness down the long echoing shaft of incredible weariness, holding captive a fragment of his awareness.

"Set it down right here," said London. "And you'd better get back. Who's watching the ship?"

"Mici."

"I want to know the minute they file a flight plan. Make sure someone's monitoring port control at all times."

Retreating sounds as Kaya went away, and then a slither of cloth and clink of instruments as London worked. Careful hands cleaned his side and sprayed a cool foam over the wound. The pain instantly fled, though it took his clenched muscles much longer to register the fact. A round disk pressed into his neck, a click and a hiss signaling an injection. Slowly the darkness retreated, pushed back by returning strength as the stimulants did their job.

"All right, Mr. Hac," she told him. "In a minute we can talk."

His eyes opened, focused to a bluish-white haze of ceiling surrounding London's face.

The face smiled, wry, encouraging. "Feel better?"

"Much," he managed through dry lips. "Thank you."

"Thank the people who put my first aid kit together. Now why don't you tell me what's going on? Who shot you? And what were you doing on the *Stellar Drake*?"

"Since you're watching the ship, I would assume you know."

"We receive orders, but not always explanations. I had no idea you were involved. Where's your partner? Where's Mier?"

"Still on board." But he kept the details to himself. When Brian refused to help Mier, both he and the SIA forfeited any future claim to Hac's services or loyalty. Which was why he needed to reach someone from Geo-Mining. He knew he couldn't take the ship on his own. "I need to make a call."

"It can wait. Brian Palo is anxious to talk to you."

"I've already spoken to him. It's important that I make the call." Hac lifted himself up to a sitting position, back propped against the wall. Though still weak, he no longer felt faint, and miraculously, the pain didn't start up again with the movement.

London's eyes watched critically, weighing his request for a moment. "Who do you need to talk to?"

"That's something you don't need to know. But it is important," he repeated. "You can trust me, you know."

"I'll make a deal with you. Agree to see Brian, and afterward I'll give you access to my comlink."

"Call first. Brian after."

London rose from her chair, shaking her head. "I don't think so. Rest for a while, and think about it," she suggested, and was gone, a lock clicking after her.

Hac drew a deep breath, taking stock of his wrecked body and his resources. The effects of the stimulant wouldn't last long, so whatever he did had to be soon. But what was it he had to do?

Return to the ship.

Rescue Mier.

Mier.

His feelings for the agent refused to be defined—or was it that he really didn't want to acknowledge them? Today he defended her against one of his oldest friends, and he had placed himself in danger for her sake. He was also, it seemed, prepared to go against the best interests of Gemsbuck, of his family.

No, that wasn't so; there was no tridenite on Tori. The report made by the geologist attached to the first mission indicated that the planet had a number of minerals, but not the distinctive deposits that allowed the formation of the triple-valence denite. Tori had proved itself a dry well. Gemsbuck Mining would have to look elsewhere for tridenite.

And Mier? How did she . . . no, *why* did she figure so prominently in his interests?

His mind slipped around the answer again.

He didn't owe her anything. True, she had taken him along on the mission, but then, she had been under orders to do so.

Orders.

SIA.

Poor Mier.

"You really got caught up in it this time, didn't you?" he told her, speaking softly to himself. The head of the agency a traitor, your supervisor ready to sacrifice you for a nonexistent treaty, and me . . . The feeling of bitter laughter in his mind. I made a fine android. I played my part so well that, even though you must have seen enough proof to convince you otherwise, you chose to believe what you had been told. Or did you, like so many wards of our government, trust that your superiors would never do anything against your best interests, would never hurt you? That's the problem with a paternalistic society; people trust authority figures just as they would a parent, incapable of believing that either one would ever turn on them. No one would believe that as there is no man completely free of self-interest, there is no such thing as a benevolent government.

And Mier stuck in the middle.

Unless she was dead by now.

Had the injection done its work? Would she wake up, sane and whole? Or would she evade the parasite by choosing the one-way path down into death?

There was no time for these thoughts, no time to waste. Hac carefully pushed himself to his feet and went to the door. Nothing as simple as a lock had ever stopped him before.

CHAPTER 44

Mier lay still as death, only the steady rise and fall of her chest indicating that she was only deeply asleep. Ttar paced, back and forth, feet silent on the costly rug, careful to stay away from the bound and gagged guard. His fingers, shoved deep in a side pocket, played with a small cylinder, while his mind went over and over a series of thoughts.

He had to get out, had to take advantage of this chance. If Hac got out . . . But he had no way of knowing this was true. Did he get safely away? Would he come back as promised?

Ttar stopped at the bedside and looked down at the unconscious agent. She could wake up with her mind stripped, completely mad, and useless to him. She'd been under the parasite's influence for longer than any of them. Sweat beaded his brow as he remembered the insinuating presence, relentlessly exploring the innermost secrets of his mind, exposing them as it . . .

He yanked his thoughts hastily away. His hand clenched on the cylinder.

No!

He whirled and began pacing again. She could help, if she was awake. He might not have another chance. If she was awake and not mad.

And that was a problem; he had no way of knowing.

He went to the door, and after listening, ear against the panel, eased it open a crack. Stillness. An empty corridor lay before his eyes. The time was now. This might be his only chance.

But two could be better than one . . . two people running from the ship, confusing things. He pushed the door closed, and went back to Mier. On the other hand, she might hold him back. She might be too weak to run.

Should he or shouldn't he?

What if they didn't make it? What if they got caught and the Professor took them back to Tori anyway? Who would help him then? Who would save him?

Damn! He had to keep that from happening. He had to get away while there was still time.

And Mier?

She had friends, the people she worked for. They wouldn't let anything happen to her, would they? She'd be all right.

But, maybe, just maybe, they'd go easy on someone who helped her escape. Yeah. That was it. He would save her and she'd make the authorities go easy on him. It wasn't like he'd really done anything—except murder Began. And that was self-defense, even though he couldn't prove it.

Mier had to help him!

Ttar removed the cylinder from his pocket. It lay in his hand, blue winking in the light, as he made his decision. With a frown on his face, he retrieved the hypo from the bed, moving swiftly, not giving himself a chance to change his mind. With a click, the spent green ampule ejected, bouncing on the carpet, and the blue snapped in place. A hiss sounded as he pressed the injection home.

Now he was committed . . . now he would know if she woke in possession of her mind, or helplessly insane.

Nothing happened.

Ttar set the hypo aside and wondered what he expected. Hac had awakened immediately when he got the last shot. Did it work differently for everyone?

He waited, anxiety mounting as seconds passed, a minute stretching into two.

Mier didn't so much as twitch.

"Hey," he called, reaching out a hand to shake her shoulder. "Wake up."

Nothing.

"Mier." He raised his voice as much as he dared. "Wake up!"

"Damn!" He shook her again, harder this time, and when that didn't work, slapped her face. "Wake up, damn it! Mier, wake up!" He shook her yet again, beginning to panic. She lay limp in his hands, and he let her go, not knowing what else he could do.

Mier lay still a moment longer; then her lids fluttered and her eyes came open.

"I know he doesn't want to see me!" Brian exclaimed as he followed London to the modern apartment serving her as a temporary base, his grin replaced by a frown of concentration. "I handled him badly the last time. I know better now. Did you contact the empath?"

"Leah Roget should be here anytime. She wasn't too happy with your summons either. You're going to have to learn to be less high-handed, Brian."

"I know. I know."

She stopped and faced him. "Remember, he's still pretty weak. Take it easy, will you?"

"Open the door."

The rumpled bed held scattered bits and pieces from the first aid kit. London couldn't be sure of everything that was missing, but SIA agents were issued fairly substantial stimulants, and these were gone.

So was Hac.

"Call your agents in," Brian snapped, leaving the room at a fast walk, talking all the time. She had to trot to keep up. "Have them meet me at the port. Call the authorities and report a kidnapping. Tell them the people on the *Stellar Drake* are harboring a fugitive. Tell them to detain that ship!"

"Why aren't you insane?" Ttar demanded.

"Why aren't you?"

He frowned, not wanting to touch on the subject when it pertained to himself.

She knelt beside the bound guard, going through his pockets, appropriating anything she thought they might need. "How long has Hac been gone?" A pistol, a rifle, a vibrodag lay beside her, as well as extra ammunition.

"I don't know. Couple of hours, at least. What—what was it like?"

"What was what like?" She turned over a keycard, reading the fine print.

"The parasite. It talked to us, you know. I mean, you talked to us, but it was the Torian."

Mier sat back on her heels, looking at the redheaded man beside her. "You're not going to leave it alone, are you? All right. It wasn't particularly pleasant, having someone else in my mind. But then, I'm from Tamerin Three."

"Tamerin Three?"

"You don't know anything about the planet?"

"Not really."

"The original colonists were gene-altered. One of the side effects was a limited telepathic ability. It was most strong between mates and family members."

"You're a telepath?"

She sighed. "No. Not a telepath. Not even an empath. But for many years I was linked with another exile from Tamerin. You might say I'm used to sharing another mind. The Torian was weird, and it took over, but it couldn't hurt me. You see, I can close off parts of my mind. I . . . Whatever it is that was essentially me, went inside that place and shut down."

"That's why I couldn't wake you up?"

"You got it. Now, if you've satisfied your curiosity, can we get out of here?"

"Yeah. But, you didn't know anything that was happening?"

"Not— No." She closed her lips firmly, and turned her attention back to the weapons. "If we're going to get out of here, let's get going."

Three things happened as Ttar reached for the rifle.

* * *

"What do you mean, I can't have access to the company link?" Hac asked, keeping his voice calm despite a growing need to yell at someone. Stimulants kept him upright and clearheaded, but he didn't know how long they would last.

"Well, how do I know you are who you say you are? We can't let just anyone come in here and use company property!"

"I told you: I am Haverland Cary. Head of Security for Gemsbuck Mining. Check it."

"How? You don't have any identification. And you . . ." He looked disdainfully at his visitor's torn and stained jumpsuit. Was that blood? Really, the man was a mess. "You certainly aren't dressed for the part."

"I've been working undercover, and I had an accident. How many times do I have to explain this to you? And there are other ways of verifying identity, vacuum brain."

The man flushed at the words, but if anything, they made him more determined not to give in. "Use of offensive language will get you nowhere."

"If you think that was offensive, you may be in for a severe shock."

"Look, Mr. Whoever-you-are, you cannot expect me to waste my valuable time, trying to verify the identity of every tramp who wanders in here . . ."

"If you don't start immediately, you'll lose this precious job and find you have nothing except time to waste."

"Threats!" The portly little man bustled to his feet, a picture of indignation. "I'm sorry, but you're going to have to leave. Or . . ."

"Or what?"

"Or I'll call the authorities!"

"Good. They know who I am. What's their number?"

The rep hesitated, hand hovering over the keyboard in his desk. Hac couldn't imagine what clerical error had gotten such a character assigned to Stonewall. The local jack miners were among the toughest crews in space; they'd eat someone like this alive. The visual picture of a crusty miner nose to nose with the fussy little rep lightened Hac's mood, despite his continued anxiety for Mier.

"Maybe you should count," he suggested. "You know, ten to one, building suspense until zero when you dial the authorities. I should be quivering with fear by then."

"You don't—"

"What 'I don't,' " he snapped, "is intend to waste any more time while you dither and whine." Hac came around the desk, moving purposefully.

"Don't you touch me!"

"I won't, don't worry. Hope you have a ticket home, because both you and the incompetent who hired you, have just joined the ranks of the unemployed. Vacate the office."

"You can't . . ." His words trailed off in rising hysteria as he backed away from the advancing form.

"I just did! Now go, while you still can."

The man fled, leaving the door open so Hac could hear him screaming for help. Smiling grimly, his assailant seated himself in the vacant chair. Keys began clicking beneath his fingers, and shortly a holocube formed above the desk. A handsome female face peered forth.

"Hello, Mother," he said. "Call out the reserves. I need some help."

CHAPTER 45

"Professor! Sir, what are you doing here?" Mier asked.

"Hello, Mier." He strolled through the doorway, completely at home. "It's good to see you well again."

"I thought you were away on leave. Where's Brian?"

"Off on other business. I've taken charge of this case." His benign gaze took in Ttar, securely held between two guards. "Take him away. I have things to discuss with Agent Silver. Private things."

The redheaded spy looked from one to the other, thoroughly bewildered. "No," he began, "Mier, you don't—"

"Silence!" the Professor bellowed. "Get him out of here!"

Ttar fought wildly, his mouth open to speak when one of the guards struck him down. Heels left twin grooves in the carpet as the limp form was dragged away.

Mier, too, was confused, but at least she had something familiar to work with. "I'm glad you're here, sir. I suppose this means we've managed to take the ship?"

"Yes. I am in command here." Quick to see how she could misconstrue the circumstances, he was equally fast to take advantage. A plan formed in his mind; a nasty little scheme that would tie things up very neatly indeed. If he played this right—and he would—it would clear the way for his success. *Aide-toi, le ciel t'aidera!*

"B-but the guards—their uniforms . . ." she stammered.

"My people—our people, undercover. Do you know where Hac has gone?"

"Hac? No. I haven't seen him."

"Hmm. I had him deactivated. Ttar must have discovered a way to reverse the field. Anyway, he's gone."

"What's been happening, sir? I seem to have been out for some time."

"I realize that," he said gently, keeping himself well under control. "We did try to do everything for you that we could, but you were so deeply in a coma. It's fortunate I arrived here before Ttar could tell you some more lies."

"Lies?"

"What exactly did he tell you?"

"Nothing. Hac had been here, and then went for help. But he's been gone too long, so we were going to try to bust out. Guess we were lucky that you took the ship when you did."

"Very lucky. Hac won't be coming back with help or otherwise."

A chill worked its way up from her gut. "I can't believe that."

"I know it is disappointing; however, it often happens that way."

"But why? Why did he do it? I thought he worked for . . . belonged to Gemsbuck Mining!"

"Greed, I would imagine. Except in his case, it was perverted programming. Gemsbuck may have owned him but someone else—whoever programmed him—was probably bought. In all the time you were together, you still didn't discover the truth?"

"No, sir."

The Professor sighed. "*Experto credite*, my child. Hac was a double agent."

"All that time, and he was the spy I was trying to find?"

"He was the spy. He tricked all of us, I'm afraid. Even Brian, who recommended him."

"What part did Ttar play in all of this?"

"I assume he was Hac's accomplice. I'm sorry to say that they were using you, Mier."

Her mind in turmoil, she thought out loud. "Hac was the one who insisted we rescue Ttar when his ship started to break up in the Stone Field."

"You're starting to remember incriminating incidents, little clues to his perfidy, aren't you?"

"Yes." She sighed, not liking this new discovery even a little bit. Then a positive thought intruded. "But he brought me back. He could have left me on Tori, you know."

"He didn't bring you back. He brought back a host body for a Torian. He didn't care about you, you just happened to be the one carrying a parasite, a convenience, nothing more."

Her face fell. "Is that how it was?"

"Yes. I'm very sorry. And be careful, Mier. If he finds out that you know the truth, he'll try to kill you."

"So he's still alive?"

"One of the guards shot him as he was trying to escape from the ship."

"And the body?"

"We couldn't find it. There was a trail of blood to one of the maintenance hatches, but by the time these incompetents discovered it, he was gone."

"What do you want me to do?"

"Find him. Find him, Mier. And then kill him. That's your new assignment."

CHAPTER 46

Ttar felt horribly ill when his eyes came open. His head hurt, and the back of his throat burned with bile. But he knew he couldn't give up.

He opened eyes to darkness where he lay curled on his side, wrists tied behind his back. Wrists tied, he realized, not arms. And with a piece of heavy cord.

He almost laughed out loud. How careless!

Hopeful despite his predicament, Ttar took a minute to gather strength and arrest his nausea. Then he went to work, bending his body even further, rolling onto his bottom arm, pulling his hands past his tucked feet and up in front of him. Stretching out into a less cramped position, he worked the knots with his lips and teeth. Tight they were, but not impossible. Minutes later he rubbed the circulation back into his hands before climbing carefully to his feet and exploring the prison. It was another cabin, lights deactivated. So he was still on the ship, still apparently considered important enough to take back to Tori.

That's what they thought!

All right, where was the door? He was alone, no one to tell him what to do, no one to worry about, and, most important, no one, this time, to stop him from trying to escape. He would die before he went back to Tori!

Help was on its way. Gemsbuck employees on Stonewall had been called in. But would they arrive in time? Hac wasn't sure, and he didn't intend to stay around and wait. He couldn't, he thought, using the third and last of the stimulants he'd purloined from London's first aid kit. When this one wore off . . . He didn't want to think about it. By then it would be all over, one way or another.

He took a cab to the port, watchful for authorities, or anyone connected with the SIA, or the Consortium. It made a long list of people who might try to stop him, most of whom he wouldn't know by sight. A daunting thought. Anyone who looked suspicious or even vaguely threatening might be a danger. Still, what else could he do? Once the *Stellar Drake* left the planet, his task would be even more difficult.

The ship stood on its pad, the immediate surroundings deserted. Hac walked toward it, well aware that he moved in full view of its sensors. He stopped beside a parked tractor, looking up at the yacht's sleek sides.

"Hello on the ship," he called.

The answer came immediately. "Hello, yourself. What do you want?"

"I need to talk to the Professor."

"You are, my friend. You are! Mier, do your job."

Mier? A slit appeared in the ship's side, widening to a door framing a hard-faced woman he almost didn't recognize. The intent of the pistol she held, however, was unmistakable. "Mier? What are you doing?"

"Killing you." Her finger tightened on the trigger.

"What?"

"Mier! *No!*" Brian's voice rang through the hangar, punctuated by running footsteps as the SIA agents arrived in force.

Hac took the moment's distraction to dodge behind the bright yellow machine, the slug from Mier's gun stripping paint where he had been standing. "Mier, what in hell's come over you?" he yelled.

"Truth, Mr. Double Agent," she called. Brian and his men had halted, well out of her line of fire. "The Professor told me who you're working for. You and Ttar."

"The Professor? Mier, he's the double agent! He's been working for the Consortium for months!" Hac argued.

"Mier! Hac, what in hell's going on here?" Brian called.

"Work your way around behind him, Brian," Mier

replied. "He's your spy. He's working for the Consortium."

"Hac? You're crazy. Do you know who you're talking about, Mier?"

"More than you do, it seems."

"And what's this about the Professor?"

"He's behind it, Brian," Hac called. "He's on the *Drake* right now, probably getting a big thrill out of watching us kill each other."

"Good, blazing . . . The Professor? That fits." Brian swung to Mier. "Put your weapon up, Silver. Hac's on our side. I can prove it."

"Don't listen to him, Mier," the Professor called, his disembodied voice coming from the ship. "He may be in on it. I often wondered why he was so determined to include Hac on the mission. Kill him, too."

The muzzle of her pistol wavered. Kill Brian?

"What are you talking about, Professor?" Brian called. "What are you doing here when you're supposed to be on Terra? And especially, what are you doing on a Consortium ship?"

Behind Mier the hatch disgorged a troop of guards, slugs tearing at the plasticrete. Men scattered, taking what cover they could. Shots were returned and guards fell.

Brian saw one of them pulling Mier back into the ship despite her argument. He ducked under the tractor where he came face-to-face with his old friend. "Aren't you armed?" he demanded.

"No," Hac replied. "Unfortunately I'm not. You?"

"Shit, no, or I'd be shooting back. What in hell'd you do to Mier?"

"Me? Nothing. But it looks like the Professor got to her. What do we do about it?"

Brian shrugged as well as he could lying on his stomach. "Either convince her of the truth or kill her. I know. I know. You don't want anything to happen to her. So we try to talk her back to our side. But remember, she usually hits what she aims at. And I'd rather it wasn't me. The Professor!" He flinched as a slug hit the tractor above his head. "I mean, he was on the list, but I never really suspected him."

"He's not only turned," Hac explained. "I think it's driven him mad."

"You mean he's unbalanced?"

"Without a doubt. By the way, I want to thank you for not telling him who I really am. I think it saved my life."

"You're welcome. It's pretty quiet out there."

"Think it's over?"

"Yeah. Sounds that way. I wonder if we won."

"Only one way to find out." Hac started to move, Brian right beside him.

"Brian Palo?" London called, stooping to look under the tractor.

"Yeah." He flushed with embarrassment. "Be right there."

"Interesting little display of pyrotechnics," the Professor's voice came from the ship.

"Professor?" Brian called as he got to his feet. "Why don't you come out so we can talk this over."

"That doesn't sound particularly productive. In fact, it sounds rather dangerous. Although I have just wasted a perfectly good security force, I still have the advantage."

"What advantage? You can't lift off without assistance from Port Control. And we can camp out here for months if necessary. You're trapped."

"Poor Brian. How shortsighted you are. Despite your protests, I can lift whenever I choose."

"He can?" his onetime assistant asked under his breath.

"I'm afraid he can," Hac said, dismayed, realizing exactly how he could arrange this. "I think you'd better let him go."

"But he's going to Tori. We can't let that happen!"

"Well," the Professor called, impatient with their silence. "Do I lift, or do I blow up half the planet?"

"What's he talking about?" a new voice inquired. It belonged to Sardo, chief of the Stonewall Authorities. This time she scowled at the ship as well as at the group of agents, ready to arrest them all if necessary.

"The ship," Hac supplied. "If we don't let him lift, he'll turn it into a bomb."

"And risk killing himself?" the woman asked. "He'd have to be mad."

"You missed that part of the conversation," Brian told her. "He is, most certainly, mad."

"Oh, great!" She turned on her men. "Michels, Cork, get me a patch into port authority. What," she asked Brian, "is the reason that you're so unwilling he should leave Stonewall?"

"He's a traitor to the Federation. He's been selling agency secrets. His *own* agency."

"That's all?"

"That's enough. He'll be sentenced to rehab for sure."

"All right. Sentence him. But catch him somewhere other than Stonewall. I don't want him on this planet a second longer than necessary. And get your men out of here before I arrest you all."

"But you can't . . ."

"I can and I will."

Brian looked at Hac, a question in his eyes. "Are we willing to let it go at that? I'm asking you as a representative of Gemsbuck."

"I've told you over and over again. There is no tridenite on Tori. The Professor's welcome to the planet."

"There's one thing—"

"Are you two going to stand here all night talking about it? Or are you going to get your army and go?" Sardo interrupted.

"We're leaving." Hac took his friend by the arm and started away from the ship.

He obviously hadn't seen the guard pull Mier back on board. "Hac, wait. Mier's . . ."

"Where is she?" He looked to the left and right, suddenly apprehensive.

"On board the *Drake*."

CHAPTER 47

"What are you trying to do? Why didn't you let me do my job!" Mier demanded, furious. Dragged back into the ship and disarmed, her mind a conflict of questions, she wasn't in the mood to be the least bit civil. Especially not with two armed guards standing just inside the hatch.

"Patience, my child. Patience," the Professor said soothingly, turning the pilot's chair around to face her.

"No. It's time for some answers. You haven't been truthful with me."

"Mier, Mier. Is this any way to behave? Everything I've done is for your own good. They would have killed you out there."

"The people out there were SIA agents. Why did you open fire on them?"

"I didn't go after them, Silver, they came here. What is this? You rebelling against me, too? You're not a traitor."

"No, I'm not a traitor, but suddenly I'm not so sure about you."

"I am the most loyal person you will ever know. However, the definition of loyalty may be beyond you."

"Loyal to yourself? Is that what you mean?"

"Very good! Kimmy, Grace, take our guest to her cabin, and see that she remains there. I have important matters requiring my attention, but very soon we must continue this conversation. You seem to have a much better grasp of ideas than your fellow agents."

"What are you going to do?" Mier asked, refusing to budge.

"I have several options. Everything depends on the people out there. Now, go along, Silver. Cooperate with me, and you won't find the experience unpleasant. On the other hand," he added when she remained stubborn, "I could make the experience extremely unpleasant."

She didn't like the connotation, she didn't like the situation, but there didn't seem to be any alternatives, yet. The man called Kimmy gestured with his rifle for her to proceed down the corridor, alert for any chance.

The SIA agent had already left the port, but Hac and Brian remained, arguing with Chief Sardo.

"I don't care if it's kidnapping. My responsibility is to preserve the peace and protect the property of Stonewall. If he jiggers the engines on that ship, we'll lose more lives than one. I'm sorry."

"Just let me talk to him," Hac said. "I might be able to get on board before he lifts."

"And then what?" Her patience dwindled fast.

"Have you reached a decision?" the Professor's voice boomed from the ship's speakers.

"Port Control . . ." she began. "Let go of me!" she snarled, pulling free as Brian grabbed her by the arm. She turned on him, speaking with awful emphasis. "Don't ever, *ever*, do that again!"

"You don't know what's at stake here," the SIA man told her. "He's betraying the Federation. He's trying to—"

"I don't care who or what he's trying to do! All I care about is the threat to this port. Now, both of you, clear the area!"

Hac broke away and started forward. "I want to talk to Mier," he yelled as Sardo's men closed in on him.

"She's not available at the moment," came the reply. "Your devotion is commendable. I must assume from the recent evidence that you are not, as I was led to believe, an android?"

"Believe whatever you want." Hac struggled to free himself, but was borne steadily backward.

"Who are you, then? Someone known to Brian, of course. But not, I think, a Federation official. No, if that were the case, I would have recognized you before this. No, you are obviously someone of importance to . . . to Gemsbuck Mining! Ah! Is it possible I am addressing one of the family? One of the mighty Carys? Brian! I commend you! This was a very clever deception. Bringing in someone with a bionic limb . . . real enough to convince anyone that the rest of the man is artificial as well. Excellent, my boy. I see now that your association with me has benefited you. You should do well. Not well enough to defeat someone of my caliber, but good enough for the ragtag crooks roaming the galaxy.

"But enough talk. Time is running out. I will begin self-destruct countdown in precisely ten seconds. If any of you care to preserve life, you now have fifteen minutes to evacuate the area."

Sardo whirled. "Michel, check on the evacuation. And get these two out of here." She took several steps toward the ship. "Port Control has you in the computer for lift-off soonest. They're preparing a window now. Will you please give them time?"

"Time? Time, my dear?" The Professor laughed. "I'll give them all the time in the world. However, they'd better hurry. You have five seconds left. Four, three . . ."

"Port Control!" Sardo all but shrieked into her wrist com.

In response the cover to the *Drake*'s landing tube gave a grating sound and began to open.

The Professor applauded. "Very good! I am beginning countdown for lift-off. Be reminded, though, I can change it to destruct with the most infinitesimal pressure of my finger on one, little button."

Fumes began to rise from the base of the *Drake*, rolling through the level, as he started warming the engines prematurely. The ship swayed lightly in its gantry as the elevator began a ponderous ascent to the lift area.

"Good-bye, Brian. No doubt we will meet again. Sharpen your wits before then—you'll need them if you hope to defeat me!" He roared with laughter.

CHAPTER 48

Mier dragged the unconscious guard into the tiny cabin that was to have been her prison, and bent over to remove his weapons. Footsteps sounded, light and hesitant in the corridor, and she pressed back against the bulkhead. The sound ceased as whoever was out there became suspicious of the open door. Seconds passed, the trembling of the ship measuring time that was not to be wasted. Mier sprang as a figure came hurtling toward her. They grappled less than an instant before recognition came.

"Mier!"

"Ttar?"

They spoke in unison, hands releasing, stepping back. A beat of silence, and then they both spoke again.

"We have to get out of here . . ."

"He's going to blow the ship . . ."

"Yeah," Ttar told her. "But listen, there's something you have to know."

"Not now. There's no time."

She picked up the guard's rifle before peering around the doorway. Empty corridor stretched in both directions.

"No, Mier, you have to understand," he insisted. "The Professor's the traitor. I heard him . . ."

"I know. I heard him, too. And we have to stop him."

"*No!*" He grabbed her arm. "He's crazy, Mier. And

the ship's moving. We don't have time for a confronta-
tion. Let's just leave!''

"We can't let him get away with what he's done.''

"He's got guards. Even if we managed to fight our way
through them, we'd never get to him in time! Come on!
There are other ways to stop him.''

"Such as?''

But at that moment they both became aware of the
sound of many feet, moving fast, and bolted away from
them.

"Great Lunar craters! Now we've had it,'' Ttar complained between breaths, trying to keep up with the swift
agent. "The main hatch's behind us.''

She dodged into a maintenance tube and slid down,
Ttar's feet right above her head. "There are other ways
off the ship.''

"If we can get to them in time." He managed to stop
himself and roll out of the tube after her. "Where are
we?''

Mier gazed at the stacks of cargo filling every available
inch of space between a bewildering forest of pipe and
conduit, and shook her head. "I have no idea.''

The noise of engine filled their ears.

"What's this?'' Ttar yelled, standing before a panel
that had been pulled from a bulkhead. "Countdown sequence,'' he read more softly to himself.

Mier pushed him aside, and after a quick survey of the
instruments, gave a wide grin. "Nice. See if you can find
a loading hatch somewhere.''

"What are you going to do?''

"There's no time for discussion. Come on, Ttar! Get
going. Or do you want to go back to Tori?''

Those were the magic words. Ttar scrambled past a
webbed stack of crates until he found a small doorway.
The locked latch yielded under his skillful fingers, and
an opening appeared, admitting fumes that roiled around
the cargo and quickly filled the area.

"Mier! Come on! I got it open.''

No response, and he couldn't see through the dense
fog that filled the maintenance bay.

"*Mier!*''

Hac stood, scowling at the ship from the wide doorway of level six, Stonewall's sun hot on the back of his neck. Despite Sardo's orders, he refused to move any farther until Brian reached him. "I'm sorry, Hac. But Mier knew what she was in for when she took the job."

"He'll take her back to Tori."

"If they get that far. The Stone Field . . ." Then he realized his remark was tactless. "Sorry."

The elevator carrying the *Drake* had risen perhaps six feet when Sardo gave an excited shout. "You'd better see this," she called.

Hac ran to her side, Brian close behind.

"Is that your kidnap victim?" the security chief demanded.

A small dark patch appeared on the *Drake*'s side. A mad swirling of the fumes marked movement as someone clambered from the ship and dropped to the elevator platform and was lost from sight.

"Mier!" Hac yelled, racing forward, Brian and Sardo pounding after.

The elevator continued its steady ascent as someone . . . no, two people swung over the edge of the moving platform. The platform was nine feet up and still rising when they dropped. Hac reached them first. "Mier?"

A fit of coughing doubled her over, and he supported her toward the door and open air. She had twisted her leg when she fell, and limped badly, tears running from burning eyes.

"I'm fine . . . fine," she gasped. "I just . . . just can't stand fog!"

Outside she stopped and leaned against him, eyes tightly shut. Despite his aching side, Hac wrapped his arms around her.

"No," she gasped, pulling back. "I have to talk to someone in authority."

"That would be me," Sardo said, coming forward.

"You have to let that ship go. Whatever you do, don't delay it."

"Don't worry, it's going."

Mier seemed to relax, but she wasn't finished. "Is there someplace where we can monitor the lift-off? There's something I have to see."

"You want to make sure the ship's gone? Or do you know something you're not telling me?"

"Please?"

"A professional courtesy, maybe?" Brian interjected, coming to Mier's assistance.

Sardo looked at him, eyes calculating, a faint smile touching the corners of her mouth. "It might be arranged, although I can't imagine why I or my government owe you anything."

Brian answered her with a grin. "I might be able to come up with a reason."

"Brian, now!" Mier insisted.

Sardo spoke into her comlink, and within seconds an aircar hovered at her side. It was a tight fit for all of them . . . all of them, that is, except Ttar. He took advantage of the confusion and slipped back into the port, intent on making himself invisible. No one noticed when he left nor remembered him until sometime later.

The car rose straight up to the rooftop landing level, where, piling from the vehicle, they followed the security chief into a grav tube and up to an observation tower. Enormous windows showed the field where the *Drake* was just lifting. Banks of monitors were below this, several of them following the vessel's progress. Sardo and her companions stood clear of the busy techs clicking at keyboards and speaking softly into mikes. The ship rose, penetrated the atmosphere dome, and continued her ascent into dark space.

"The son of a bitch is getting away," Brian intoned sadly.

"I don't think so," Mier replied.

"You did something," Sardo interrupted. "You did something to that ship! If you've endangered . . ."

There was a flurry of activity as one of the techs pointed at the screen. "Something's happening to the *Drake*."

The ship shimmered, seeming to grow large until, in a flash of light, it exploded. Flaming debris shot off in every direction, streamers of color blotting out the stars. In an instant it was over. In the control room machines hummed serenely, going on with their jobs.

"You don't have to worry about the Professor anymore, Brian," Mier told him, breaking the silence.

"Guess not," he replied, stunned. "When did you decide on this drastic course?"

"Don't begin to congratulate yourselves just yet," Sardo interjected. "What I was about to say was that if you have endangered any of the ships or satellites currently in orbit above Stonewall, you'll face the consequences, and I don't care who you work for."

"I think you'll find the *Drake* was far enough out. I timed the explosion very carefully. I remembered how long it took the *Corsair* to get beyond the orbital lines."

Sardo scowled and went to speak to one of the techs.

"Well done, Babe," Brian whispered.

"All right," the security chief told them when she returned. "As far as we can tell, there's been no damage. You'll have to come with me. There are reports to make out."

"I think I can handle that for you," Brian suggested. "Reports are my job. Mier's part in all of this is finished."

Sardo glared at him as she took a deep breath and then let it out in a snort. "Very well. Follow me, please." Her back was stiff and disapproving as she left the room.

"I think the two of you should make yourselves scarce," Brian suggested in a low voice. "I'll handle everything from now on. Angry security chiefs are what I do best. Especially if they're female."

"And my vacation?" Mier demanded.

"You've earned it. Hac, I'll talk to you later." He looked at his old friend. "I'd get that tended to, if I were you. You look awful."

"Thanks. I will." But Brian was gone, an anticipatory grin on his face. Hac shook his head and then sank down into a vacant chair. The stimulant was wearing off and exhaustion reached him.

Mier stood stiffly, suddenly uncomfortable.

"We should get out of here," he suggested. "It seems to be all over."

"What happened to you?" she asked, eyeing the ruin of his jumpsuit.

"Slight damage to the chassis. Nothing irreparable, I assure you."

Anger flared in her eyes. "Chassis? Irreparable? You dare remind me of your deception?" She gripped her lips tightly together for a second. "I don't know you. I don't know who you are. I don't even know your name, damn it!"

"It's Hac."

"Hac? Human Analog Computer, right?"

"No," he said patiently. "Haverland Andrew Cary. The fourth. But everyone calls me Hac."

She drew a deep breath. "It's too bad you're wounded. After what you did to me, I'd like to . . ."

Too aware of the interested techs, he stopped her. "Mier, wait. Yell at me all you want, but later. Right now I'm very tired. Think we could suspend hostilities long enough for you to help me get somewhere more private?"

"You seem to have managed quite well on your own up to now!"

"Mier?"

She wasn't immune to blue eyes.

"Damn," she softly said.

ABOUT THE AUTHOR

Johanna M. Bolton was born an Army brat in New York City, and moved for the first time at six months of age. She has lived in Japan and Germany, as well as a number of the states, a kind of gypsy childhood she would recommend to anyone. She has studied fine art, biology and mathematics, taught pre-school, high school and college, ridden dressage horses, written for newspapers, trained show dogs, bred tropical fish, traveled on her BMW motorcycle through the Rocky Mountains, and tried being married.

She now lives in Florida, which she calls the antechamber to Hell. Her household includes a giant dog called Max, two cats (Maus and Joseph), tropical fish and a bay, Thoroughbred horse named Gunner. She plays the flute, piano and guitar, practices karate and Tai Chi, collects dragons and one day she will learn to fly.

Introducing...

The Science Fiction Collection

Del Rey has gathered the forces of four of its greatest
authors into a thrilling, mind-boggling series that no
Science Fiction fan will want to do without!!